Pretty Bright

Author of Deadly Decisions & Deadly Decisions II

MiMi Renee

Ink Game Publications

This book is a work of fiction. Names, characters, places and incidents are products of the author's imagination or used fictitiously. Any resemblance to actual events or locales or persons, living or dead is entirely coincidental. Any and all locations existing are mentioned in the book to give it a feeling of reality.

ISBN 978-0-615-39536-4

LCCN: 2011900336

Cover Design/Graphics Charlie Big Six Hustle/www.120designs.net
Author: Mimi Renee
Editor-in-Chief: Jill Alicea/savafiend76@roadrunner.com
Proofreader: Niccole Simmons/www.21streeturbanediting.co m Interior Design: Glenda A. Wallace/ bookinteriordesigns@gmail.com

I dedicate this book to all the readers, the writers on the grind, and to all the people who have continued to love, support and believe in me! This one's for you...and it's only the beginning of what I have in store for you...

The Writer Chick

Acknowledgments

First I'd like to say thank you to my Heavenly Father, for giving me the craft, the passion and the ability to write my dreams into reality. You are an incredible God, and I love you wholeheartedly! To my daughter, Aonesty a.k.a Poo Bear...Like I always tell you, sweetheart; continue to fight for your dreams...NO MATTER WHAT! It's your destiny and I love you more than life itself! Big Whoadi, I thank you and love you for your continued support. You are and have always been the back bone to everything that I do. Together we move mountains, and I love and appreciate you very much!!! Shout out to my parents, Melvin and Nadine and my siblings, Melvenia, Melanie and Melvin Jr...I love you guys soooooo much and thanks for always being there for me. I don't know what I would do without you guys! Shout out to my industry friends who have been more than just a little help to me: Shaifire (Debbie Deb) K'wan Foye, Terry L. Wroten, Latia D. Johnson, and a special shout out to my girl Cha'Bella Don!! You have had my back through this journey, and I want you to know that I am forever grateful for you...Now get back to writing!!! Lol. I would also like to say, thanks to my editors, Jill Alicea and Niccole Simmons from Twenty-First Street Urban Editing for helping me with the delivery of my second book born. My cover designer, Charlie a.k.a Charlie Hustle for seeing my vision and delivering it. I appreciate all of your hard work and time, and I thank you all very much!

Shout out to all my family, the Burkes, the Anderson's, the Adkins, the Linder's, the Harvey's, the Way's and the Harris family! I love you all very much! Last but not least, I want to say THANK YOU to all the readers and supporters...Without you, my stories go untold. I truly appreciate you all and from the bottom of my heart I want to say THANK YOU for all of your continued love and support! I hope you'll all enjoy!

Sincerely,
The Writer Chick, Mimi Renee

Spring 2005

Part One

"What it do, bitches?!? The female that they love to hate is in the muthafuckin' house!" Bright said upon entering the house of her best friend Treasure that lived in a house a couple of blocks from her.

"What's good, bitch?" Treasure stood to greet her friend. "Balling ass niggas!" Bright spat, popping her collar. "And I'm ready to get faded tonight too. How you doing?" Bright asked, striking a sexy pose and then slapping Treasure a high five.

"You is a fool," Treasure said, recovering from laughter. In the middle of small talk, Treasure busted out with the drama. "Why that nigga Chrome call me last night, Bee?" Treasure called Bright, Bee for short. "And yes, I let that nigga have it!" Treasure said, seeing the expression on Bright's face. "He talking 'bout, 'I wasn't tryna talk to Bright on the low, she was tryna holler at me!" Treasure said, twisting her lips up. She didn't believe a word he had said to her. He was a dog ass nigga and Bright was her girl, and she trusted her more than anything.

Bright laughed. "Yeah right! I tried to holler at his ass? It was just like I told you, Treasure. That fool was tryna holla when I came out of the bathroom, nigga grabbed my ass and shit like I was too faded to resist, or like I would be on some grimy shit with my homegirl's so-called boyfriend. Fuck him!" Bright said, getting heated all over again. Chrome was cool, but he wasn't fine enough nor did he have enough money for her to play her homegirl like that.

"I'm already knowing, Bee, that's why I gave it to his ass again when he called me a few minutes ago...and I gave his punk ass the dial tone!" Treasure said, nodding her head. Chrome had been her dude for three months. Treasure really liked him, and she thought he liked her too, but when Bright told her what he had done to her, Treasure picked up the phone, called him, cussed him out, and then dumped him. Just like that.

"He ain't shit," Bright said, seeing the disappointed look on Treasure's face. "You a fly ass bitch, and niggas come a dime a dozen to females like us - da Norf's baddest bitches. Fuck him!"

"Exactly, fuck him!" Treasure added. "Now what's the agenda for the night?" She said, trying to get her mind off of Chrome.

Treasure was an only child. She and her mother, Jackie, shared a home with her grandmother, the same home that Treasure's mother was raised in. Treasure was a straight-A student, and because of it, both her Mom and Grandma put up a big fuss over her, and whenever they had extra money, they'd give it to her. Treasure played the good girl role in front of her Mom and Grandma, but she was a wild rebel outside of their supervision. And since they were both at work, the two girls carried on as they did in the streets.

Bright, on the other hand, was the oldest of five siblings that her mother had borne between three different men. Bright had her own father, she was the daughter of a deceased, white, rock star. Deja and Cordell shared the same Latino father, and finally Ramon

Her mother worked around the clock in order to support her and her five children. And though she was never really there, she tried to be the best mother she could be in the situation.

Her mother Rosette told her she named her "Bright" fresh out of the womb, once she had seen how light her complexion was. She would always tell her that she had told the doctors, "Damn, she's a bright baby, I'ma name her Bright!" Feeling the pressures of her home life, it wasn't that Bright hated her life. She just wished she didn't have to play the mother role, or have as many responsibilities as she did when her mom was out at work. Honestly, that was the reason she was unable to keep her grades up in school, it seemed like she never had time for homework.

Both girls were beautiful with different, unique looks. But because Bright possessed more exotic features than Treasure, Bright was declared the more dominant beauty of the two. Bright was the product of a bi-racial love affair between her white rock star dad and her African American mom. Blessed with a rare beauty, she stood five feet five inches tall. Bright was straight up model material, and was packaged with just enough of everything on her small frame. She had big green eyes, golden brown hair, and she beamed like a shining star wherever she was. That alone was fifty percent of the reason why most girls hated on her, and the other fifty percent was from her screwed up attitude.

Treasure held her own in the beauty department. She had honey-brown eyes that complimented her copper brown complexion. She had soft, jet black, shoulder-length hair that stayed neatly trimmed in a wrap. Standing a half of an inch shorter than Bright, Treasure was more on the thick side, and she possessed the body of a ghetto bombshell. She had ass, hips, and breasts for days, and when she walked past any crowd, both male and female, would always have to take a double look at her. "Damn, that bitch got a bomb ass shape,"

Treasure would hear a lot of girls say when she passed them. However, unlike Bright, Treasure didn't let her beauty get to her head, and she was actually a very intelligent and down-to-earth girl, that was liked by most. But because she lived by the same rules of the game that Bright did, which was "Getting niggas with money," the two got along well.

Treasure and Bright had been best friends for five years, and would be seen together all the time. Being North Long Beach residents, they both attended school at David Starr Jordan High School, and considered themselves Da Norf's baddest bitches (DNBB). Using their looks to their advantage, they got just about anything they wanted from the opposite sex - money, clothes and jewelry - and they never had to ask twice. Because Bright wasn't mentioned in her father's will, or acknowledged as his child, she was determined to live the rich and luxurious lifestyle that she felt she was robbed of. She would always tell her friends, "I'm Bright; I was born to be rich bitch." And she meant it.

Caught up making plans for the night, their little homegirl Samantha, a.k.a. Suge, knocked on the screen door. "Hey Suge, come on in!" Treasure said with a smile on her face.

"What's the bizzness?" Suge asked, happy to be in the presence of her big homegirls.

"You tell me, what that shit do, young?" Bright smile.

After giving both of her girls love, Suge sat down and joined in the conversation. Suge was only in the ninth grade, but because she had an older mentality, both Treasure and Bright took an immediate liking to her that eventually lead to them kicking it with her and schooling her.

Suge was taller than both girls, standing five feet seven inches tall, and she had a cute face to go with her curvy shape. However, with all the physical, mental and verbal abuse that she took at home from her mother, Suge had low self-esteem and believed that her chocolate skin made her ugly. Her mother would beat her for things like needing help with homework that she didn't understand, or for any other excuses she could think of when she was having a bad day. The physical abuse hurt, but it was the verbal abuse that scared Suge and made her feel bad about herself. Her mother was the worse ingredient in her life, and she would often tell Suge that she was so black and ugly that nobody would ever want her. Suge was the reflection of her mother down to the core, but she hated Suge for being everything that she used to be before her life was ruined and she gave birth to her. It was so bad that Suge hated her own skin, and secretly wished it was lighter. But with Bright and Treasure always telling her how cute she was, and then after different guys at school started asking her out, she begin to love her dark skin just a little bit more.

"My little bitch looks hot!" Bright smiled, checking Suge out. It was obvious that Suge had low-self-esteem and wasn't confident in her beauty, but Bright didn't understand why, being as gorgeous as she was. So whenever the opportunity presented itself, Bright made it her duty to praise and compliment Suge. She would constantly school her and tell her that confidence was both sexy and beautiful, and that a lack of it was a turn off. Bright learned early in life that guys picked beauty over brains any day, and that good looks plus confidence equaled a woman getting whatever she wanted from a man. Meanwhile, the ugly and insecure only got what they could.

"What man wants an ugly ass woman?" Bright would always say to her friends to make logic out of her theory.

"Thank you, Bright," Suge smiled, feeling confident and happy at the same time that she was up to her big homegirls' standards.

"So we kicking it with some college guys tonight, huh?" Treasure asked after downing a half of can of Pepsi.

"College basketball stars," Bright added.

Treasure folded her arms across her chest, "Okay, but unless they got wealthy ass parents, you better know them college boys be broker than us," she laughed. "But I don't have no plans, so I'm wit' it." she said.

"All I'ma say is, "Larry Lane…UCLA star ball player...top dog! " Bright said, popping her collar. "That's guaranteed future money right there, baby," she said, putting emphasis on it.

Trying to recall the familiar name, Treasure began to repeat his name over and over again, until she remembered him. "Larry Lane, Larry Lane, Larry Lane, Larry Lane," she recited. "Oh, that nigga!" Treasure smiled nodding her head. "Oh yeah, he is fine, and he betta have some fine ass baller friends there for me too!" Treasure warned.

"I told 'em I was coming with two bad bitches, so he gone have a homeboy there for you, and a little homeboy there for Suge," Bright said, then she threw her long hair back behind her shoulders. She had it all mapped out.

"I hope these college dudes got some dough, 'cause my fine ass is broke!" Treasure laughed, heading to her bedroom to grab her knock off Gucci bag.

"Y'all ready to hit the mall?" she yelled out to them.
"Super ready," Bright replied. "I seen some hot-girl

outfits that I wanted from Forever 21," she said, standing up from the sofa.

"I saw some cute stuff too," Suge chimed in, followed by a soft giggle.

Treasure called her mother at work to let her know that she was going to the mall with her friends. Then they all walked out of the house to the bus stop, talking about what each girl wanted to wear, and what store they wanted to boost from. Almost every other weekend, the girls hit the mall and hit different stores boosting. Bright would distract the sales associates while Treasure detached the sensor devices from the clothes and Suge would put them in her bag. They had great team work, and that was probably why they never got caught.

After getting off the bus on Lakewood Blvd. and Candlewood Ave., the girls talked about their night's plans as they walked through the mall's parking lot. Approaching the Subway entrance, Suge decided to enlighten Bright on some information she had on Larry Lane.

"I know, Larry's, sister, Linda Lane," Suge announced. "She used to be in my seventh period class, before they moved out of Long Beach. And the way she be talking, girl, Larry got a lot of girlfriends, Bright," Suge warned her.

"Ha!" laughed Bright. "Do you think I really give a fuck?" she said with arrogance and attitude. "I'm, Bright, lil one, and in case you didn't know, I gets what I want, when I want it, and not a second later!" She barked in diva mode. "These other hoe's tryna get like me," she said, feeling herself.

"Hell no! And why should I, when her nigga gone be the one spending monies on me and doing what I want him to do and when I want him to do it," she said, dusting her shoulder off. "His bitches are his problem, not mines! And on the real, it ain't my job or concern to be worrying about his bitch or bitches in the first place!" she stressed. "That's his job, not mines, and when I take him from all them bitches he so-called be dealing with, he ain't gone never cheat on me, cause I know how to keep and please my man," she said confidently.

Suge was confused. She understood why Bright only messed with guys that had a lot of money, but dealing with a guy knowing he had a girlfriend, that was a different story, and she didn't agree with it. She thought girls were supposed to have each other's backs and not play doggishly.

Seeing the confused look upon Suge's face, Treasure jumped in the conversation. "I don't like fucking with dudes that have girlfriends either, Suge. But like Bee said, that's dude's problem to be worrying about his girl, not ours!" Treasure laughed. "It's not like she's yo fucking homegirl!" She said in Bright's defense, recovering from laughter.

"Exactly, Treasure!" Bright agreed, then she turned her attention to Suge. "Youngster, you still have a lot of growing up to do, and a lot to learn. But we got yo back, so you gone be good. All you have to do is watch, listen, and learn," she assured her little homegirl. Then she wrapped her arm around Suge's shoulder and continued to spit more game to her about niggas with money and how to get it.

Inside the Lakewood Mall, Treasure and Suge worked like professionals, boosting their new outfits while Bright kept the staff busy getting her different clothes to try on. Coming out of the dressing room at

Forever 21, Suge slid straight out of the store with a knock-off bag full of stolen items without being noticed. Afterwards, with the little money that the girls did have, they all decided to sit down for lunch at the mall's eatery. Then, once they finished eating most of their meals, they walked around the mall a little while longer, collected a few numbers from various guys, and then headed back to the bus stop to go home.

****

Later on that night after her mother's boyfriend Vince stopped by, Bright was able to break free from home without her mother asking her too many questions. She told her mother that she was going to Treasure's house to watch movies. Knowing how close the girls were, Rosette didn't see a problem with it, and she waved Bright off.

On countless Friday nights while their parents thought they were at each other's houses, they would be posted in different hoods, showing their natural black asses. Dressed to impress from head to toe in their stolen designers clothes, they'd be out drinking, smoking weed, shaking their asses, and talking fly.

Bright being more of an asker and taker than Treasure, she always asked the guys she dealt with for money. She would always tell her girls, "Them niggas don't mind pulling they dicks out to get it, and I don't mind pulling my hand out to get they money." So if money wasn't thrown her way quick enough, she'd put her hand out and ask for it.

Treasure, not being as forward, liked to be offered and given things, and she had a cute way of making guys want to give her without appearing to be a gold-digger.

Though she wasn't getting as much money as Bright got from guys, she was definitely getting hers.

Once Bright made it down to the corner liquor store on Artesia and Long Beach Blvd., she called Treasure and told her to meet her there, where Larry Lane and his boys would be picking them up.

"Here I come, Bee," Treasure said, looking out the window to see if Suge was on her way down the street. "Young game still going with us or not? Cause she ain't here yet," Treasure asked hurriedly, as she made her way to the bathroom to give herself a quick look-over. Seeing that she looked good, Treasure waited on Bright's response.

"She said she was," Bright remembered. "Just grab her up on your way over here, and hurry up. Larry should be here any minute, and I don't wanna hold him up too long," Bright said.

"Here I come," Treasure said, before hanging up the phone.

On her way down the street, Treasure ran into Suge coming up her block.

Once Suge apologized for being late, both girls rushed down the street and to the corner store before Larry Lane got there.

While the girls were talking, Larry Lane pulled up in a Ford minivan full of guys. The girls began to look sideways at the van and mumbled amongst themselves about the type of vehicle he was driving. Bright could have sworn he was riding in a Mustang when he pushed up on her. However, because he had a promising future ahead of himself and he was just a college student, Bright decided she wouldn't diss him too hard. But she did want to know what happened to his car.

"Let's just make the best of the night," Bright quickly said to her girls before Larry was in earshot.

Replacing their mugs with pleasant smiles, they agreed, and then climbed in the van after Larry parked and unlocked the doors for them to get in. Seeing Larry's handsome face put a big smile on Bright's face. He was tall, dark, and handsome, and it was his winning smile that won Bright over the day he had pulled over and asked her for her number.

Larry didn't have much money, nor did he pretend to. He had come from a family full of hard workers, and when he got accepted to UCLA they all came together and purchased him his dream car just as they had done with others in the family before him.

"Where yo ride at, Larry?" Bright asked after getting comfortable in the passenger seat.

"It's in the paint shop. I'm changing my blue paint to yellow," he said, looking into her sexy green eyes.

"Sounds good to me," Bright said, blushing from the way Larry was looking at her.

"And you gone look good riding in it too, wit yo fine ass!" Larry told her, pulling out of the store parking lot.

Bright smiled, "Well good, cause this old van is not with the business!" she teased. Larry laughed, and then they continued to laugh and talk until they reached his house.

Over at Larry's house in Westwood a city right below Beverly Hills, Bright wasn't impressed at all. His house was everything that she expected it not to be. It was an average-sized three bedroom house. His mother and sister Linda had their own bedroom and Larry and his brother Desmond shared a room. The furniture was nothing to brag on, but they did have a nice big screen TV in the living room.

Their house was immaculate, and it was much cleaner than Bright's three bedroom apartment. Their kitchen sink stayed full of dirty dishes, the kitchen and bathroom floors were hardly ever mopped, and dirty clothes were scattered throughout the apartment. To top it off, their apartment smelled like the excessive beer and cigarettes that her mother faithfully drank and smoked after a long day's work. Bright was, to say the least, extremely embarrassed about their filthy Section 8 apartment, and it was the reason she never invited anybody over, including her best friend Treasure. And although Bright could have helped out more around the house, she came up with one excuse after another, when her mother would be on her head about cleaning.

"Ma, why do I always have to do everything around here?" Bright would always complain. However, theonly thing she was worried or concerned about was herself, her gear, how good she looked, and keeping up with (NWM) niggas with money.

Though the kickback at Larry's house was nothing like Bright had expected it to be, or even worth the outfit she was wearing, Larry was doing a good job entertaining and keeping her interested. Larry was different from the other guys that Bright messed with. He was goofy and very playful, but in a way of trying to impress her. And no matter how hard Bright tried to act as if he wasn't funny, she continued to find herself in deep laughter throughout the night.

"You good, you having fun?" Larry asked Bright, and then he dove in and kissed her lips before she could answer him. Bright smiled; she was really starting to feel Larry. She didn't have to try and impress him; instead, he tried to impress her, and he worked hard to keep a smile on her face.

For once, she was just able to be herself. "I'm having a good time, Larry. You having fun chilling with me?" Bright asked as she draped her arms around his shoulders and looked him in the eyes.

"A very good time," Larry replied, looking Bright back in her beautiful green eyes as he continued passionately kissing her.

"Look at these niggas, acting like they all in love and shit," Larry's homeboy Reggie said as he came from the restroom and passed Larry's room.

Removing his lips from Bright's lips, Larry wrapped his arms around her waist and told Reggie to keep it pushing. "Get up outta mines, playa," Larry said, then slammed his bedroom door shut in Reggie's face so that he and Bright could get a little closer.

Low-key, Reggie was jealous because he hadn't got that far with Treasure yet. Because she was accustomed to niggas jocking and chasing her down, and he was used to having girls throw the panties at him, it made their connection all that more difficult. But since his rod was beginning to stiffen at the sight of Treasure's fat ass and her luscious lips, he decided to give her the attention she desired in hopes of getting some by the end of the night.

Back inside the bedroom, Larry had Bright butt naked on top of him while he fucked her brains out.

She was a much easier catch then he had expected her to be. He thought he would at least have to take Bright out on a real date, meet her mother, or at least spend some money on her before she gave him some. But he figured that like most girls, she too couldn't resist Daddy Lane and his sweet game.

He kissed on her belly, rubbed her ass, sucked on her nipples and slid her clothes off of her within five minutes of being alone with her. Excited about the big piece of meat before her, Bright wanted to slob all over his knob and force it down her throat, but Larry told her to get on top.

Climbing off of her knees and on top of his stiff meat, Bright forced every inch of him inside of her tight pussy and then began to choke it, squeezing her pussy muscles real tight on him. "You got some good juicy pussy," Larry moaned as Bright rode him, making her breasts jump up and down in a constant rhythm.

Fiending to have her nipples back inside of his mouth, Larry began to massage Bright's breasts and squeeze her hard nipples in between his fingers.

"I like that big dick, Larry, you got the biggest dick I've ever seen before," Bright moaned honestly, looking him in his eyes. She didn't know a dick could get as big as Larry's.

"You like that dick, Bright?" Larry asked, pumping himself deep inside of her. Her fuck faces drove him wild.

"I'm loving the dick, baby," Bright moaned as the pain turned into pleasure.

"Taste this dick, baby," Larry said, not wanting to cum so soon. He could tell that she had wanted to suck it earlier.

"You gone taste this pussy?" She asked, slowly making her pussy pop and talk to him.

"Sit on my face, sexy, and lets sixty-nine it, baby," Larry said as he helped Bright off his waist.

He wanted to kiss her sweet lips once more before she gave him head and he ate her out. Pulling her face to his, they got lost in a passionate tongue kiss and then Bright introduced her pussy lips to Larry's tender lips and wet mouth.

Larry gently sucked on Bright's pearl tongue and instantly sent chills up her spine. She moaned, throwing her head back. Fulfilling her end of the bargain, Bright leaned down and made her way down to his penis. Facing off with it, she removed the rubber that Larry had on and then hungrily took him down in one deep slurp as she grinded her pussy on his face. Working their hardest to satisfy one another, Larry made Bright cum several times before he told her that he was about to cum. That turned Bright on because she liked to suck the cum right out of a dick. She had never had an orgasm before; she was sprung. Using both of her hands, Bright stroked Larry's penis and then sucked and slobbered all over it until he exploded in her mouth. Larry let out a moan like never before; he had never had his dick sucked so good. After Bright spit the cum on a towel he had on his bed, they laid down to recuperate.

After ten minutes of heavy breathing and silence, Larry rolled over and stared at Bright lying comfortably in his bed, then broke the silence. "The pussy is good, and you got some bomb ass head game baby, is it all mines? You gone be my girl or what?" he asked. Bright sat up on the bed and covered her face as if she was embarrassed, and played the innocent role. It was a role she played with every guy that she slept with on the first night.

"What's wrong?" Larry asked her, removing her golden hair from her face. He thought, *Damn is she acting like this because I asked her to be my girl?*

Bright spoke, "I've never done this before Larry," she cried. "I feel like such a hoe, this behavior is way out of character for me. I can't believe I slept with you on the first night," she lied, letting phony tears fall down her face.

"Look at me," Larry said, turning her face to face him and wiped her tears away. "Sometimes shit happens, it was natural and maybe happened so fast because it was meant to be. So don't be so hard on yaself, baby. It doesn't make me think or look at you any differently than I did before. I'm feeling you and I really like you, Bright, which is why I asked you to be my girl in the first place." He kissed her on the cheek, then gently sat her on his lap and asked her to be his girl again as he planted kisses down her back.

Smiling to herself, Bright thought, *Got ya ass right where I want you, nigga!* "I do like you, Larry, I don't have a boyfriend either, so yes, I would love to be your girl as long as you can promise me that you won't hurt me, lie to me, or cheat on me," she said, looking back at him and deep into his eyes.

"I ain't gone have no reason to cheat with a girl like you on my side," he said. "You the finest girl I ever been with, and I enjoy being around you. I thought you was gone be some ditty, uppity chick that was gone have her nose all up her ass!" he teased.

"Whatever!" Bright spat then hit Larry upside the head with his pillow. "Never that, homeboy, I'm amongst the realest of realest females out here, and don't ever forget it," she said, falling into his arms for a hug. After a hug they took a shower together, put their clothes back on, and then joined the others back in the living room.

When everybody finished eating, Bright helped Larry wash dishes and straighten the kitchen back up. Treasure and Reggie, on the other hand, were in the bathroom getting it in, while Suge and Larry's little homeboy Blake kicked it in the front yard talking and listening to music.

After Larry dropped them back off, Bright confessed to her girls that she was really feeling Larry Lane and how he had asked her to be his girl.

"Don't be turning sucka on us, Bee," Treasure teased.

"Never dat!" Bright said. But for the first time she couldn't wait to get home to call Larry. She was missing him already and wanted to hear his voice.

Part Two

Over the weeks, young Bright had fallen hard for Larry Lane, and every chance she got to ditch and hang out at his house, she did. He loved keeping his head in between her thighs and sexing her in a doggy style position. They had gotten so comfortable with each other that a few times they didn't even use condoms, and Bright didn't care or complain. All she knew was that she wanted to be Larry's girl and have his baby. She just prayed she'd hurry up and get pregnant before he was drafted to the NBA.

During their nutrition break, Treasure, Bright and their full-figured homegirl at school named Nicole linked up and purchased beverages and snacks like they normally did. Nicole was what Treasure and Bright called a know- it-all. Nicole was a senior and an honor roll student, cute, and had the biggest confidence in the world. Nicole was light-skinned with short jet black hair that she wore in various trendy cuts. She had tight brown eyes, a tiny waist, and a big ass with thick thighs that she liked to call "grown lady curves." She was one of those types of girls that went with her conscience on everything that she did and always had to be right. However, because she was a virgin, they hardly ever kicked it with her outside of school because they would always disagree on celibacy. But they liked her because she was a realist, and she spoke what she felt, and didn't keep up drama. Once they grabbed a seat on the pole that they named and certified the G-pole across from the science building and restrooms, they started snacking and yapping.

"What's up Bee, can I get a taste of that?" David, her ex-boyfriend from Lindbergh Middle School, asked her.

"Boy please, you already know if you ain't about dollars, you ain't tasting this," she quoted her own philosophy and laughed.

Knowing that Bright was all about the money, he pulled the three dollars he had out of his pocket. "I got a few dollars to spare," he teased back.

Bright laughed. "Ha, a few too less...keep it pushing," she said, waving him off.

Walking off, David said, "It ain't always about money, Bright, and remember that money can't buy real love." He smiled.

Bright smiled back at him. "But it sure buys me happiness and it make my panties wet," she whispered, pointing at her gold mine. "Now shoo!" she said, waving him off in laughter.

Laughing Treasure waved, "Bye-bye David," adding more injury to the insult.

David nodded his head, "You shouldn't be like that, baby, but it's all good," he said, disappearing into the crowd.

"Y'all ain't right," Nicole teased, watching David walk off.

Since Bright had gone to Lindbergh and Treasure had gone to Hamilton Middle School, they had both dated all of the hottest guys on campus, and had sex with a few of them too. By the time they reached high school, they no longer had interest in cute guys that got lunch money from their parents, and had no other money. So after Treasure's big break-up with her old high school sweetheart named A.J., she agreed with Bright that high school boys were just a waste of time. After recovering from laughter, Nicole came out of left field and said, "Bright, you keep missing school, yo ass gone get held back and then ya fine ass won't look so sexy then."

"And if you don't drop a few pounds, you want be looking so sexy either!" Bright snapped. She didn't like her grades being mentioned because it made her feel stupid.

"Shit, you a lie!" Nicole said. "I could stack twenty more pounds on this one hundred and eighty pound frame and still get it!" she laughed. "I keep telling you looks ain't everything, but beauty and brains will conquer the world!"

"Whatever, fat ass!" Bright spat, dumping her slice of pizza in the trash. She was becoming irritated with know-it-all Nicole.

"I prefer to call myself "Big Sexy," and all the niggas know it too, just ask ya boyfriend," she teased.

Treasure burst into laughter, "You is a fool, Nicole." She was laughing so hard that she felt like she was about to pee on herself.

"I doubt if my dude would ever mess with somebody like you!" Bright shot, becoming defensive. She was so upset that her face was turning red.

"Too late! Been there done that! I had to drop his ass two weeks before he got with you. He said he was looking for a girl that sucked nuts and licked ass. I told him I wasn't that type of girl, but then he found you!"

Nicole said, busting up laughing with Treasure. Nicole had been known for her comedian spirit and she didn't mind throwing daggers when the opportunity was presented either. To her, it was all in good fun, but anything personal she handled in a totally different manner.

"Bitch, fuck you!" Bright snapped, stepping to Nicole's face. She was growing tired of the insults.

Nicole and Treasure both stopped laughing and looked at each other, they were confused. They clowned all the time and it was never a problem; in fact, it was Nicole's personality that had drawn them to her in the first place. There was never any harm intended, so to say the least, she was flabbergasted by Bright's behavior. But now that she was in Nicole's face, she wasn't going to back down to her, and Bright should have known that.

Bee, are you freaking serious?" Treasure asked, holding her back by the arm. She didn't know what had gotten into Bright; they roasted each other all the time.

"Naw, fuck her, fuck that!" Bright yelled as she, snatched her arm from Treasure's hold. Then she started yelling and screaming in Nicole's face, drawing a crowd around them. "You always got some shit to say about somebody, and I'm tired of the shit!"

Looking at Bright pointing her finger and jumping raw in her face, Nicole spoke calmly, but firmly. "You know you my homegirl and all. I never meant anything by it, we all fuck around like that. But if you don't take it down a few notches and get yo hands out my face, Im'a beat yo ass, Bright," she warned.

"Y'all tripping, I'm not gone let y'all fight!" Treasure yelled, stepping in between the two. "Back up, Nicole, let me holler at Bee, 'cause this is some BS right here."

"Yeah, I'll do that, Treasure, and I agree this is some bullshit," Nicole replied, and then she walked away as the bell rang.

"Fuck, the bell rang, we'll talk after class, Bee," Treasure said, wishing she had more time to speak with her.

"Man, fuck this, I'm outta here, I ain't gotta deal with this shit! Nicole got me hot; I'm going to see Larry. You going with me, Treasure?" Bright asked.

"I can't go, I got a test. You should stay too, though, Bee," Treasure implied.

"I probably should, but I'm not. Look, I'll come to your house later, Treasure," Bright said, then she walked off. Treasure watched her friend walk off a few feet, then she ran to class before the tardy bell rang.

Bright walked over to Burger King, hoping thatshe'd see one of the homies to smoke a blunt with her, when Chrome rolled up on her, bumping his music.

"What yo hater ass doin', Bright?" he said, turning his music down with a blunt in his mouth.

"Minding mines, wit' yo lying ass! Why you was lying to my homegirl, Chrome?" Bright asked.

"Look, on everything, I was faded as fuck and I was tripping, but you didn't have to tell, Treasure. You know I loved that girl!" he said, then passed Bright the weed. "Hold on to that, I'ma pull into the parking lot so we can talk. You gotta help me get Treasure back," he said.

Bright hit the weed, then walked into the Burger King parking lot to talk with Chrome. *He came with the weed and was right on time,* Bright thought. When Chrome pulled into the parking lot, Bright hopped in the car with him.

"Damn, didn't nobody tell you to smoke all the weed, Bright!" Chrome said, grabbing the roach of the blunt from her fingertips.

"My bad, I had a fucked up day thanks to this fat bitch that wish she could be me named Nicole! So yeah, I was pulling on that shit," she said.

Chrome laughed. "You crazy! But anyways, how you gone help me get my baby back? I miss that girl like crazy," he admitted. He didn't have no time for Bright and her drama. He was concerned with getting Treasure back.

Bright was used to being the center of attention, and for some reason, she was getting jealous hearing Chrome make such a big deal out of Treasure, instead of him trying to hit on her. Bright got lost in her evil thoughts, hummm. *Treasure does always speak on how good he fucked her and how big he was, and since they're no longer together and she doesn't want anything to do with him anymore, and she has moved on with Reggie, I might as well find out what all the hype was about. I have a few hours to kill before school is out, so why not?*

"Look, Treasure has moved on, she fucking with this other nigga now. You know you wanted to fuck with me first anyways, so let's quit wasting time and let's go fuck," Bright said, then licked her lips.

Chrome was appalled at Bright's behavior and at the lack of loyalty that she had for Treasure. And for her to even say or think he wanted her first was a lie; to him, Treasure was much prettier and sexier than Bright. At that very moment, Chrome wanted to kick Bright's ass right out of his car, and he even wished he had recorded her to let Treasure hear the truth for herself. He knew Treasure would never believe him over Bright; to her Bright's shit didn't stink. But since he hadn't recorded Bright's comments, and Treasure had moved on with another guy, he figured fuck it, this bitch want dick, I'ma give it to her. A devilish smirk came across Chrome's face, then he rubbed Bright thigh.

"I doubt you can handle this dick like Treasure," he said, nodding his head. "I ain't never had no sex as good as hers. And the way she sucked it, paleaseee!" He said to assure that she would be ready for all of the degrading things he had in store for her.

The truth was that Treasure wasn't really into oral sex. She had good pussy, but she wasn't all that great in bed either. Chrome appreciated her inexperienced bedroom skills; to him, it proved that she hadn't been around and he took pride in teaching her. He liked her not only because she was beautiful with a hot body, but more so because she was a smart girl and had a good head on her shoulders. He had been peeping her out his full senior year at Jordan last year, but they were both in reputable relationships on campus. He hated how he had messed things up with her.

"Who you think taught Treasure what she knows?" Bright asked, unzipping his pants. She felt she could show him better than she could tell him. Once Bright stroked his penis until it got rock hard, Chrome took the pleasure in shutting her up, by pushing her head down and forcing his penis deep down in her throat.

****

After fourth period, Treasure felt bad for leaving her girl Bright hanging. And since she had completed her test, she gathered her things to leave school for the day to find Bright and be there for her. She had never seen Bright get that angry over Nicole's jokes in the past, so she wanted to find out what was really going on with her. After sneaking out of the school gates, Treasure headed to Burger King to see if she could find Bright. She knew that was always her first stop after leaving school.

Standing at the light to cross the street, Treasure noticed that her ex-boyfriend Chrome was parked in the parking lot, so she decided that if she didn't find Bright at Burger King; she'd ask him to drop her off at Larry's house, since that's where Bright said she was going.

But before she could get across the street, Chrome had pulled out of the lot and headed in the opposite direction. Across the street Treasure checked inside of Burger King for Bright, and then all over the lot for her...she was nowhere in sight. Getting ready to exit the parking lot, Treasure was approached by district truancy officers, and tried to talk herself out of being taken to off-campus suspension for the remainder of the school day. Not going for her story, they told her to get in the backseat, hauled her off to OCS, (off campus suspension) and then called her mother to come pick her up.

"Fuck, I should have stayed at school," Treasure huffed standing in the OCS detention.

****

Bright had never had a guy cum all over her face and piss on her before, but since Chrome was adamant about how good Treasure did this, and how good Treasure did that, her competitive side just had to prove that she could do it better. After hours of hardcore sex, Bright was happy that it was all over with. She was sore and was in need of a good bath, but a shower would do until she got home. Climbing out of the bed, Bright yelled for Chrome to give her a wash cloth and a dry-off towel.

"We ain't got time for all that, I got somewhere to be in the next ten minutes," he said, talking with his back turned to her.

After everything they had just done, Bright gave him

a look of disbelief. "You trippin', Chrome, I have to take a shower before we leave here! Now where are your towels at?" she asked.

"Ain't no shower popping off today, Bee. Get ya shit on so I can take you home," he said, facing her with a look of disgust on his face. Though he was a dude, to him this type of behavior was frowned upon. Bright was not only a snake, but a trick ass bitch, and he was going to treat her as such. He didn't have any love for her.

"What the fuck is ya problem, Chrome?" Bright snapped, giving him attitude back.

She didn't understand him, but she planned on having a shower before she left his house, point blank period. Not giving him a chance to answer her question, she looked for the towels herself. Once she found the towels in the hallway closet, she went to the bathroom, turned the shower water on, and climbed inside.

Pissed off that he heard the shower water running, Chrome walked inside the bathroom, pulled the shower curtain back, and then went off. To him, not only was Bright a trick, but she was also a disrespectful trick.

"Bitch, I told yo tramp ass wasn't no showers popping off up in here today! Get the fuck up outta there!" he yelled, and then he threw her out of the shower and onto the bathroom floor.

Tasting the blood from her lip, Bright went off and tried to fight Chrome as if she was a man. But her punches and kicks were nothing up against his one hundred eighty-five pound, six foot three inch muscular build. When she kicked him in the groin area, he backhanded her, sending her flying through the hallway and onto the living room floor without wings. At the moment, Bright was afraid of Chrome and what he would do to her; she felt her life was at stake. Having the opportunity to run to his room to lock herself inside, Bright got up off the floor and ran for her dear life.

"Bitch, you gone make me hurt you!" Chrome yelled, chasing after Bright. He was within a few inches of grabbing Bright by her hair when she slid inside of his room and locked the door. Using her body as a weight to keep him from entering the room, Bright began to yell and scream for help. Tears streamed from her face, and her body shook nervously and uncontrollably. She didn't know what had gotten into him or what she should do next. Chrome was still yelling and he had kicked the door so hard that Bright had fallen off the door and onto the floor. He had turned into a mad man! Seeing the cordless phone on the nightstand, Bright quickly crawled on her knees, grabbed the phone, and then dialed 911.

"911, what's your emergency?" A man's voice echoed through the phone.

"Helppppppppppp, I've been raped!!!" Bright yelled and sobbed through the phone. "And he's gonna kill me! Can you please send somebody over here?" she cried. Then the line went dead. Chrome had disconnected the phone cord in the living room, and he planned on beating Bright's ass.

"Bitch, you gone lie and say I raped you? You's a lying ass bitch!" Chrome yelled, charging down the hallway and then kicking the door down and off the hinges. Frightened, Bright crawled into the corner and folded into fetal position. She knew Chrome was gonna beat her; she just prayed that help would come quickly. "You little lying bitch!" he yelled as he kicked and stomped at her defenseless body. Bright begged and pleaded for him to stop.

"Please stop, Chrome, please!!!" she cried.

Out of control, Chrome yelled, "I ain't gone stop until you fucking die, you stupid bitch! I hate hoes like you!" he said, then he took his thick leather belt off and began to whoop her. Not able to endure the painful slashes and wrath from the belt, Bright suddenly regained enough strength to kick, and she swung at Chrome as hard and as fast as she could while she begged and pleaded for him to stop. Bright was now purple and blue, and she could feel her skin splitting apart with each lash and whip of his leather belt.

"STOP, YOU CRAZY MUTHAFUCKA!!!!" Bright screamed. She was kicking to save her life.

"If I'ma go to jail, it's gone be for beating ya muthafucking ass, you lying, trifling whore!" Chrome yelled psychotically. He hadn't planned on beating Bright or any other woman again in his life. He had been going to anger management and domestic violence classes regularly for the past six months, and he tried his best to avoid trifling females like Bright. But since he had priors and Bright was gonna throw rape on top of that, he knew he would be going down for a very long time. And he was gonna see to it that his prison term would be well worth the sentence. After five more minutes of torment, the police kicked in Chrome's front door, beat him, arrested him, and then sent an unconscious Bright to the emergency room. She was in bad shape.

The next day, Bright's hospital room stayed swamped with doctors, nurses, law enforcement, and both her family and friends. Pictures were taken of her beat-up and bruised body and many different tests were run on her. Blood and urine samples were taken, as well as both oral and genital swabbing for her rape kit.

None of this would be happening if Chrome would've just let me take a shower and then drove me home, like he was supposed to do. But instead, he beat my ass and I had to call the police on him and file not only assault, but rape charges on him too, Bright thought. She would have been honest and just pressed assault charges on him, but what excuse would she have to give to her best friend, Treasure, about being at his house in the first place? Bright had never lied or cried rape on anybody before, but after the way Chrome did her, she had no sympathy for him, and she felt he was going to get what he deserved. Bright was inside her hospital room talking to Treasure when her nurse walked through the door with detective Mary Shutter.

"Bright, Detective Mary Shutter is back to take your report," Nurse Adkins said. Nurse Adkins was a beautiful, short, black and Mexican nurse that had consoled her and made sure that Bright's stay was comfortable. She had even given her a good shower after she got the samples they needed for her rape kit, and she had sat and prayed with Bright when she was afraid to be in the room alone. When Bright didn't respond, Nurse Adkins asked her if she was going to need more time.

"I'm fine, Nurse Adkins. I told the nice detective lady yesterday that I would be ready to talk today, and now I'm just ready to get it out and over with," Bright said, fighting hard to hold back her tears. She had never felt so violated in her entire life.

"Good, honey," Nurse Adkins said. "Now if you need me, I'm just a buzz away, my dear. I'll be right across the hall," she said, giving Bright a warm andsincere smile.

"Thanks, Nurse Adkins, my best friend Treasure is here now, so I'll be fine," Bright said, returning a warm smile. Nurse Adkins winked at Bright, and then she stepped out of the room and closed the door behind herself to give them privacy. Bright painted this award-winning rape picture of Chrome, whom she lied about by saying he had lured her inside of his house, forced himself on her, and made her have both anal and oral sex with him. She also told the detective how he tried beating her to death. The detective stood to leave the room and assured Bright that she would see to it that Chrome got the maximum amount of time for what he had done to her.

Later, after Treasure left the hospital, Bright's mother Rosette made it back to the hospital in time to help Nurse Adkins give her daughter a shower. Gale told Rosette that she would look after the kids for the night so she decided to stay the remainder of the night with Bright in the hospital. Tired after almost two days of no sleep, Rosette fell asleep shortly after Bright's shower. But for some reason, sleep didn't come that easily for Bright, so she stayed up all night, watching TV and talking on the phone with Larry. At first she was too embarrassed to say anything, but she later decided to tell him.

He was devastated, and he told Bright that he would never let anything ever happen to her like that again. Then, when the sun rose, she was finally able to close her eyes and go to sleep.

Part Three

Three months into their relationship, Bright and Larry were getting serious. He'd take Bright to the movies, dinner, amusement parks, skating, bowling, the beach, or any other social events they could go to together. And when their money was right, they would spend an entire day in a motel room, playing house and making love to each other. Not to mention, Bright never missed any of Larry's basketball games; she was his biggest fan in the crowd, rooting him on and yelling his name. Rosette adored Larry Lane too, and not only because she saw big money in his future, but because Larry was clean-cut, well mannered, and respected her and her daughter Bright to the fullest. Besides that, any guy that could help Bright get her grades up in school was alright with her. He'd help Bright with her homework, and he would always explain the importance of having a good education to her. In their world there was no "I" in "We." They were very much in love, and would do anything for each other.

On the last day of school for summer break, Bright, Treasure and Suge mobbed up in Wal-Mart to steal Bright a pregnancy test. Her period was late, and she was not only hoping, but praying that she was pregnant. As soon as Bright made it home from school, she rushed to the restroom, peed on the stick, and then took a quick shower. Once Bright rinsed off, she grabbed her bath towel to dry off then climbed out of the shower to read her pregnancy results. *"Please let me be pregnant,"* Bright said to herself before picking up the pregnancy test.

"Bright, the telephone, its Treasure!" her little sister Deja said, knocking and yelling through the bathroom door.

"Fuck! Give me a minute, Deja!" Bright yelled back pissed off that her pregnancy test read negative. Swinging the door open, Bright snatched the phone from her sister's hand then walked inside her bedroom and slammed the door behind her. "What's up, Treasure?" Bright said with an attitude.

"Damn, bitch, what done crawled up yo ass?" Treasure snapped back.

"Apparently not a baby," Bright said, almost becoming emotional. "And I'm pissed off!"

"Don't even trip, Bee, you still young, and when it's time, it will happen...trust me!" Treasure said.

Before Bright could respond, her mother had opened her bedroom door and told her not to be slamming any doors in her house. "And what's your problem anyhow, Queen Bee?" her mother asked, seeing Bright on the verge of tears.

"It's nothing, Mom; I'll talk to you once I get dressed, and after I finish talking to Treasure."

Rosette threw her hand on her hip. "I have a better idea: we'll talk after I use the little ladies room. I have company on their way over, and a dirty ass kitchen to clean, so tell Treasure goodbye," she said, and then she closed the door.

Forgetting that she had left the pregnancy test in the bathroom, Bright quickly told Treasure that she'd call her back, then ran out of her room, passed her mother in the hallway, then locked herself in the bathroom to discard the pregnancy test.

Rosette was furious. "What the hell is your problem, Bright? You almost knocked me over like you either on drugs or got a serious mental problem!" Her mother yelled. "What the hell is going on with you?" Rosette demanded to know.

Bright opened the bathroom door after she threw the pregnancy test and box under the bathroom sink behind the cleaning supplies and then flushed the toilet. She knew it would be safe there for the time being. "I'm sorry Ma, I had to pee," Bright lied, stepping out of the bathroom.

"You've been acting real strange lately, Bright, and we're gonna get down to the bottom of it too!" her mother said, closing the bathroom door behind herself fussing.

Inside her room, Bright dried off then threw on a pair of low rise shorts, a white tank top, and a pair of Old Navy flip flops, and then she threw her hair in a neat ponytail. Happy that her mother's drinking buddies and card partners had arrived, and that she wouldn't have to explain herself to her mom, Bright picked up the phone and dialed Treasure back.

"You alright now?" Treasure asked once Bright called her back.

"Yeah I'm good, I'm over it, you know I don't let anything keep me down for long," Bright said, looking at herself in her bedroom mirror. From as far back as when she was a little girl, Bright was always good at erasing or blocking things from her head that made her feel down and out.

Her mother would always say, "Girl, you gone be a cold little heartbreaker when you grow up." But if only she knew the things that Bright had to endure to get that type of mind set...

"So it's Friday, we ain't got no jobs," Treasure teased,

impersonating her best Chris Tucker voice from the movie *Friday.* "So what's up? And what we getting into tonight?" Treasure asked.

"I'm rolling with Larry. His mother is out of town so we have the house to ourselves," Bright replied. "He wanna fuck me, feed me and let me slob on his knob," Bright teased.

"Bitch, you just been kicking me and Suge to the curb!" Treasure said, sucking her teeth. Though she respected the fact that Bright had a man, it seemed like they hardly ever kicked it anymore unless they were at school. And they were supposed to be tighter than that. "I can't believe Ms.Sprung.com is playin her homegirls for some nigga. They come and go, remember?"

"Larry ain't just some nigga, Treasure, and you know ever since that shit happened with Chrome, he's been real protective of me. So please don't get it twisted, I'm not never putting a dude before my girls; I just have a real boyfriend now," she said.

"Yeah, I hear you, Bee, but that thing with Chrome happened months ago, and his punk ass is in jail! Speaking of that, fool he wrote me a letter, but I ripped that shit up and threw it in the garbage can. I wants no parts of his low down dirty, grimy ass!" Treasure said, boiling inside. She hated him for what he did to her girl and how he had portrayed her.

Bright held her chest and took a deep breath. She was relieved that Treasure didn't open the letter. She didn't want Treasure second-guessing or questioning her side of the story or friendship. She already had to come up with a good excuse as to why Treasure didn't see her in the car with Chrome when he pulled out of the Burger King parking lot. She told her she was probably picking up her purse when it had fallen on the floor of Chrome's car. "I hate that nigga!" Bright said thinking of the ass whooping he had given her.

"Me too!" Treasure said, disgusted at the mention of his name. "But anyways, peek game, Ice been coming around here looking for you," Treasure said, changing subjects. "He rolling a tight ass Escalade on some twenty sixes too, so don't fuck up and luck out on ya money, honey. You already got Larry sewed up, so you might as well shake him for the night and come handle yo business, and see what Ice talking about. You know Larry ain't balling like that, boo," Treasure said in one breath.

Disregarding Treasure's last comment about Larry being broke Bright tried to recall the unfamiliar name. "Ice?" Bright asked, confused. The name didn't ring a bell.

"Terrence, Bee!" Treasure said, refreshing her friend's memory by giving her Ice's government name.

"Oh, that nigga...eastie eastside Ice!" Bright said, instantly seeing dollar signs. Terrence was not only a reputable Crip from the eastside of Long Beach, but he was also fine, a baller, and had a collection of clean-ass low riders that Bright loved.

"Yeah the one and only Ice," Treasure laughed. "What other Ice do you know?" Treasure asked.

"Girl please, you know I don't be calling these niggas by they nicknames. I call them by the names they mamas gave 'em," Bright said with her hand on her hip. Other than her looks, being privileged to call guys by their government names made Bright feel more superior than other females.

"Bright, Bright, Bright," Treasure laughed, nodding her head. She always had to do things to make herself stand out more, or be different from other females.

Bright stood there and weighed her options. Damn she thought to herself, *Ice is a big nigga on the block, he fine as fuck too and he got that real dough! But on the other hand, homie is known as a big time playa, and he got too many bitches! But fuck that, his money runs as long as the Hudson River and I can definitely use some of that,* she thought.

"So what you gone do, Bee?" Treasure asked impatiently.

"Bitch, I'm 'bout to come get my money!" Bright laughed. "I'm just thinking on how he used to have ole girl, Netta, shining back in the days before she started smoking that dope!"

"And she was just one of his females." Treasure added, hyping Bright up. "It's yo time to shine, girl!"

Pumped up, Bright said, "I'm main chick status too, I know I can come up." She was thinking of a way to break her date with Larry.

"Well come on, Bee," Treasure said excitingly. "He said he was gone be back in an hour, and that was about forty five minutes ago," she said.

"A'ight, good looking, Treasure, I'm on my way!" Bright said, ending the call.

Then she dialed Larry up.

"Hey baby," Bright said after Larry answered the phone.

"Hey boo-boo, I'm on my way to pick you up in about five minutes," he said, assuming that was the reason for her call.

"That's why I called you, baby, I can't go. My auntie on my father's side is in the hospital, and my dad is coming to pick me up. They say it's not looking good either," Bright said losing her train of thought and the original story that she planned on telling him. It was odd, but for some reason it was hard for her to lie to Larry.

"Your dad is picking you up?" Larry asked in a surprised but confused tone.

"Yeah, my dad, baby," Bright answered.

"Bright, I thought you told me that your dad passed away?" Larry said.

Bright began to stutter, "I meant to say my godfather, baby, my bad. My biological father has been gone for a long time, and for years I've called my godfather my dad." She laughed, hoping he believed her. The truth was that Bright didn't even have a godfather.

Larry laughed, "You had me worried for a minute there, boo-boo, I thought you were lying to me. I hope your auntie gets better though, call me and keep me updated on her status. I'll probably be here for a little while," Larry said. He was really looking forward to spending the evening with Bright. He had already cooked dinner for them, and later he planned on breaking her off, then cuddling up to watch movies.

"I will, love," Bright said, blowing kisses through the phone, and then she hung up.

****

After Bright threw on some more appropriate-looking clothing, she grabbed her purse, kissed her mother on the cheek, and told her that she would be back in a few hours.

"Where you going?" her mother asked.

"To hang out with Treasure and Suge, we gone have us our own girls night," she laughed.

"Okay, but be back by midnight, and I haven't forgot about our little talk either. We'll talk about it over breakfast!" She said, balancing a cigarette in between her lips while she dealt a deck of cards.

"Okay ma, see ya later!" Bright said, exiting their apartment. When she got outside, she thought, *Please God don't let Larry call back while I'm out, PLEASE! Speaking of, Terrence gone have to buy me a cell phone and quick!* Catching a ride from one of her many admirers from her neighborhood named Rat, Bright asked him to drop her off at Treasure's house since she wasn't in the mood to walk.

Rat didn't mind at all. He was actually honored to drive her over to her friend's house. Taking the longer route and the opportunity to parade Bright around the neighborhood like she was his girl, Rat took his sweet time and stopped and hollered at every hustler and player he saw in the neighborhood. Bright began to grow impatient.

"Rat, I'm in a rush right now!" Bright snapped, interrupting his conversation. "My dude is on his way to Treasure's house to pick me up. You the homie and all, but if he catch us in the car together, he gone be hot, and we might have some problems...problems that I'm tryna avoid. So can you please drop me off right quick?" She said loud enough for everybody to hear. She didn't want anybody getting the impression or misunderstanding that they were messing around.

Looking dumbfounded, Rat put his foot on the gas pedal, then hit the corner to drop Bright off. When he pulled up in front of Treasure's house, he tried to get Bright's digits before she got out of his car. Ignoring him as if she didn't even hear him, Bright kept it pushing to Treasure's front door without saying thanks or even good bye. *He has no money or fame and for those reasons alone, he would get no love from me,* Bright thought as she knocked on Treasure's door.

He was one of the few nobodies whose name she never even bothered to ask.

"Bitch!" Rat yelled out to her as he drove off the street. Bright was so caught up in her own thoughts that she didn't even hear him.

"What you doin' rolling with that broke fool Rat, for, Bee?" Treasure asked, stepping out of the house and onto the porch.

"Girl, I just asked his raggedy ass to drop me off over here 'cause I didn't feel like walking, but girl, tell me why I almost had to cuss his ass out?" Bright replied with her hands on her hips.

"He was tryna get his in, huh?" Treasure laughed, and then she took a seat on the porch steps.

"Girl, you know he was! I only asked him for a ride because I didn't feel like walking. But you should of seen how happy he was when I asked him for a ride!" Bright laughed.

"I'm already knowing, Treasure said.

Right when Bright was preparing to take a seat next to Treasure on the steps, Terrence rolled up, bossing, bumping Dr. Dre. "Damn, is that that fine-ass female they call Bright right there?" He asked, sticking his head out of his truck window, looking Bright up and down. Though Long Beach was known as the city of Crips, the tension between the east and north side Crips stayed on the rise. But because Terrence had respected family from the Norf and he was about getting money, they didn't press him so hard when passing through.

"Knock it off, Ice," Treasure laughed, calling him by his street name. Then she directed her attention to Bright. "You better hurry and leave before my mama or grand-mother come out here being nosy and start asking you a gang of questions," Treasure warned.

"I know, huh?" Bright said, quickly walking toward the fenced gate. "I'll probably stop back by after I finish up with Terrence, so be looking out for me, and answer the phone!" Bright said, walking out of the gate.

"I might hook up with, Suge and leave. It's Friday night, I'm not tryna be cooped all up in the house," Treasure replied, standing on the porch.

"I'll call you in thirty minutes to see what's up!"

Bright said as she climbed inside of Terrence's Cadillac Escalade like she belonged.

"Hey, Terrence," Bright said once she was secured in the passenger seat.

Terrence laughed. "So me and you that tight now, that you can just call a nigga by his government name?" he asked, turning his music down.

"I guess we are, 'cause I don't do the street name, nickname thing," Bright said with her nose in the air.

Terrence smirked, then nodded his head. "Well, since we ain't tight like that, but you fine as fuck, I'll give you a pass to call me by my government name when we're alone. But in public it's, Ice, a'ight?"

"Bet," Bright said, then reclined her seat.

Looking at Bright all laid back and comfortable in the passenger seat, Terrence smiled. "Yeah, go on and get all comfortable, beautiful," he said, then turned his music back up, driving off Treasure's street.

Terrence reminded Bright of the rapper Jim Jones, but he possessed the swag of the rapper Snoop Dogg. He had a caramel complexion, with nice wavy hair that was kept neatly braided or laid in a slick ponytail.

After a few moment of silence, Terrence spoke. "So what is it that you would like to get into tonight anyways, Miss Sexy ass, beautiful Bright?" Terrence asked, putting emphasis on the word "sexy".

"I'm rolling with you, so you tell me," Bright replied in a soft, flirty tone.

Terrence rubbed his hands together, smiled, looked Bright up and down, and then undressed her with his eyes "Shit, don't leave it up to me, I'm a nasty nigga," he replied, softly rubbing the side of Bright's face with the back of his index finger.

Bright laughed. "I guess that makes us a perfect match then," she smiled, sensuously biting on her bottom lip. Months ago while on the bus, Bright had found an ID card of a twenty-two year old lady that looked almost identical to her and decided to keep it. And since she had it in her possession, she suggested going out for dinner and drinks.

"Cool, I been making moves all day, and I ain't ate either, so grabbing a bite to eat sounds good," Terrence replied.

"Let me grab this cheese from my dude on the eastside, then we off on our merry-ass way," Terrence said.

Ten minutes later, they ended up on the eastside of Long Beach off of Pacific Coast Highway and Pine Street for Terrence to collect his paper. The east side of Long Beach wasn't Bright's favorite place in the world to be, especially after she had gotten jumped in the ninth grade by a group of females from Long Beach's Insane Crip gang over a dude that she used to kick it with named Issac. So from then on, whenever Bright was on the eastside, she'd keep a blade and pepper spray in her possession for her protection. But now, since she was riding with eastie Ice, she had no fear.

After collecting his paper and knowing he couldn't creep in Long Beach the way he wanted to, Terrence hit the 91 freeway east and headed to Buena Park, and then asked Bright what she was in the mood to eat. "They have a lot of different restaurants on Beach Blvd., what you in the mood to eat?"

"Let's do Claim Jumpers," Bright said, she heard they had good food. Then she asked him if she could use his phone. She wanted to call Treasure to find out her plans for the night. After getting Treasure on the phone, she told Bright that she and Suge were going to a party that Nicole had invited them to, and then gave her the address just in case she wanted to meet up with them later.

Walking in the parking lot to the restaurant, Terrence asked Bright how old she was. "I'm seventeen, but according to the fake ID I have, I'm twenty-two," Bright said, not being completely honest. She was only sixteen years old. "And how old are you?" Bright asked, hoping that age wouldn't be a big problem for him.

"I'm twenty-six," he quickly answered. "But when will you turn eighteen?" he asked curiously. It didn't sit well with him that Bright was underage.

"I'll be eighteen in three and a half months," she lied.

"A'ight cool, I guess I can creep with you for a few months," he smiled.

He figured she was practically already eighteen and three and a half months was no time. "But I must warn you, though," he paused. "You can't get any of this dick until then, and not a second before...been told this shit is addictive!" he teased.

However, he already had plans on breaking her off right after dinner.

"Who said I give my treats out that soon, anyways?" Bright said like she was hard to get.

"Hold on," Terrence said stopping in his tracks. "You just said you were nasty like me, though."

Bright laughed, "I am, but that didn't mean you were gonna find out anytime soon."

"Let's go get our grub on," Terrence said recovering, from laughter.

Inside, after busting out her ID, Bright had the waiter bringing her drinks back to back. She had quickly taken down three Top Shelf Margaritas and two shots of Patron while they waited on their food. By the time dinner was served, it was fair to say that Bright was fucked up.

"You not gone eat ya food?" Terrence asked, seeing that she was feeling herself.

A wicked smile appeared across Bright's face. "I'm saving my appetite to eat you," she said, licking her lips and squinting her eyes at him.

Terrence cleared his throat, then threw his arm in the air, "Check please!" he said, signaling their waiter over. After he paid for their food and drinks and tipped the waiter, they made their way to his truck.

Inside the truck, Bright didn't waste any time getting the party started. She got on her knees, unbuckled Terrence's pants, pulled his penis out, and then told him to drive. Terrence didn't hesitate; he started his truck up and pulled out of the parking lot. He loved getting head on the road. Bumping Aaliyah, Terrence moaned softly as he gently guided Bright's head up and down the shaft of his hard penis. In the bedroom, Bright was more of a giver then a taker, and enjoyed performing oral sex more than anything.

"This shit is the fucking best, baby! Don't stop though," he moaned, rubbing his hand through her hair.

Aiming to tease, Bright said, "That was just a little sample." Then she got off of her knees and back into the passenger seat.

"We almost there, baby," Terrence said in a sexy and composed tone, then he increased his speed to the motel.

Pulling up in the parking lot of the Motel 6 in Long Beach off of Downey Ave. and Artesia Blvd., Terrence parked his truck then went inside to pay for a room while Bright waited inside his truck taking puffs off of the Granddaddy Kush that he had provided. A few minutes later, Terrence was tapping on the passenger window, signaling for her to get out. After she dumped the remains of the blunt in the ashtray she climbed out of the truck and followed him up a flight of stairs to their room.

"You need somethin' from the store?" He asked Bright once they were inside the room. He wanted to make sure Bright was as comfortable as possible before he fucked the shit out of her.

"I'm good," Bright said. "Just feeling nasty and all X-rated." She bit down on her bottom lip and moaned as she gave him her sexy face. "You wanna help me out of my clothes?" Bright asked Terrence, standing and looking at him over her right shoulder. She was ready to perform and satisfy.

"Give a nigga a strip tease or somethin'," he said, licking his lips. "Take 'em off...slowly." He paused, then reached in his pocket and retrieved a bundle of money. "I'm tipping," he smiled.

Turning to face him, Bright put a sexy smile on her face. "Take it off slow like this?" Bright demonstrated, slowly removing her top off.

"Yeah, like that, Sexy Bright," Terrence said as he began to throw twenty dollar bills in her direction. As Bright continued to inch each piece of her clothing off like she was a seasoned dancer, Terrence couldn't take his eyes off of her. He was hypnotized by her deep beauty, flawless body and her ability to fuck a man without touching him. Once she got down to having nothing but her G-string on, she stood directly in front of Terrence, bent over, then slowly removed her G-string as he squeezed and slapped on her ass.

"Spank me, Ice," she said, stroking his ego, knowing he liked the way she moaned his street name. Making her ass giggle, Bright was infamous for her dance skills; it was what taught her how to perform and please a man. Her peers would always tell her that she would make a killing in the strip game, but Bright was more interested in having a baller take care of her, and in return she'd take care of him. Up until having sex with Larry, Bright didn't really understand what sex was supposed to feel like for a woman, nor did she take the time to try and learn it. In her opinion, sex was overrated and was primarily for the pleasure of a man. But since she was great at it and loved to perform and please, she considered it her most precious weapon to gain anything from the male species.

Not able to take anymore, and wanting desperately to get inside of Bright, Terrence begin to roll a condom on his swollen penis. Seeing that, Bright stopped him from putting the condom on, and then fell on her knees to taste it again.

"No baby, I wanna suck it some more," she begged. Even more than performing sex, Bright enjoyed giving oral sex more than anything. It was something about sucking on a fat piece of meat that turned her on and made her moist.

"Get that dick, Sexy Bright," Terrence moaned, letting his head fall back from the wrath of her warm, juicy mouth. He loved the way her soft lips sucked and nibbled on the head of his penis.

As Bright worked overtime sucking and slurping on Terrence penis, then softly biting on the head of it, Terrence began to moan heavily.

"Oh shit, suck that dick, girl, I'm about to bust," he moaned, holding the back of Bright's head as she deep throated him.

"Give me that nut," Bright managed to say after coming up for air. She sucked and bit on the head of his penis a few more times, then said, "Give it to me baby." Terrence had never had his dick sucked so good before, or by a girl as young as Bright. She sucked his dick like an art that she had a deep passion for, and the noises she made were toe-curling. And no matter how hard he tried prolonging the pleasure and from erupting in her mouth, he couldn't help it. It shot out like a space shuttle going to another planet.

"OHHHHHHH, SHIT!" Terrence moaned, holding Bright's head as he released in her mouth. "Oh shit that was the fucking best," he said, recovering from his orgasm while Bright sucked him dry. "Aw shit!" he continued to moan.

After Bright spit his semen out in a wash cloth, she smiled, knowing she had him right where she wanted him. Then she climbed on top of him, rested her head on his chest and whispered, "I love sucking on yo dick, Terrence, and if I was your girl, I would suck it all the time, day or night."

Terrence rubbed through Bright's hair breathing heavily; she had sucked the breath straight out of him. "You my girl then," he said, then kissed Bright on her forehead before falling asleep. An hour later Terrence woke up to a sniffling Bright crying in his arms. "What's wrong with you, baby?" Terrence asked, lifting up to see her face.

Playing the innocent girl role, Bright cried, "I don't know what got into me, but I can't believe I gave you head on our first date. I feel like such a hoe and I don't normally get down like that," she said as she began to sob even harder. "It must have been the alcohol." she said in between cries.

Terrence grabbed her face. "Sometimes shit happens, baby, and it don't make you no hoe either." Then he teased, "You damn near got a nigga all in love and shit, with all that good head you just gave me. So as far as I'm concerned, you my baby, and I'm yo daddy." He wiped her eyes and then kissed her on the nose. "You one sexy ass bitch," he said, not able to get enough of her beauty.

Bright moaned, then Terrence spread her legs apart, strapped it up, and slowly inched his penis as deep inside of Bright's wet pussy as he could until he exploded again. Then before leaving the room, he fucked her doggy style like there was no tomorrow as he pulled through her long golden hair. After that he took her home before his wife started blowing him up.

Summertime

Part Four

"Bitch, so you telling me that ya boy, Ice, got a little dick?" Treasure asked Bright the next morning inside of her bedroom.

"Yes, it's on the itty-bitty side, he ain't got nothing on Larry," she said, nodding her head. "But he did break the girl off, and I know I'll be getting a lot more of that" she laughed.

"I bet you will be too," Treasure teased. "Big pockets for little things!" Then they both fell into laughter.

****

Bright's mind was consumed with Larry Lane and Terrence's money. And even though she felt bad about cheating on Larry, she knew that the money would make up and compensate for the guilt. After helping her mother around the house, Bright hooked up with Larry and played the PlayStation at his house, and later on, she treated him to dinner and a movie. But before he dropped her back off at home, they sat in the back seat of his Mustang at Huntington Park, wrapped up in each other's arms, kissing and telling each other how much they loved each other.

Larry was the only guy Bright was ever able to be herself around. He made her laugh, smile and feel happy inside. She didn't have to pretend in bed and swallow his nut to turn him on. He actually catered to her, and made love to her. Being with Larry made Bright feel mushy; it was sincere, and it felt very real. But if Bright hadn't known from the gate that Larry was a future basketball star, she would have never given him the time or the day, and would have probably missed out on real love. Her infatuation with money and the material things that it bought her kept Bright cheating and creeping, and she didn't plan on stopping until Larry was on top.

Pulling up in front of her apartment building, Larry had to pry Bright off of him. He took his lips from hers and smiled. "It's getting late, baby, and we don't want Moms to catch us out here like this."

"I hate leaving your side, Larry Lane." She kissed his lips once more, then climbed out of his car.

"I keep telling you, I'ma marry you and make you my wife!" he winked, then pulled off of her street.

Feeling like it was all a big dream, Bright skipped into the apartment playing house in her head and fell asleep with a big smile on her face.

****

Here it was almost the middle of summer, and Bright was still balancing both her money man, Terrence, and her lover boy, Larry Lane, without getting caught. Stretching, then sitting up in her bed rubbing the sleep from her eyes, Bright planned on going out to buy and surprise Larry with a fresh pair of Jordan's, like she did whenever guilt would consume her for cheating on him. She would constantly reason with herself that Terrence was only temporary until Larry caught his big break, but until then she was gonna continue to milk him dry.

"Wake it up, Queen Bee, it's time to clean house," her mother yelled through the apartment. Rosette gave her daughter the nickname Queen Bee because she acted as if she were royalty and had what people called a diva attitude.

Bright thought to herself, *When did they ever have to clean? Their houses stayed nasty.* "Maaaa!" Bright yelled as she walked to the living room to see what was going on.

"Don't 'Ma' me," Rosette snapped back. "It's time to clean house!" she said kicking through a pile of dirty clothes on the living room floor.

Bright sucked her teeth, "Ma, when does anybody ever clean up around here?" she asked.

"Well if your high yellow ass wants somewhere to lay yo head, I guess we'll all be cleaning up this pig's sty today!" she said with her hands on her hips. "Section eight inspectors are coming out Tuesday morning."

"Mama, but it's Sunday though," Bright whined.

"Why are we cleaning so early?" She knew that since they were up for inspection that there was no escaping housework, but she was confused as to why they had to clean up two days in advance.

"Yes I know its Sunday, smart ass!" her mother said, giving her a dumb facial expression. "But it's gonna at least take us two good days to get this place in order!" Rosette paused to catch her breath. "Look around here Queen Bee, this place is filthy," she said seriously.

"Man, I have to do everything around here," Bright said, marching back to her bedroom for a change of clothes. "Ma, are the rest of your kids going to be participating in the family festivities today?" she yelled, changing clothes in her bedroom.

"Until I can find they lazy, trifling asses, I guess it's just me and you. Now come on, and let's get to it! Oh, and by the way, your Highness, Larry called for you while I was cleaning the bathroom," she said sarcastically. "So hurry up and call him back right quick so we can clean up this house up!"

"Larry?" Bright asked, peeping her head out her bedroom.

"Naw, Larry!" her mother said giving her another dumb facial expression, and then threw her hands in the air. "What you be smoking on, Bright?" Her mother asked her, then quickly nodded her head. "Never mind, don't even answer that. Just hurry up and make your phone call, so you can get in here to help," she said.

Bright made her way to the cordless phone in her room. "I hope ya lazy kids find their way back home by the time I get off the phone, Ma. It's already unfair enough that I gotta play mom when you're gone to work and then have to turn around and do they house work too," Bright fussed.

"Well tough cookie, big sister! 'Cause guess what? I go to work to take care of you too, and on top of that I give you more than I give the others, and I make it possible for you to have your own bedroom when I should be the one with my own room. I shouldn't have to be sharing a room with my two youngest daughters. But I do that to compensate you for all the extra shit that you have to do around here! So quit complaining before I start complaining on how high ya ass be walking up in here, and the different hours of the night you be walking up in here!" Rosette paused, seeing that she had Bright's full attention. "Now I like Larry a lot, don't get me wrong, but I'll even start cutting his time short too! Do you understand, Queen Bee?" her mother said sarcastically.

"I know, Ma, I know, I was only kidding...and I don't be smoking no weed either," Bright lied. "I just want Deja, Cordell, Ramon and Ryonna to help around here too, 'cause you work hard and should be able to come home to a clean house sometimes," Bright said, hoping to get her mother off of her tail.Rosette thought, *I knew I'd get her to shut her big mouth up!*

It wasn't that Rosette didn't care about the things Bright was doing, she just really didn't have the time to be home and enforce the laws of her home to her child- ren. She worked twelve and sometimes twenty-four hour shifts at a time at her nursing job, in order to provide for her children. So she knew there were some things she wouldn't be able to stop without the help that she didn't have. And since it was only weed, and Bright wasn't a high school dropout, a drug addict, or a pregnant minor, she didn't feel like her smoking weed was such a big deal.

After Bright got off the phone with Larry, she ran out and found all of her siblings, then brought them back home to help clean up. Once her mother gave everybody jobs to perform, she thumped her 1980's mix smooth groove CD, and got to work. Bright prepped the laundry for the wash, while Deja and Ryonna had trash detail they had to collect trash from every room in the house. Cordell and Ramon were on wall detail scrubbing the walls from top to bottom.

Rosette worked in both the kitchen and living room, cleaning underneath the surfaces, trying her hardest to make her house look like a home. When the girls were finishing picking up trash around the apartment, they went to assist Bright, hanging and folding laundry, in the on-site laundry facility. Then finally by eight p.m., the house was spotless and dinner was served. Rosette fried a batch of chicken wings, baked some French fries, and made a hearty house salad. For once in a long time, they sat down and ate dinner together like a family, in their clean apartment. It was a proud, long-overdue moment for Rosette and everybody was happy.

Two Weeks Later

After Rosette fixed dinner and gave her children orders to follow, she headed to the door to go to work. She was so proud of how her children were keeping the house up, that she worked extra hours at her second job to put new furniture in the house. Rosette bought everyone new beds and bought a new flat screen TV for the living room. Now all she needed was a brand new living room suite and dining room table, and after her next paycheck, she would be able to do just that.

"I love you guys! Be good, and listen to your sister while I'm gone. I'll take you guys to McDonald's for breakfast in the morning, okay?" she yelled before leaving the apartment.

"We will!" They all yelled back in unison, taking turns on their Xbox in the living room.

"See you later, Ma, these kids know better than to try me, 'cause I'll beat'em!" Bright teased, yelling out of the kitchen window to her mother as she was getting in her car. Rosette backed out of her parking stall laughing. "You better be nice to my babies, Queen Bee," she said as she drove away.

After a shower, Bright told her sisters and brother to stay inside and play the Xbox until she got back, and that she would bring their favorite treats backs from the liquor store.

"Can we eat dinner if you're not back by five?" Deja, the next oldest in line, asked.

"Yeah, and make sure they don't get in any trouble too, Deja. You're the next oldest, so I'm depending on you to have my back and watch theirs," she told Deja, and then passed her a ten dollar bill.

"I'm on it, big sis!" Deja, smiled, assuring Bright.

"I'm depending on you, Deja. I'ma make a quick run with Larry, then we'll be outside sitting in his car, so don't y'all try to pull off no slick stuff, either," Bright said, walking out the door.

Sitting in Larry's freshly painted Mustang after grabbing strawberry-banana smoothies from Jamba Juice, Larry and Bright were caught up sharing a juicy tongue kiss when Bright noticed Terrence rolling up her street. She hadn't seen or called him in a couple of days, so she was sure he was looking for her. *Fuck, Bright* thought, *this nigga can't be popping up on me like this, I should have asked him to buy me a fucking cell phone to avoid all of this.* Feeling as if she was about to piss on herself, Bright dropped down in her seat and yelled for Larry to go. She was hoping and praying that Terrence hadn't seen her.

Larry sped off then yelled, "Why the fuck am I speeding off for, and why are you hiding, Bright?" Larry kept an eye on his rearview mirror and on his surroundings. "What the fuck is goin on, Bright?" he asked, growing frustrated.

After thinking up a quick lie Bright blurted out, "My Uncle just drove up the street, Larry, and if he sees me with a guy, he gone be tripping big time," she said nervously as she peeked over her seat to see if Terrence was following them. The last thing she wanted was for Terrence to bust her out and put her on blast. If Larry found out what she was up to, she knew she would lose him for good. "Is he coming this way? Did he see us, Larry?" Bright asked.

"Who dude in the Escalade on them twenty six inch rims?"Larry asked her.

"Yeah him, is he following us?" she quickly asked.

"Naw, he kept going straight. Now get up, Bright,"

Larry said, giving her a ridiculous look. "You got me thinking we about to get sprayed or something." Larry paused for a second to figure out what direction he was going to turn, then he turned right on Butler street. "If that's yo Uncle, Bright, why didn't he park and go inside instead of just driving by?" he asked suspiciously.

"I have no idea why he didn't stop, Larry, I thought maybe he seen us," Bright said, making sure Terrence was clear out of sight. "But it's not unusual for my uncle to check on us while my mother's at work, he does it all the time," Bright said getting back into her comfort zone.

"I can understand your uncle's position, Bright, fly ass niece like ya self, he probably wants to make sure dudes ain't just all over you," Larry laughed. "But me and Unc gone have to meet, moms like me, so I'm sure she'll put a good word in for me. I'm a reputable kind of guy," Larry teased.

"You don't know my uncle, Larry, he's crazy! He still gives my mother a hard time about dating, and he definitely doesn't want me seeing any guys right now," Bright said convincingly, nodding her head. "He just wants me to focus on school and worry about boys later." "Well, after we get married it's gone be all good, I'll be part of the family...you know what I mean?" Larry said proudly.

"Yes baby, just me, you, and our babies," she fantasized. "But until then, we're gonna have to be careful, because that fool rolls around with a pistol," Bright said, hoping to pump fear in Larry's heart.

Uncomfortable with the idea of going back to her house and chancing another run-in with Terrence, Bright talked Larry into going to his house, since his mother wasn't scheduled to get home until nine p.m. inside; they fooled around and made love for hours. When they finally came up for air, it was close to five p.m. "You want something to eat?" Larry asked. "I could make us some burgers or something," he said after he stepped out the bathroom, drying his hands off on a paper towel.

"No," Bright moaned. "I just wanna lie in your arms for a little while longer and look in your eyes," Bright said, wanting to feel the comfort of being in Larry's arms again. When she was in his arms, she felt whole and complete.

"Larry laughed, "That's funny, I was just thinking of doing the same thing." Larry swept Bright off of her feet, then laid her back in his bed, and held her tight in his arms. Bright was his boo, and he had very strong feelings for her.

"I love you so much, Larry Lane," Bright said, looking deep into his eyes.

"And I love you too, Bright Lane," Larry replied.

Then, after a passionate kiss, the two got lost in deep conversation.

****

"Deja, go inside the house with that knife now!" Treasure yelled, trying to contain the situation that had arisen between Deja, Ryonna, and a group of girls that were trying to jump on Ryonna.

"Those bitches gotta a problem with my sister, then they got a problem with me!" Deja yelled, holding her knife in stabbing position. She wasn't gonna stand for anybody thinking they were going to punk or jump on her little sister. And just like she told the group of rowdy fifth graders before one of the other neighborhood kids ran over to get Treasure for help, if they touched her sister, she was gonna get to slicing and dicing, and she meant it.

By the time Treasure and Suge made it around the corner, the little girls' parents and older family members had already made their way over to the scene. Seeing Deja with a knife in her hand caused an eruption from the parents who felt their children's lives were being threatened. The chaos and loud noise that were taking place was loud enough to wake up the dead, and even with Treasure and Suge on the scene, the problem still seemed to grow bigger and bigger.

"That little bitch better be lucky that she didn't use that knife on my baby!" An angry parent yelled, pointing and yelling at Deja, causing uproar from the other parents.

"I wish she would have used that muthafucking knife!" Another chimed in.

Deja had tears in her eyes. She was so mad that shewanted to fight, stab, and swing at the next person that yelled at her. "If that little bitch would have touched my sister, I would have sliced her ass up, so she better be lucky!" Deja yelled back to the lady that called her out of her name. *How dare that grown lady call me, another woman's child and a little girl, a bitch?* She thought, growing angrier and angrier.

"Take Deja in the house, Suge!" Treasure yelled, trying to calm the situation down. Once she had seen Suge take the knife and grab Deja up, she directed her attention to the angry mob of people in front of her. "Why would you call a kid out of her name? That was so fucking immature!" Treasure began to yell in the direction of the woman that called Deja a bitch. "Yo grown ass out here going hard on a little kid like y'all wouldn't have done the same if y'all were in the same position. All five of these little girls were trying to jump on one little girl and her big sister came out trying to defend her. She wasn't gonna stab anybody, she was just tryna scare them off of her sister!"

"These kids' mama ain't never here, and they little bad asses always out here getting into shit, cussing and disrespecting adults, especially them damn boys. So I'll call the little bitch what I want, especially if she even thought she was gone stab my child!" The woman yelled with an attitude, popping her neck and stepping into Treasure's direction.

"Lady, don't come get up in my face, cause I don't mind fighting adults, and sending they asses to jail either. So to avoid all this extra shit, get y'all kids, and I'ma get mines. And if y'all have a problem, come holler at they mama and my auntie Rose in the morning!" Treasure snapped back with attitude.

Before long, Treasure and the lady were face to face yelling and arguing when Bright and Larry pulled up.

"What the fuck is going on?" Bright yelled, breaking through the crowd with Larry on her heels. She had received a call at Larry's house from her mother, yelling and screaming at her for leaving her sisters and brothers unattended.

"Your fucking sisters and brothers are the problem!"

The lady yelled, then pushed Bright out of her face and onto the ground. Bright falling on the ground sparked off the forceful blow that Treasure took to the lady's face.

"Bitch, no you didn't!" She yelled, igniting a block fight.

Larry helped Bright off the ground and without saying another word, she begin to swing in the direction of the angry crowd that was attacking and trying to take Treasure down. Seeing this, Suge, Deja, and Ryonna ran down the stairs to aid them. Suge fought her way through the crowd to help her friends while Larry tried to break the fight up and pull Bright off of another girl. Deja grabbed the water hose and begin whipping it at the crowd to get them off of her sister and friends. When Cordell and Ramon ran up and saw Deja whipping the crowd with the water hose and Ryonna fighting two girls, they instantly jumped into the fight to help.

"What the hell is going on?" Rosette said, climbing quickly out of her beat up 1995 Honda Accord. The sound of the police sirens began to break up the fight and made the adults who had children snap back into reality and grab their kids.

Rosette grabbed hold of Deja, who was now swinging the water hose on a group of little girls who were jumping on Ryonna. One of the little girls was beaten pretty badly and had blood all over her face from the lashings that Deja had given her.

"Oh Lord, what have you done, Deja!" Rosette said, going to the aid of the wounded little girl on the ground.

"They was tryna jump on Ryonna, Mama, and like you told us, if one fight, we all fight!" Deja said, not feeling any remorse for the little girl.

The girl's cousin, catching a glimpse of her little battered cousin, ran over to check up on her. "Is my cousin okay?" she asked, falling to her knees with Rosette.

"Call the paramedics, somebody, this little girl is hurt!" Rosette yelled, holding the little girl in her arms. "Cordell, Ramon, Deja, and Ryonna get yawls tails in the house right now!!!" Rosette ordered with so much authority that the whole scene had quieted down. Once the police got there, they begin arresting everyone on the scene that was involved in the fight. Children and adults were thrown into the back of squad cars and taken to jail, all beside Rosette and Larry, who had both been trying to break the fight up.

Inside the house, Rosette called her job to explain the urgency of her leaving, and was fired for insubordination. She had left one of the elder residents in bed at the convalescent home that she worked at without the railing pulled up, resulting in him falling out of bed and later being sent to the emergency room for treatment. Disappointed, Rosette hung up the phone, held her tears back, then left her apartment to check on her children.

Later that night, all of the juveniles were released from juvenile detention except for Deja. The adults that were involved in the fight were all awaiting their court dates. Deja had beaten the little girl so badly that assault and battery charges were pressed against her. Deja had broken the little girl's nose, cracked three teeth, and had opened flesh wounds all over her head that had to be stitched up. The girl was in poor shape.

Bright, Treasure, and Suge were released the same night, and sadly, the minute Suge made it home, her mom beat her so badly that she would need weeks to heal. Treasure's mother Jackie was very upset at first, but she felt it was necessary for her daughter to help her friend and family in such a situation. She warned them both to turn the other cheek in the future. Rosette, on the other hand, was very upset with Bright for leaving her children unattended, causing her to lose her job, and more so because Deja was still in juvenile detention. She restricted Bright's phone usage and limited the time she spent with Larry. But Rosette knew once she found herself another job that Bright's punishment would go right down the drain.

Part Five

Rosette had been off from work for over two weeks and because of it, both the landline and cable had been turned off. Not able to tolerate it any longer, Bright called Terrence to break her off. "Hey boo, come through and drop me off some money, my cable and home phone is off, that's why I haven't been able to call you," she said, standing on the corner of Long Beach Blvd. and Artesia, using the pay phone.

"No hi, hello, how you doing' or nothing, just give you some money, huh?" Terrence said back into the phone.

"I'm sorry baby, I just been stressed out," Bright sighed. "My little sister is still in juvenile, my mom lost her job behind it, and I don't have a phone to call you or any cable to watch."

"Yeah I see you been goin' through it, baby," Terrence said, happy to hear her voice. It had been almost a week since they last spoke, and over three weeks since he last hit it. But since she had a good reason for not calling him, he decided to go easy on her and not curse her out like he had planned on doing. "Give me about twenty minutes, and meet me by the elementary school, I'm leaving the eastside of Long Beach right now."

"Cool," Bright said, then hung up the pay phone. After grabbing sodas from the donut shop, Bright walked across the street with Treasure to Starr King Elementary School to wait on Terrence.

"I can remember my elementary school days at Starr King like it was just yesterday," Treasure said, reminiscing.

Elementary!" Bright said, laughing. "Now them use to be the days when we lived in the Carmelitos!" Bright said, "I remember it used to be a gang of fine ass little boys up in there back in the day." The Carmelitos was a known housing project in North Long Beach that Bright and her family used to live in during her elementary school years.

"Whatever, but it was my Starr King ass that saved yours when ya yellow ass got transferred to Hamilton Junior High School!" Treasure hissed.

"Yeah, yeah, yeah," Bright teased. "That's crazy how you came to my rescue that day in the locker room. Maria and them were gonna jump me. You was like 'ain't none of y'all gone jump her, let the new girl catch a fair one," Bright remembered.

"Yelp, cause they only wanted to jump you 'cause you were new, pretty, and the talk of the school straight hating!" Treasure said.

"Man, I was so happy to see you step up for me too," Bright said, remembering the day clearly. "But you see it wasn't no punk in me either, cause I was about to fight every last one of them females by myself. Even though they were gone probably beat my ass!" Bright laughed.

"I wasn't gone let 'em though," Treasure said, "cause they tried to pull that same bullshit on me in sixth grade. And trust when my mother called my auntie from Compton, her and all her bad ass kids came and turned that school upside down! And I ain't never had no more problems out of them haters since," Treasure laughed.

"Ain't no cute scary females over here!" Bright said.

"Real talk!" Treasure added.

"Heyyyy Sexy Bright and company!" Terrence yelled out of the window of his Escalade as he hit the corner.

Bright smiled and begin posing like a supermodel.

Treasure laughed. "Will y'all knock that shit off," she said, shaking her head at Bright as she proceeded to act like America's Next Top Model.

"That's my baby right there," Terrence said as he sat back in his truck, smiling, watching Bright work her fancy.

"Hey, Daddy," Bright said upon climbing in the passenger seat to kiss Terrence's lips. "You gone take me to get a phone today, Ice?" Bright said, holding up to her end of the bargain by calling him by his street name in the presence of others.

"You know I'll do anything for my baby boo," Terrence said as he started his truck back up. After Bright told Treasure to get inside, they made their way to a local Cingular wireless store to get Bright a phone. Grabbing one of the hottest phones on the market, Bright walked out of the store with a brand new Razor cell phone. Once they got to Treasure's house, Treasure climbed out and Bright headed to the motel with Terrence to break him off before he dropped her back off.

"Why don't we ever go to your house, Terrence?" Bright asked, wondering why they always ended up at sleazy motels to fuck. She had never stepped foot in his house.

"Cause I'm always out in the city grinding, and ain't no use in taking you to my house way in the valley just to turn back around to take you home."

"I guess," Bright replied, then Terrence climbed out of his truck to go pay for a room.

Inside the room, Bright worked Terrence a few times before she hopped in the shower. When she got out of the shower, she heard a loud commotion going on outside.

"Terrence, what's goin' on out there, daddy?" she asked as she threw her clothes back on. When she didn't get a reply, she stepped out the bathroom and called Terrence's name again. He was good for falling asleep after some good sex.

"What the fuck," Bright said out loud to herself. "Where the hell is Terrence at?" Once Bright was fully dressed, she grabbed her cell phone and called Terrence, then she looked out the motel window to see what was going on. Catching a part of the action, Bright's mouth flew wide open as she watched a madwoman swing a bat repeatedly at Terrence truck, while she yelled and screamed at the top of her lungs at him. She was a sickly looking woman that stood about five feet seven inches tall; she was dark-complexioned, with what appeared to be a long, jet black wig, and had a skinny frame. Bright thought, *Damn, is Terrence out here turning bitches out on dope or something? First Netta, now this bitch outside...what the fuck? I popped an E pill with him a few times, but I'ma need to start watching what this nigga be putting in the weed before I be next.*

"Tell me what room you got this little bitch hiding in right now, Terrence, or I'm taking all these windows out!" She demanded in a loud squeaky voice. "Does the bitch know you're a fucking married man!" she yelled in his face.

"Tameka, put the fucking bat down, baby, I ain't here with no fucking female! I keep tryna tell yo ass that... I'm here on business, and you making me look bad out here," he said trying to calm his wife of eight years down.

"Business, my ass!" she yelled, hitting the hood of his truck, leaving dents with each blow. "I told you if you cheated on me ever again I was divorcing yo sorry ass,

I'm fucking tired of this shit and I can't believe you'd do this to me after everything I've been going through!" she yelled, punching him with her free hand.

"Hit my muthafucking car one more damn time, Tameka, and you gone make me hurt you out here!" Terrence said heatedly as he grabbed his cell phone from his pants pocket. It was a good thing he ran an operation out of this particular Motel 6, otherwise he would have been stone cold busted. Terrence called his homeboy and asked him to come outside to holler at his wife, because she thought he was at the motel cheating instead of handling his business. After his homeboy came outside of the stash room and met them in the parking lot, Tameka cooled off and apologized to Terrence for her behavior. Then she hopped in her Beamer, and left the parking lot.

"Damn, all this for a fucking piece of pussy," Terrence said, looking his truck over with his homeboy.

His boy nodded his head in agreement. "You should have taken that shit from her my nigga, 'cause on the real, babygirl fucked yo shit up. You gone end up having to buy another one," he said.

"On everything!" Terrence said, boiling on the inside.

Bright had had enough. She knew she had a man and was playing Terrence, but how could he go on seeing her without letting her know that he had a wife? Feeling betrayed, Bright sucked up her anger, grabbed her things, and then made her way out of the room. She had already called a cab to take her home, but she needed to grab some money from Terrence before she cussed his ass out and left.

"Ice baby, come here!" Bright yelled out to him from their motel room.

"Fuck! I hope she didn't see or hear that shit Tameka

came over here with," he sighed, backing away from his

partner, before walking back into the room.

His homeboy just nodded his head.

Terrence walked in the room observing Bright closely. "What's up Beautiful? What you doing?" he asked, not sensing any animosity from her.

"Nothing," Bright smiled. "Just got out the shower.

"You ready to take me home? It's almost time for my mama to go to work." she said as a devilish grin appeared across her face.

Terrence looked at the time on his cell phone. "Yeah it is about that time, huh?" He was familiar with her mother's work schedule.

"Yelp, you still gone give me that money before we leave?" she asked with her hand out.

"You already know I got you, baby, but you gone have to take a cab home," he said, shaking his head in disappointment. "One of my homies' girls came up here tripping, thinking that my truck was his truck, and she fucked my shit up, thinking this nigga was cheating on

her...and I'm heated too!" He said.

"Really? When did all this happen?" Bright asked, playing it off as she looked out the window to observe his truck.

Terrence passed her four one hundred dollar bills. "Is that cool right there, baby?" he asked Bright. He was obviously still very disappointed.

"The phone bill is three hundred alone, the cable is one-eighty, and I need some money for me," she said, rubbing his back. He gave her an additional five hundred dollars and then told her to keep the rest for herself. Bright put the money in the pocket of her jeans.

"You have a twenty so I can pay the cab? They may not have any change for these big bills," she said with her hand out. Terrence peeled off a couple of twenty dollar bills and then passed them to her. Bright tucked it in her bra. Then, without further words, she hauled off and slapped Terrence into the next week and headed to the door.

Stopping himself from slapping her back, he yelled, "What the fuck was all that for?" He grabbed her by the arm to stop her from leaving the room.

Bright yanked her arm from him. "Get ya fucking hands off of me and go home to yo wife, you fucking liar!" Then, once she heard the cab driver honk his horn, she slapped him again then made her way out the room and to the cab.

"Come here, let me holler at you, baby!" Terrence yelled out to Bright. "I love you, baby, let me explain!" he said, hoping that she would stay and give him a chance to come up with a good excuse and clear everything up. Bright didn't look back; she just climbed in the cab and told the driver where to take her. She knew that playing the hurt role would benefit her in the long run, and that Terrence would be throwing money her way- money that she wouldn't even have to fuck for or ask to get.

****

Needing her bestie to talk to about the drama at the motel, Bright hooked back up with Treasure, smoked a blunt, and then asked her to take the cab with her to pay the phone and cable bill. After explaining the situation, Treasure was appalled.

"That nigga got a bitch at home, Bee?"

"A wife, girl!" Bright replied nodding her head.

"And that's why I'ma milk that fool dry," she said spitefully.

Bright was the child of a mistress and a married man, a filthy rich white man at that, who died from a heart attack and didn't acknowledge her or even mention her name in his will. At his repast, when her wicked grandmother introduced her to the rest of the family, the looks and things they said behind Bright's back hurt her deeply. Here she was, an innocent child, yet everybody saw and treated her as a disgrace. Growing up, Bright hated when her mother would allow her to spend the night at her white grandparent's house. While she thought Bright was having a great time meeting and mingling with her father's side of the family, she was being hidden in their house, and terrible things were happening to her things that she had never spoken about and tried hard to erase from her memory. But them both dying of heart conditions, one shortly after the other, was enough payback for her.

Bright didn't hate or blame her mother for it, she just wished she had a father like her siblings did. Deja and Cordell's father was sentenced to life in prison, and even they spoke to him a few times a month, whenever their mother asked for help which was hardly ever, his family helped out as much as possible. Ryonna and Ramon's father called them from time to time too and sent them money from Texas every birthday and Christmas. But Bright was the fatherless child, and she had no family other than her mother and siblings. And no matter what, or how old she got, it continued to be an on-going issue that would haunt and taunt her. That was reason number one why she promised herself to have kids by a wealthy man, she wanted them to have everything that she was supposed to have growing up as the child of a rock star. She would say, "My pussy ain't for sale, but it damn sure isn't free either." Bright knew her future was secured, she had a future NBA star and she knew once they got married and had children, she would never have to want or need for anything ever again; and her children would have something that she never had: a father.

Once Bright paid the phone bill, on the cab ride back home, she and Treasure had a real heart-to-heart talk about both of their family lives. When the cab dropped them off in front of Treasure's house, they rushed inside to freshen up before her mother and grandmother made it back home. The last thing they wanted to do was to get caught smelling like weed by Treasure's mom, Ms. Jackie.

"Damn, bitch, I gotta pee!" Treasure announced, unlocking the door, then she ran inside the house to release her bladder. "Grab the mail, Bee, and put it on the entertainment center," Treasure yelled from the bathroom.

Bright grabbed the mail, and surprisingly, the first piece of mail she noticed was a letter from state prison to Treasure from Jonathan Carver, A.K.A. Chrome. Feeling anxiety, build Bright quickly grabbed the letter, folded it up, put it in her back pocket, and then placed the rest of the mail on top of the entertainment center like Treasure asked her to. When Treasure came out the bathroom, she looked through the mail, then they headed back out to the porch. Since the letter was burning a hole in Bright's pocket, she made up a quick excuse to go home so she could find out what Chrome was trying to tell Treasure.

"I'm about to bounce, Treasure, it's laundry night," Bright announced, then headed out the gate.

"A'ight, bestie, Reggie supposed to be coming over in a few, and I have a movie date with this fine ass boss gangsta from Compton named Lil Boo. He balling out of control and is rolling a slick ass Benz...yeah Bee, he so fly!" Treasure yelled down the street to Bright.

"Balling...have fun, girl, and if ole boy got a friend, holler at me! Hit me on the cell when you get back home and tell me all about it!" Bright laughed, then continued walking home.

"I will!" Treasure yelled back then ran inside the house.

****

"Bright, talk to your sister," Rosette yelled, passing Bright the telephone when she walked through the front door. Bright couldn't stand the fact that Deja had to spend the rest of her summer in Los Padrino's Juvenile Hall, and even more so that she wasn't at home watching them like she was supposed to have done in the first place.

"Hey Dejaaaaa, baby!!!"

"Hey Queen Bee," Deja teased, calling Bright the name their mother called her. Bright was so happy to hear her sister's voice, that she planned on speaking to her until her phone time was up.

"Me and Larry gone come see you in the morning, and remember, don't let them little girls try to turn you out and take ya snatch from you, you hear me?"

"I already know, sis," Deja laughed.

"The first female that try you, you bust her right in the mouth," Bright instructed her seriously.

"Don't be hyping Deja up to get into any more trouble, Queen Bee...I want my baby to hurry up and come home!" Rosette yelled out from the kitchen, where she was preparing dinner.

"Maaaa, I'm just telling Deja to protect herself in there, that's all," Bright yelled back to her mother from the living room, then she whispered into the phone. "Like I said, bust any of them bitches that try you fresh in the mouth. You cute with long hair, and them dykes gone be on you."

Deja laughed. "These girls know what I'm here for, and trust me, they don't want it, Bright."

"I love you, sister!" Ryonna yelled, hanging off of Bright's lap.

"Me too," Ramon and Cordell chimed in.

"Mama loves you too, Deja, and you behave yourself in there so you can hurry up and come home!" Rosette said, becoming teary-eyed and emotional.

"I love y'all too!!!!" Deja yelled after Bright put her on the speaker phone.

After the phone call with Deja, Bright went into her bedroom, tore open the letter that Chrome wrote to Treasure, and then began to read it to herself.

Dear Treasure,

I hope this letter reaches you in the best of health and spirit possible. As for me, not that you may really give a damn, I'm managing and hangin' in there, and trying to accept the fact that I may have to spend the next fifteen years of my life in prison over your fake ass homegirl and her lies. And even though you and this whole fucked up judicial system may never believe me, I swear, I never raped your friend. I admit I did beat her ass up, but I NEVER RAPED HER and I'm telling you what God loves and that's, the truth! That rat gave that shit up to me openly and willingly, and the ONLY reason I fucked her stanking ass in the first place was because she told me you had moved on with some other nigga. After that she started throwing the pussy at me and gave me head in the front seat of my car in the Burger King parking lot. I wouldn't even waste my time writing or lying to you, Treasure, if I wasn't telling you the truth. I feel I owe at least that much to you. And even though I know there will never be a chance of us getting back together ever again in life, I just honestly want you to know what type of back stabbing ass homegirl you rolling with. She thinks she's better than you and will try to sleep with any dude you may have future relations with just because she thinks she's all that. So you watch out, Treasure, cause Bright ain't nothing but Poison and she's not that true friend that you believe or that she portrays herself to be. That girl doesn't care about nothing or nobody but herself. P.S: If you write me back, just to let me know that you have received my letter, I will promise that I will never bother you again.

Sincerely, Jonathan Carter

"I am Treasure's true friend, stupid ass nigga!" Bright said out loud to herself. Then she ripped his letter up to shreds. Happy she hadn't torn the envelope up with Chrome's address on it, Bright smiled. "Treasure gone write yo ass back alright, Mr. Carter," she said devilishly, reaching for the notebook and pen that sat on top of her night stand. After writing Chrome a short, sweet, "I don't give a fuck letter," Bright forged Treasure's name on it then searched for an envelope around the apartment. Unable to find one, Bright tucked the letter in Chrome's envelope until she could get her hands on one, then tucked it under her bed and went about her evening.

****

The next morning as promised, Bright and her siblings went to visit Deja at the juvenile hall center in Norwalk. Larry borrowed his mother's van so that he could drive them all over for the visit. Afterwards, Bright treated everyone to lunch at Friday's in hopes of cheering Ryonna up. She was extremely sad that Deja couldn't come back home with them. When Larry pulled up in front of Bright's apartment, as usual she dreaded parting ways with him.

"I'll be back to pick you up after practice, boo boo," Larry said as he kissed on Bright's soft lips.

"I love you, Larry Lane," Bright told him as she exited the van.

"I love you more, Mrs. Lane," he said, then drove off.

"Ryonna and Ramon, go take y'all showers. Cordell, take yours before you go to bed," Bright ordered upon entering the apartment. Since Cordell was the next oldest sibling in the house, Bright felt it was time to stop treating him like the youngest two and start giving him a little more leeway. "Tie your hair up, Ray," Bright said, calling her sister 'Ray' for short. "And when you get out of the shower, pick your Bratz Dolls up off the living room floor, and go to bed." Bright took a stretch, then walked in her room to relax and count her money. She wanted to buy Larry a few new outfits and another pair of Jordan's. In the middle of counting her money, Terrence start blowing her cell phone up, and instead of ignoring his calls as she had done for the last couple of days, she decided to answer and play the victim role so that she could start collecting her money in full.

"Hello," Bright answered as if she was miserable and depressed.

"Baby, this Ice, what's wrong, why you sound like that?" Terrence asked, concerned. "Why you haven't been answering my calls, baby? I need to talk to you, I miss you," he pleaded. "Do you miss me too, Bright?" he asked.

Bright sniffed into the phone. "Why you do this to

me, baby? You should have told me," Bright said, then begin to cry.

"I wanted to baby, I did... and matter of fact, I was gone tell you, but it was hard for me, I was scared I was gone lose you, and I love you baby, I don't ever wanna lose you." After a few moment of listening to Bright sniffle and cry, Terrence asked, "Do you still love me, baby?"

"I need time right now, Terrence. I'm tryna come up on some extra money to go visit my grandmother in Vegas, I need to clear my head," she cried in between sobs.

"Let me give it to you, baby, I did the shit to you, and I'm willing to do anything in my power to make it up to you baby. I love you, Bright," he said in a comforting and sincere tone.

"No, I can't see you right now," Bright cried. "It's gone be too hard to face you Terrence. My heart is so broken," she cried.

Terrence felt bad and didn't want to lose Bright, so he told her he would drop the money off to Treasure and that when she got back he wanted to see her. Bright hung up the phone crying. An hour later, Treasure called Bright and told her that Terrence had just drove over in his 64 Chevy Impala low-rider and dropped an envelope full of money off for her. Bright began smiling, then after putting her shoes on, she told her brothers and sister to watch cable in their mother's room until she got back, and for them not to answer the door for anybody. Then she made her way over to Treasure's house.

"He broke yo ass off!" Treasure said after they counted out twelve hundred and fifty dollars. "And you should have seen that fool too, Bright, he said 'tell my baby that no matter what, I love her, Treasure.' He was looking all sad and pitiful," she laughed.

"Girl, I put it on good too. I was crying and sniffling, and he was like, 'Bright baby, I love you girl, do you love me?" She teased, trying to disguise her voice like a man. "He just don't know he about to get milked for all that money, messing with me," Bright said, then passed Treasure two hundred dollars. "I'm going to spend half of this on Larry tomorrow at the mall, then I'ma call that nigga Terrence in a few days and milk his ass again," Bright laughed.

"Thanks, girl," Treasure said putting the money in her purse. "I'm going out with that suwoooo nigga from Compton again tonight, he such a boss that I wanna spend all my money on him," Treasure teased.

"Damn, like that?" Bright laughed. "Looks like you got a Larry on ya hands," she teased. "You said his name is Lil Boo?" Bright asked.

"Yeah and he fine as fuck, all thugged out and shit," Treasure said, really feeling him.

"So I guess you not rolling with us to the frat party tonight, huh?" Bright asked, disappointed. "Reggie gonna be there," Bright said, hoping that Treasure would change her mind.

"I like Reggie too, Bright. But you already know how I get down when I really like a guy. I let them chase me around and give 'em the cold shoulder so that when they get my time, they will appreciate and value it," Treasure said, honestly.

Bright rolled her eyes and nodded her head. She didn't believe in or use that method to get or keep a dude. She believed the more she gave, the more she'd get. "Yeah, yeah, yeah, Treasure, what's up with Suge though?"

she asked. She hadn't seen or heard from her in over a week.

"She still on punishment," Treasure said, shaking her head in disbelief.

"Poor Suge," Bright said, missing her little homegirl. After talking for a few more minutes, Bright went home to get prepared for her evening with Larry. Once her mother came home, she called Larry to pick her up so that they could go out and get their party on.

Part Six

A week after Treasure's seventeenth birthday, Lil Boo had picked her up to take her out to the movies. She was enjoying herself with her suwoooo gangsta from Compton. He was indeed one of the most swagged out guys she had ever been out with. Dressed sexy in a fuchsia tube dress, sliver sling backs, and her hair pressed out in a silky wrap, Treasure and Lil Boo were having a great time. After they left the movies, he invited her back over to his house.

"I'm cool with that," Treasure said, then gave him a sexy smile.

"Lil mama, you sexy as fuck, I can get lost looking in them pretty brown eyes of yours," he said, followed by a wink. "Hope yo man don't mind me stealing you for the night?" Lil Boo teased.

"I don't have one, unfortunately, the creep that I thought was mine ended up raping my homegirl, now his loser self is in jail," Treasure said, trying not to lose her classy edge.

"Damn, I'm sorry to hear that, Lil Mama," Lil Boo said, then he grabbed her hand. "You better off without a nigga like him in ya life anyways."

"I guess you're right," Treasure said as tears fell from her eyes. She still felt hurt and bitter over the situation.

"Are those tears I see in ya eyes?" Lil Boo asked once he pulled into his driveway.

Treasure nodded her head and closed her eyes. "I'm cool, I guess I didn't realize how much I've really been affected by this."

Lil Boo wiped her eyes. "Ain't no crying with me, baby, let's go inside and get ya mind on something else." He climbed out of his Benz and then walked around the car to open the door for Treasure to get out.

Treasure smiled. "You are just too sweet."

"Even better than diamonds, I'm a girl's best friend, sweetheart." He grabbed her by the hand and led her into his house.

Inside, Lil Boo gave Treasure a full-body rub down. He enjoyed rubbing on her fat ass, and her eyes pretty brown eyes reminded him of his baby's mama, Keisha Cones eyes. "Damn blood, you have some beautiful ass eyes...I can just look in 'em all night long."

"Really?" Treasure asked, giving him a soft, sensual smile.

"They look like diamonds." Lil Boo rubbed his index finger down the spine of her back, then softly in between her booty cheeks, looking her directly in the eyes.

"I feel like I've known you for a million years." Then she sat up and gave him a soft, passionate peck on the lips.

"Can I have some more?" Lil Boo asked, holding Treasure tight in his arms.

She felt secure there, and even though she promised herself that she wasn't going to continue to sleep with different guys within the first few dates...tonight she was breaking her own rules, and she wasn't gonna hold anything back.

"You can have whatever you want from me tonight," Treasure purred.

He held her face with both of his hands, kissed her lips, and then whispered in her ear, "I promise I'll be gentle with you." He sucked, kissed and bit on every inch of her body. She had never had a real orgasm before, and Lil Boo had made her cum twice even before he ate her out or penetrated her. The way he sucked and blew cool air on her hard nipples made her yearn for his touch.

"You like that?" he asked as he put a condom on his swollen penis. Treasure had never been with a guy with a penis as big as Lil Boo's before. She got excited, expecting, he'd be just as good with his tool as he was with his hands and mouth.

"Yes, I like that, baby," Treasures said, spreading her legs apart, welcoming Lil Boo inside of her. After he put the condom on, he climbed on top of her, and took slow, deep thrusts inside of her as he looked into her pretty brown eyes. "I told you I could get lost in them eyes," he said in a heat of passion.

"Ohhhh, that feels so good," Treasure moaned, running her manicured nails through his back and rubbing all over his chest.

"It does?" Lil Boo responded, pecking her soft lips after each stroke.

"Yesssss," she moaned, throwing her pussy back at him, fiending for his lips to touch hers and for him to go deeper and deeper inside of her. "It feels so good," she said, pushing him off of her, so that she could get on top of him.

"That's what I like to see, take that dick, brown-eyed girl," he moaned as he filled both of his hands up with her breasts, then he squeezed her nipples between his fingers to keep them nice and hard.

"Ohhhh, brown-eyed girl got some bomb ass pussy," Lil Boo said as she dropped and popped her jewels on him. "Make them titties jump, brown-eyed girl," Lil Boo begged, on the verge of erupting.

Excited to make him feel as good as he had made her feel, Treasure moved up and down his love stick, making her titties bounce. Lil Boo flipped her over and put her in a doggy style position, then rode her hard and deep as he slapped her fat ass.

"Oh, Lil Boo!" Treasure said, continuing to scream and moan as she called out his name.

"I'm right here baby, let that shit come again," Lil Boo said, stabbing her G-spot and making her cum all over herself. Treasure thought she'd suffocate for a loss of air, as she screamed and moaned, gasping for air, her body buckled in an orgasm to a point of ecstasy that she had never been to before.

"Get it baby, get it," Lil Boo said, then he erupted holding on to Treasure's trembling body. This would be a night that Treasure would never forget.

****

"Bright, I ain't never-ever got served like this before in my life bitch!" Treasure explained as they walked over to Suge's house. They hadn't heard from her in a while and were worried about her.

"Damn, so baby got it goin' on huh?"

"Man!!!" Treasure yelled, getting hyped, nodding her head. "On everything I love, Lil Boo is the best dick I've ever had."

"How old is he?" Bright asked curiously.

"Like twenty-five, I think," Treasure said, trying to remember clearly.

"How old you tell him you were, Treasure?" Bright asked.

"I told him I was nineteen," Treasure said as she knocked on Suge's front door.

"Is Suge here?" Treasure asked after her mother answered the door with a cigarette hanging from her mouth.

Suge's mother removed the cigarette from her mouth and gave them both nasty looks. "Suge can't hang with y'all fast asses no more, so don't call or come over here for her no more!" she said, then slammed the door in their faces. Bright and Treasure looked at each other in disbelief with their mouths hanging open.

"What the fuck?" Treasure asked, breaking the silence.

"That bitch don't know anything about us, how she gone come at us like that?" Bright said as they headed out of the yard.

"Treasure, Bright!" Suge yelled out of her bedroom window, then waved them over once she grabbed both of their attentions. After making sure the coast was clear of Suge's mother, they both crept back into the yard and ran around to the side of the house to Suge's bedroom window. Suge looked awful.

"Damn boo, what's goin' on?" Bright whispered loudly enough for only Treasure and Suge to hear her.

"This bitch been fucking me up y'all, for no reason either," Suge cried. "I'm running away tonight. She knows where you stay at, Treasure, so I need to come to your house, Bright. Just for a few nights, until I call social services on her ass or something. It was obvious from the bumps and the bruises that Suge was being abused.

Bright nodded her head in agreement.

"I feel like goin' in there and kicking your mother's ass!"
Treasure yelled. "How could she do something like this to her own damn daughter?" Treasure fumed.

"Shhhh, she may hear you, Treasure," Suge warned, looking toward her bedroom door.

"Let her," Treasure said. "I'm really hot right now about how she got you looking."

Trying to get their plan together before they were caught by Suge's mother, Bright spoke quickly. "Where you want us to meet you at? And what time you planning on escaping from this bitch?" Bright said nodding her head in disgust.

"At about nine o'clock; just meet me at the end of my block," Suge sniffled, wiping her nose with the back of her hand. "I may need y'all to help me carry my stuff." Bright blew Suge a kiss.

"We'll be there, Suge, don't worry about it," Bright assured, grabbing Treasure's arm to creep back out of the gate. She was afraid Treasure was about to explode and do something crazy. Her mouth was twisted up, nostrils flared, both of her fists were balled tight and she was breathing so hard that you could see her chest go up and down. Suge nodded her head in agreement and then closed her bedroom curtain. After talking about Suge's situation a little longer, Bright made tracks home because she knew her mother had to leave for work in less than a half an hour and she wanted to ask her if Suge could stay with them for a few days.

"Maaaaa!" Bright yelled upon entering their apartment.

"I have a headache, Queen Bee," her mother said, coming out of the kitchen from preparing a dinner. Seeing her mother resting her head in the palm of her hand and squinting her eyes, Bright took it down a few notches.

"Sorry Ma, what's wrong? Are you okay?" she asked concerned.

"Just a hangover, too much damn tequila last night," she said. Rosette turned the pilots off from under the corn and mashed potatoes and then put the lids on top of them.

"I guess you and Vince had a good ole time," Bright laughed as quietly as she could.

"I guess we did," she said as a slight smile appeared across her face. "But that's why I only stick to drinking my beer, no hangovers at all," she laughed. "Now I just hope this aspirin kicks in before I get to Mrs. Yates house, all that woman does is yell and scream," she said, taking a seat to put her work shoes on.

"Poor baby, you'll be alright," Bright said, sitting on the arm of the couch. "Oh yeah, Ma, can my friend, Suge spend a couple nights over here? Her mom's a workaholic like you and she's always home alone bored," Bright said.

"Yeah, I don't have a problem with it as long as her parents don't. Just make sure you guys keep the house nice and tight. And before I forget again," Rosette remembered, massaging her temples, "Please bring that Xbox back out of the boys' room, it seems like ever since it's been there, Ramon and his little friend stay locked up in the room hogging the game."

"Aight, Ma, I will, and now that you mention it, he does always be locked up in the room by himself or with his little friend. The other day, Cordell almost had to kick the door down to get in there. I thought I heard Cordell tell him to bring the game back in the living room, too" Bright said hunching her shoulders. "But don't worry about the house, you know I been staying on top of it especially since it took us forever to get it this clean," she laughed. Besides that she didn't want, Larry stepping into a fitly apartment when he came to visit her.

"Okay, the corn and mashed potatoes are on the stove, and the chicken is in the oven. I'll see you in the morning," her mother said after she kissed her on the forehead. Then she headed out to her twelve hour nursing shift.

After Bright rounded her siblings up, she made the youngest two take early baths and told Cordell to take his before going to bed. With Deja still in juvenile detention, Cordell had really stepped up and helped Bright out around the house. He was maturing, and she had hardly ever had any trouble out of him anymore.

"Why we have to take showers early tonight, Bright?" Ryonna asked her. After the big fight that sent Deja to juvenile, Ryonna had pretty much lost all of her neighborhood friends, and now that she had some new nice playmates, she wanted to stay outside longer to finish playing jump rope with them.

"You can play longer with your friends tomorrow, Ray, but I have a lot to do tonight, boo butt. Now go on and get in the bathtub before Deja calls." The mention of Deja's name instantly made a smile appear across Ryonna's face. Happy, she skipped down the hall to take her bath singing out loud, "I'm gone talk to Deja, I'm gone talk to Deja." Bright smiled, looking at her little sister. She remembered being a happy-go-lucky little girl just like her before. Then suddenly her smile turned into a frown when unhappy and unwanted memories began to fill her head.

Later on after everybody took their showers, Bright fixed their plates, put them on the table, and told them to come eat while she cleaned the kitchen.

"After y'all finish eating Ray, wipe the table off like

mama showed you with the glass cleaner and napkins. And Cordell, since you the next oldest in line, put the movie on y'all agreed to watch and chill until I get back. Don't open the door for anybody, and if Mama calls tell her I'm in the shower and then call me." Bright said.

"Okay, okay, we will," Cordell said, with a mouth full of food. "I got's this."

Bright grabbed her cell phone then ran out to meet up with Terrence. She hadn't seen him since the motel incident, and he said it was important that he speak to her. And since she was low on money she decided she'd give him a few moments of her time. When he pulled up in his black low rider, Bright climbed inside and buckled up. She assumed that since he was driving his cherished low rider, that his truck must have been getting worked on.

"How you feeling, Beautiful?" Terrence asked cautiously as he rubbed his finger down the side of Bright's face.

"I'm alright, I guess," Bright said, forcing tears to burst from her eyes.

"Look baby, I'ma keep it real with you right now. Since everything is out on the table. I am married, and have been for eight years now. Tameka is my high school sweetheart, so yeah, she does mean a lot to me, and a nigga done took her through hell and back, cheating on her and shit. But I ain't been seeing nobody else since me and you been fucking around. I love you and wanna take care of you. Tameka ain't gone be around too much longer no how, so bear with me, Bright, I need you," he said, becoming misty-eyed.

"So what, that mean you about to divorce her?" Bright asked, looking at him, wondering why his eyes were watering up.

Terrence nodded his head no. "I can't do that, Bright, Tameka has cancer. She had surgery an er'thing but the shit just keep growing and spreading all over the place. The doctors told us she had two months to live, so understand when I tell you that this shit is complicated. I can't leave her in her time of need, but I don't want to lose you either, so I'm just asking that you bear with me, baby. I got you, you hear me?" he said, pulling over in the alley behind the Shaky's Pizza on Paramount Blvd. and South Street to kiss her lips.

"You should have told me, baby, I would have listened to you and understood. But now you got me feeling like you playing games wit me. And as much as I want to believe you right now, Terrence...I don't, baby," Bright said, wiping the tear that had formed and leaked from his eye.

"You think I'd be out here crying and shit like a lil bitch for nothing, Bright? This shit fucking hurts my heart! It's tearing me up inside knowing that my wife gone leave this earth soon and it ain't shit I can do to change that...and now I'm about to lose you too!" he said, looking her in her eyes. "Give me a fucking break, baby, I wouldn't just hurt you for nothing," he said, grabbing her face so she could look him in the eyes.

Bright took a deep breath. "I wanna believe you, baby, but you broke that trust," she said, looking him back in his eyes.

Terrence grabbed his cell phone, scrolled down to his wife Tameka's number, put the phone on speaker, and then told Bright to be quiet.

After three rings, a woman's voice that Bright remembered to be the lady's from the Motel 6 answered.

"Hey, Teddy Bear," she sang into the phone.

"Hey Teddy Mama, how you feeling right now?" he asked.

"I'm okay, Teddy, you don't have to call and check on me every five minutes," she laughed.

"I know, it's just that I wanna make sure you're alright, all the time, you know?" Another tear managed to fall from his eye. Bright wiped it away.

"When I go, Teddy, I want you to know that I've made peace with this whole thing. I'm not afraid of dying and going home to my heavenly father. I'm suffering here you know, always in pain, I won't have to suffer no more when I die."

The moment was so emotional that Bright had even begun to shed tears. To her, Tameka was a strong woman, and she felt bad about her situation.

"You say you made peace with it baby, but I haven't.

I'm hurting out here over this," he said as his voice cracked. "For me, Teddy, be strong baby, okay? You have to be strong for me like I'm being for you. I love you, Teddy Bear, and when you come home tonight I just want to hug and celebrate the time that I do have left with you. Speaking and thinking of only happy times, you hear me?"

"I hear you, Teddy Mama, I'll be home soon. I love you baby."

"I love you too, Teddy Bear."

Bright had a flood of tears streaming from her eyes. *That's why she looked so sickly,* Bright thought. Tameka's words and outlook on things were the most beautiful things she had ever heard, and she felt for the both of them. "Terrence, I'm sorry baby," Bright cried, then climbed on top of him to kiss his face and wipe his tears away. "You have been going through so much and I promise that I'll be here for you as long as you keep it real with me."

"I need you, Bright," Terrence replied seriously. Then he passionately kissed her lips, wishing they were Tameka's lips, and that it was her on top of him instead of Bright. But with all the pain that Tameka had been going through lately, sex was out of the question, and Terrence was in the need of some good lovemaking to relieve some tension.

Terrence and Bright foreplayed for over thirty minutes when he begin to raise her shirt up and suck on her nipples. Bright's pussy throbbed for him like never before. She eagerly removed her pants; she wanted him inside of her badly. Terrence put his condom on and then carefully placed Bright on top of him. Bright put her heart into it and rode him slow and passionately.

"OHHHHH, you got some good tight ass pussy baby," Terrence moaned, sucking on Bright's neck and rubbing his hands up and down her smooth back.

To avoid getting any passion marks, she moved her neck and put her titty in his mouth. "It's yours, baby," Bright moaned with her eyes closed, rubbing his face and chest as she gripped his penis inside of her. "I'm about to cum," Bright lied since she was pressed for time. She had to meet up with Suge soon, and she knew If Terrence thought she was on the verge of an orgasm that he would go crazy and explode.

"Ride that dick, baby, I'm about to cum too."

Though the space was tighter in the Chevy than the Escalade, Bright rode faster and faster, making his 64 bounce up and down as if he were hitting his switches on it. Bright made loud fuck noises and bit on his neck, making him cum with her nipple in his mouth.

"That was good baby," Terrence said after Bright removed herself off of him.

"I loved it too baby," Bright said, putting her pants back on. Terrence gave her a few hundred dollars, then he dropped Bright off at home. He needed to get home to his wife and Bright wanted to take a bath before meeting up with Treasure and Suge.

"Bright, Cordell left after you told him not to,"Ryonna said once Bright made it back inside the house.

"Where did he go? It's eight o'clock at night!" Bright said angrily.

"I don't know, but Ramon wouldn't let me use the phone to call you, he kept taking it from me," Ryonna told.

"No I didn't," Ramon yelled hoping he wouldn't get in any trouble.

"Yes you did, and I told you that I was gonna tell, Bright when she got back," she said honestly.

"Quit arguing you two!" Bright yelled frustrated.

"Soon as I give his little butt an inch, he decides to take the whole fucking mile! I'll be back don't open the door for nobody, and Ramon, you better not pick on, Ray either, are I'ma tear yo butt up when I get back home. You understand me?" She asked pointing at him. Ramon nodded his head yes.

Bright went out looking for her brother, cussing and fussing the whole time until she saw him running out of the liquor store with a few of his bad ass friends.

"Cordell, get yo ass over here and in the damn house!" Bright yelled out to him from across the street. "I told Mama on you too, and she coming home to kick yo ass!" she lied hoping to scare him.

"Well, I'm telling on you too, then!" Cordell said, parting ways with his friends and making his way across the street to his sister.

"Tell, I don't give a damn, I'm damn near grown anyways!" Fussing the whole way back home, Bright told Cordell if he said one more word that she was gonna beat the black off of him. Knowing that he couldn't handle Bright, he shut up and ran inside the apartment steaming. *If Bright thinks she's the only one that can break all the rules around here, then she has another thing coming,* Cordell thought to himself. Inside Bright snatched, Cordell up by his collar. "If you disobey me again and I catch you outside, I'm fucking yo ass up on sight! Do I make myself clear?"

"Yeah, Bright, dang! I said okay already," he said, trying to remove himself from his sister's grip. When Bright released him from her hold she pushed him to the floor.

"And that goes for all of y'all too!" she said, directing her attention to Ryonna and Ramon who were peeking from behind the couch. After they both agreed, Bright ran some bath water, and she called Treasure and told her that she was in desperate need of a good bath and to walk Suge over to her house.

Treasure laughed. "Aight funky cock, we'll be there in a few."

"Thanks deep throat." Then Bright climbed into a nice hot bubble bath. "Damn bad ass kids," she said as she lit her blunt, inhaled, and then relaxed her head on the bathtub cushion.

****

Suge had been over at Bright's for over three days without her mother finding her, and since Suge loved hanging out with Bright's siblings, it allowed Bright the time she needed to step out at night without worrying about them getting into any trouble.

"How you feeling, Young?" Bright asked after stepping out of the shower and into her room where Suge was resting in her bed.

"I'm alright, just thinking about being in a foster home, with strange people and shit. I'd rather stay here with you and your family. Your mother likes me...maybe she'll let me stay a little longer," Suge said, sitting up in bed.

Happy that Suge was comfortable, Bright smiled. "I know she wouldn't mind if you stayed the rest of the summer, but once school starts she'll want to meet your mother and everything, and you know that won't work. And if she found out she was harboring a runaway, she'd go crazy and be on my head...tough!" Bright said, throwing on a pair of cotton boxer shorts and a white tank top.

"Yeah, you're right, Bright, and I guess a foster home can't be any worse than where I've been all these years either, right?"

"Right," Bright said, moisturizing her skin. "Well, Larry's coming through with movies and a bottle, I'm about to roll a blunt up to smoke, so if you wanna get faded, we'll be in the living room waiting for you," she said hoping to put a smile on Suge's face.

Suge smiled. "Okay, I will." Then she headed to the bathroom to shower.

Earlier that day, Suge had accidentally dropped Bright's cell phone behind her bed when she noticed the letter addressed to Treasure from her ex-boyfriend, Chrome. Suge was puzzled as to why Bright had the letter under her bed in the first place, and since her curiosity wouldn't allow her leave it alone, she decided to read it and find out what was going on for herself. Inside the bathroom, Suge pulled the letter from under her shirt and pulled it out of the envelope to read. However the letter was written to Chrome in Bright's handwriting...with Treasure's name signed on it. It read:

If you need for me to respond so that you can leave me the fuck alone, I will! I read your letter, and yeah, I already know what happened. Bright told me everything, so please don't think I don't know! And even if you didn't rape her, so what! You were wrong for beating her the way you did over a shower, and you deserve all the time you got for messing with her in the first place!

P.S Please don't ever write back to me again, I hate you and hope you fucking die in prison!

Sincerely a bitch that hate you,

~ Treasure

"This is wild! What the hell is going on? And what is Bright hiding?" Suge said to herself. After putting the letter back inside the envelope, she wrapped it inside of her T-shirt to ensure it wouldn't get wet, then she climbed inside the tub to shower. Once she was all cleaned up and dried off, she dressed comfortably in a pair of pajamas, then tucked the letter back under Bright's bed where she found it. Then she went into the living room to watch movies and get faded, life was tough.

Part Seven

Bright woke up early to catch her mother before she left for work. "Ma, can Suge stay a few more days?" she asked, rubbing the sleep from her eyes. "If it's okay with her mother, I guess it's okay with me, Queen Bee. Speaking of, I haven't met Suge's mother yet, and when I get back home tonight, I'd like to at least speak to her." Rosette said, finishing up her morning coffee and cigarette before going to work.

"Okay, but I think she'll still be at work at that time. I told you, that lady is a serious workaholic like you, Ma."

"Poor woman, if she works as hard as me," Rosette said, dumping the last of her cigarette out in an ashtray. "Cause I know I need me a break," she sighed.

"You need to find you a rich man like my daddy to take care of you," Bright replied.

"That type of business don't last forever. I need some life time assurance; hell I got mouths to feed. I gotta go, Queen Bee," her mother said, grabbing her work bag to head out of the door. "Oh, and before I forget, quit smoking weed in my house, Bright! She gave her daughter a look of authority. "I don't care if you are in the bathroom with it, you ain't grown and the next thing you know they'll all be tryna smoke that shit...and It's already bad enough that you doing it!"

"Maaa! I don't be smoking no weed up in here, Cordell is lying!" Bright said.

"How did you know Cordell told me anything?" Rosette said looking at Bright with her hand on her hip. "And leave him alone too; he says you're always getting on him." Before Bright could speak again, Rosette opened the apartment door to leave then said, "I don't wanna hear it, Bright, just do what I say please." Then she closed the door behind her.

Bright huffed, "I got his little punk ass," she said to herself. Then she went to the kitchen to prepare breakfast. After breakfast, Bright told her siblings to go outside to play, and not to get in or start any trouble, then she called Larry over to break him off.

"Bright, I'ma run over to K-mart to grab a few things, you wanna go with us?" Suge asked, stepping into the living room.

"Who, you and Treasure?" Bright asked. "Yeah, she's on her way right now." Suge said.

"Naw, y'all go ahead without me, Larry's on his way over," Bright replied. "And oh yeah, Blake been asking about you too!" Bright smiled.

Suge laughed. "Blake with his cute self, tell him to call me later on," Suge said as she grabbed a glass out of the dish rack, then poured herself a glass of orange juice.

"You miss ya mama? Bright asked Suge, seeing the sad look on her face.

"Heck naw! That hoe could choke on something and die, I wouldn't give a fuck! I just been down because of this whole situation, but it's nothing a good ole blunt can't fix though." Suge laughed. "You wanna smoke one with us before we leave?" Suge asked, pulling a Swisher Sweet out of her designer bag.

"And you know this!" Bright laughed. Once Treasure got there, they all kicked back in the living room listening to music, puffing, passing the weed and talking, when a knock on the door interrupted them.

Treasure, sitting on the couch by the bay window, whispered, "Bitch the, Po-Po at the door!"

Bright instantly looked at Suge and told her to go hide in her mother's bedroom closet, then she dumped the remains of the blunt down the kitchen sink, sprayed the living room with Febreeze air freshener to kill the smell of the Kush, turned the music down, and then answered the door with a cup of orange juice in her hand.

"Can I help you?" Bright asked.

"Yes we're looking for a Samantha McGraw, is she here?" the officer asked.

"Samantha McGraw?" Bright said dumbfounded.

"Oh, you talking about, Suge," she said, nodding her head.

"Yes; she ran away from home a couple weeks ago, and we have reports that she has a friend that lives here by the name of Bright Sheldon and that she has been in the area, and has possibly been staying here."

"Wait, Suge ran away?" Bright asked, playing dumb.

"Yes she has, Miss...What's your name?" he asked her.

I'm Bright Sheldon, and Suge is my friend, but I didn't know that she ran away from home. She stopped over here last night on her way home. I mean...at least that's what she told me," Bright said, looking concerned.

"Are your parents or any other adults in the residence at this time?" the officer asked.

"No, my mother just went to work, but I can assure you that Samantha isn't here." Bright said.

"How old are you, Miss Sheldon?" he asked.

"I'm sixteen, I will be seventeen next week," Bright answered.

"Do you mind if I take a look around the apartment, Miss Sheldon?" he asked, not completely believing Bright's story.

"Of course you can, Officer Grub," Bright said, reading his last name off of his badge. "If you have a search warrant to do so," she said politely.

Officer Grub gave Bright a nasty look. "If I find out that your friend has been staying here, in this apartment, I'm sending your mother to jail and whatever kids that lives in this house to Social Services. I'll be in the area, watching," he said, making his way down the stairs.

"Okay, not a problem, and if I see her before you do, I'll let her know that you're looking for her. Have a good day, officer," Bright yelled after him, then closed the door.

The second Bright closed the door she said, "Bitch, this shit is getting serious! Suge gone have to call Child Services today! My mama will kill me if she finds out she been harboring a runaway," she panicked.

"She can go to jail too, Bee," Treasure said.

Bright called out for Suge to come in the living room as she paced the living room floor thinking of what she could do to make the situation better.

"Here comes Larry, Bee," Treasure announced, looking out of the window to see if there was any police activity going on outside.

"Okay, let him in, I'ma have Suge call the people in my room."

"Okay," Treasure replied, removing herself from the couch to open the door.

Inside the room, Suge called Social Services and explained her whole situation, about how she had ran away from home because her mother was abusing her and had been doing so for over six years. Suge told the lady that she didn't want to go home and that she even wanted to divorce her mother. Suge cried so hard when she asked the lady for help that both Treasure and Bright begin to tear up as they comforted their friend. Finalizing the conversation, it was agreed that Suge would meet the social worker at her office in one hour.

"I'll be there," Suge said, wiping her eyes.

Moments later, Treasure walked outside to survey the area. Seeing that the coast was clear she gave Larry and Bright the green light to take Suge to the Social Services office. In the backseat of Larry's Mustang, Suge laid across the seat to avoid being spotted.

"You okay back there, Suge?" Larry asked, hearing her sniffle.

"I'ma be better once this shit is all over. Thanks so much for everything too, you guys," Suge said, wiping her eyes.

"You already know it, Young, you my girl for life, through the good, the bad, and even when I don't act like it, you hear me?" Bright said, then kissed Suge on the forehead.

Suge held Bright tight. "You and Treasure have been my true family, and I'ma never forget it."

Once they pulled up in the parking lot, Bright and Larry walked Suge inside the building and waited with her until Maria Hernandez took her to the back.

"I love you, Suge, and I don't care where you go, you better keep in touch, okay!"

"Always," Suge said, as she waved goodbye to Larry and Bright.

Before going back to the apartment, Bright asked

Larry to stop her by the post office to mail off a letter to her cousin, when in fact it was really the letter she had written to Chrome.

****

Back at the apartment, Larry and Bright played around in her bed kissing and dry humping. "I love you, Bright," Larry said in between pecks on the lips.

"I love you too, baby, very much," Bright said, sitting on top of Larry, looking deep into his eyes.

Larry pulled through her long golden hair, as they dazed into each other's eyes. Yearning to be as one with her, Larry sat up and kissed her passionately. "Fuck, I can't wait to marry you so I can go to sleep with you every night and wake up and see your beautiful face every morning for the rest of my life."

"You mean that, Larry?" Bright asked, planting kisses over his face.

"Every word of it, baby, I'm fucking crazy in love with you, girl," he said, squeezing her breast through her shirt.

"Let's do it, baby," Bright said, lifting her shirt to take it off. She liked her nipples played with.

"Not in yo mama house, babygirl, she trust me too much for that," Larry said, pulling her shirt back down. "She won't know, Larry, she still at work," Bright moaned.

"But your brothers and Ryonna can come up in here at any given moment, boo boo. And I got too much respect for them to get caught up in here like that," Larry said, continuing to squeeze her breast and fondle her nipples.

"Well, stop teasing me then," Bright said removing his hands from her breasts, then she climbed off of him.

"Don't be mad, baby, you can have this dick all night, tomorrow night. You still going camping with us, right?"

"I'ma ask my mama tonight, so let me get in there and cook and clean before she gets home, I'll have a better chance of going that way," Bright said, opening her bedroom door.

Larry stood up and revealed his hard member. "He depending on you, baby," Larry teased.

"You better stop it, Larry," Bright said, hungrily licking her lips. "You know I like kissing it," she said.

"I thought you loved it," he said, biting down on his bottom lip, grabbing himself.

"Boy, you playing," Bright said as she walked out of her room.

Larry laughed, "I love you too, boo boo."

Once her mother got home and opened a can of beer, Bright and Larry asked if she could go on the camping trip with Larry and his friends. After begging and promising to behave she told them yes. Bright was extra excited. The next day, she hit Terrence up for money and went and bought her and Larry all sorts of neat camping gadgets. She even bought him some new games for the PlayStation 2 she had bought him awhile back.

"Bright, yo ass is getting fat, you sure you ain't pregnant?" Treasure asked her after she paid for her items.

"Nope! I took a pregnancy test last week, still no baby for me. This weight is all that FF time we be getting in," Bright said, grabbing her bags.

Treasure rolled her eyes in the back of her head, "You always coming up with something, Bee, now what is FF supposed to mean?" Treasure giggled, grabbing her items.

"Fucking and Feeding time, quit playing!" Bright burst out laughing.

"I like it," Treasure said. "I guess I can say my Suwooo gangsta from the CPT, Lil Boo, puts the FF time in too huh?" Treasure said, smiling and switching.

"He putting in that kind of work already?" Bright asked.

"Yep, all the time too," Treasure said popping her collar. "Oh and he's having an all-white end of the summer pool party at his house next week. You're invited!" Treasure said.

"It's a date, and long overdue. I need to know this fool that got my girl nose wide the fuck open," Bright teased.

"Where the cab at though?" Bright said out loud. "I called for one before we got in the dang line," she pouted.

"Here it come, cry baby," Treasure said, pointing at the approaching cab.

"Good, 'cause I'm tired and my funds are low, gotta call my money man, Ice to set me right," Bright laughed.

"What's up with his wife, though?" Treasure asked with concern once they were inside the cab.

"He said she still fighting, that nigga taking it hard as fuck too," Bright said.

"Can you imagine, you being her, and him being Larry? I bet it's hard," Treasure said, nodding her head. "I can't even imagine that," she said.

"Girl, you and me both! Tameka is a soldier for real," Bright announced.

"Yeah she is," Treasure said sympathetically.

When the cab pulled up on Bright's street, she paid the driver, then Treasure went inside to help Bright pack her bags for the camping trip.

****

"Come here, Teddy Bear," Tameka weakly called out to her husband. Terrence had been there for her every beck and call on his hands and knees. He had put the streets on hold, and didn't have time for anyone one but his wife.

"How you feeling, baby?" Terrence asked her, sitting at her bedside, then he began to gently rub her face.

"To be honest with you love, I feel a lot better than I look," she lied to keep him strong. Inside she felt horrible, in pain, and was ready for it to be all over with, but she just couldn't go without making sure that her Teddy Bear would be alright.

A smile appeared across Terrence's face, then he climbed in bed with her. "That's what I like to hear," Terrence said, lying next to her and then gently lifting her head to lie in his arms.

"I remember when we first got married, you said, 'Tameka, I'ma always take care of you,'" she remembered clearly with a smile on her face.

"I did that shit too, huh, baby? You ain't never wanted or needed for shit, have you?" he said, feeling proud.

"Man of your word," she laughed. "Even though you cheated a lot, I appreciate that you never put any other woman before me." Unable to bear children, Tameka blamed herself when she found out about all three of her husband baby mama's, but she stayed because she loved him and couldn't have any for him.

At the moment, Terrence felt bad for the numerous amount of times he cheated on his wife. Tameka was a good detective, and he was never able to get away with anything with her. He knew that if it hadn't been for her illness catching up to her that she would have discovered

Bright a long time ago.

"That was when I was younger, baby, letting that street life and fame get to my head, but I promise you this, none of them bitches ever meant what you meant to me. None of 'em," he said. "You've always been the apple of my eye and the blood that runs through my veins to keep my heart pumping, baby, and that's on everything I love, Tameka."

"I've always known that, isn't that what I just said to you, Teddy Bear?" Tameka said, letting out a slight laugh. "I forgave you then and still now, you've been a good husband to me," she said, shifting her head for comfort in his arms with her eyes closed.

"All I ever wanted was to make you happy, Teddy Mama, and I don't want you to ever think that I was out there on that dumb shit because you didn't satisfy me at home, because you did. I was just young, dumb, and thought I was the man because I could hit anything moving." In the past, Terrence admitted to Tameka that he cheated on her because he wanted to have a baby, but after that he regretted it, because she blamed herself for every single affair he had on her thereafter, which was far from the truth. He was just being a dog.

"We got married very young baby," Tameka admitted. "We're still young now," she laughed.

"Yeah we are baby, that's why I believe we gone overcome this cancer shit, we gone grow old together, and I promise you on my life that I'm not gone never, ever, cheat on you again," Terrence promised. His mind was made up that after this, it was over between him and Bright.

"I don't know about growing old baby, this illness hurts too much for me to keep going on," she sighed as she gently rubbed Terrence's forearm.

"You just have to keep on fighting it, Teddy Mama, 'cause I ain't ready for you to leave me yet."

"It's not your call or mines, baby, it's that man upstairs call," Tameka said, pointing her finger up. "And when he calls, baby, I'm going, and I'm okay with it, but now I need to know that you will be."

Terrence sat up in the bed. "Fuck that, hell naw I ain't gone accept shit, you just keep fighting, Tameka!" he said, raising his voice.

"Shhhh, don't be like that Teddy," Tameka said, trying to calm him down.

"I'ma be like that, so don't plan on dying no time soon,"Terrence said, looking his wife in her eyes.

"You're being so selfish right now, Teddy Bear. Don't you understand that I'm hurting right now, that I'm constantly in pain and that even this medication don't stop it?" Tameka paused to take a few breaths. "I asked God to give me more time to help you deal with this, and you're not making it easy on me at all, Teddy Bear. So I beg you, baby, please... for me," Tameka said softly patting her heart, as a tear fell from her eye. "I want to know that when I'm gone, Teddy Bear, that you'll accept that I wasn't afraid to die and that I'll be in a much better place," she said, looking him in his watery eyes.

"I can't, no, fuck that, I'm not gone accept the shit. I need you here, Teddy Mama," Terrence said as he slid off the bed and onto his knees.

No matter how much he wanted to make it easier for his wife, he just couldn't. "If God is the one giving you the extra time, then I say ask him to remove and cure this illness, baby, you too young to die. We were supposed to grow old together, Tameka. So please, just where you belong," he cried, laying his head on her chest. "I'm not ready to say good-bye yet."

Terrence had never cried in front of her before, and seeing him cry hit her even harder than the cancer did. "I can't stay any longer," Tameka said, rubbing Terrence face. "But I'll tell you what…"

"What's that?" Terrence asked, lifting his head up from her chest.

"I'd sure like some vanilla ice cream," she smiled. "Can we at least agree on that?"

"We sho can," he smiled back at her, standing up. "Now while I go grab the ice cream, you better be getting at God about getting rid of this illness," he fussed as he walked to the kitchen.

"I will, but can I get a kiss first, Teddy Bear?" Tameka smiled.

Terrence turned around and smiled at her. "Now that's what I'm talking about." Then he knelt down to kiss Tameka's soft lips slow, soft, and passionately.

"I love you, always, Teddy Bear." Tameka said.

"I love you, baby," Terrence smiled, then stood back up to get Tameka's ice cream. "Now gone and get back to God, I'll be right back," he said.

Tameka closed her eyes and smiled. "Teddy Bear, Teddy Bear."

****

Up in the Big Bear Mountains, Larry and Bright were having the time of their life. They had done so many aquatic sports in the lake that it wasn't even funny: wakeboarding, water skiing, and parasailing, all of which Bright enjoyed. Their last day there, they all agreed on renting a pontoon boat to just relax and cruise the shoreline.

During the ride, the two girls that Larry's teammates brought along got to putting on yet another freak show. Susan the Asian girl sat on Wendy the white girl's lap and began bouncing up and down on her and shaking her breasts in Wendy's face.

"Not this shit again," Bright said under her breath. They watched their freak show the first night in the cabin and she wasn't in the mood to watch them again.

Larry grabbed Bright by the behind and sat her on his lap. "Not enjoying the show, baby?" he asked, then kissed her on the cheek.

"Not at all," she said moving her hair from her face. "Is she eating her coochie?" Larry asked, looking around Bright's upper body. Bright turned her head. She couldn't believe it, Wendy was eating Susan out like there was no tomorrow, while the guys sat there and watched.

"Suck that pussy, Wendy," Larry's teammate James said, slapping her on the ass.

"Babe, what the fuck?" Bright asked in disbelief.

"They're not seriously about to do this again, are they?" "They came here to have a good time with the girls, and I came here to have a good time with my future wife. Don't pay them no mind," he said as she kept watching the show.

"Well maybe I wouldn't if my man wasn't all up in them bitches' coochies," Bright said, turning Larry's face to hers.

"Come on, baby, this shit ain't no worse than us watching porn. And besides, it's a guy thing to watch two girls get down."

Bright understood, but she liked to keep and have all of her attention especially from her own man. *Fuck Wendy and Susan,* Bright thought as she stood up and removed her bottoms.

"What the fuck you doing?" Larry said, directing his attention to his girlfriend standing in front of him almost nude.

"Getting your attention back, Daddy Lane." Then she sat back on top of him, pulled his penis out and began to stroke it.

Quickly, Larry took the throw blanket he brought along with them and covered Bright's backside.

"You like that, baby?" Bright asked as she continued to stroke his penis.

"Get on it," he whispered, "and I'ma show you just how much I like it," Larry moaned. Bright got on top and as usual did her thing. Riding him and moaning in his ears as he watched Wendy and Susan make out with each other made it all that more exciting, and within seconds he had busted inside of Bright for the seventh time that weekend.

"I think that was our baby that time, Larry," Bright whispered in Larry's ear.

Larry smiled. "You a fucking freak, girl."

"For you, I'll do and be it all," she said, easing her bottoms back on. Larry nodded his head. "That's why I love you, girl."

Part Eight

Bright had been back from Big Bear Lake for a little over a week and was still unable to get in touch with Terrence. She hoped his wife hadn't died already or that he had got caught up in the streets and got locked up. But then again, those better have been the only reasons and excuses he had for not answering or returning her calls. Deja was days away from being released from juvenile, and Bright needed money to throw her a welcome home party. Not to mention, she needed extra money for new school clothes, cause the two hundred dollars that her mother had given her wasn't going to cut it. *Where are you, Terrence?"* Bright said to herself after she left him yet another voice mail.

Her mother busted into her room. "Happy seventeenth birthday, Queen Bee!" She had a platter in her hand to serve Bright breakfast in bed. It was routine that Rosette served her children breakfast in bed, made them dinner and a cake of their choice, and at least a twenty dollar bill on each birthday. But this year, Rosette had a crispy hundred dollar bill for her eldest daughter's seventeenth birthday. She appreciated Bright for her role around the house, and though she didn't have a lot, she gave what she had where her children were concerned.

"Thanks, Maaa!" Bright said, sitting up in bed waiting for her breakfast tray. A sausage, cheese, and onion egg omelet with hash browns and toast on the side was Bright's favorite breakfast dish, and nobody prepared it better than her mother did.

"Take a picture of me serving and kissing the Queen,"

everything to Rosette, and she took as many pictures of happy moments as she could with her children. Cordell took three good snaps of them.

"What you want for dinner, Queen Bee?" her mother asked with a smile on her face.

"I'll take some of your nachos, a strawberry cake, and root beer floats!"

"You got it, Queen Bee," her mother said as she passed Bright a birthday card. "Now go on and open your birthday card up, so I can get a picture of you reading it before I go to the grocery store."

When Bright opened the birthday card a one hundred dollar bill fell out of it. "Aww, thanks Ma," she said, reaching out for another hug. Then she read the card out loud: *"Happy Birthday to the best daughter and sister that a mom, sisters, and brothers could ever ask for! We all love you and appreciate you Bright! Happy Birthday from all of us!!!!"*

"Smile, big sis, smile!" Cordell said, snapping another picture of her. Bright mustered up the biggest smile that she could, then she winked at him, initiating a truce. After Cordell snitched on her about smoking weed in the house, she had barely spoken two words to him at a time.

"That was too sweet," Bright said. "My first customized birthday card! Thanks all of y'all, and I love y'all so much too, group hug!" she yelled with her arms extended.

Later the house was rocking. All of Bright's friends came over to celebrate her birthday, and bring her gifts. Nicole had even stopped by with a gift and had a plate of her mom's delicious nachos. For Bright's Birthday, Larry got her name tattooed on his chest and bought her a

Victoria Secret Bath and Body set. Bright was happy about the tattoo and loved the fragrance that he picked for her. By ten p.m., the party had turned to her mom's normal card party when her longtime friends and boyfriend Vince stopped by.

"Aye, I'm surprised your uncle hasn't stopped by," Larry said to Bright while they sat on the living room couch. He was enjoying watching the old-timers play cards, cha-cha, and talk trash to one another, particularly Bright's Mom.

"He's out of town," Bright lied. Her spirits were somewhat down.

"Why the long face?" Larry asked, directing his attention back to Bright. "I know it's not about the baby, is it?"

After taking a pregnancy test earlier that day and learning that she was pregnant, Bright began to worry, and the reality of telling her mother and disappointing her became her fear.

"Yes, it's about the baby!" Bright responded in a loud whisper so that Larry could hear her over the loud music. "I'm scared to tell my mother now, and what if she stops liking you?" she asked.

"I seriously doubt that," Larry said with confidence. "Yo moms know that you're dealing with a good dude and that I'll always be here and have your back." He smiled, hoping to lift her spirits. "Everything will be alright, Pretty Bright." He was overwhelmed with joy about becoming a father.

His words alone raised Bright's spirits, making her smile. "I love you, Larry Lane."

"I love you more," Larry replied.

Preparing to go in for a kiss, their rhythm was broken

on and cha-cha with me, Queen Bee," her mother said as she danced across the floor and grabbed Bright's arm to dance with her. Whenever her mother had house parties, it was routine that she cha-cha with her children, mainly Bright.

"Aww Ma, I don't feel like it," Bright complained. "Gone and dance wit ya mama, girl," her mother's friends, Gale and Lyn, yelled out to her.

"I ain't in the mood!" Bright replied.

"I got you, Mom's." Larry stood up and grabbed Rosette's hand to cha-cha with her. He knew Bright was in an emotional state of mind and didn't want to be bothered, so he took the dance for her.

"Alright now, let me see if my son-in-law can handle this," Rosette teased, sliding across the living room floor doing the cha-cha with Larry.

"I got this, Mom's...what you know about this?"

Larry asked, spinning Rosette around and then dipped her down. The cha-cha was a tradition in his family, and was carried out at every family function.

"That boy think he know something, Rose," Vince said, cutting in. "Let me pluck this chicken," he added in a competitive tone.

The ladies began to laugh, drunk Lyn yelled out, "That's right Vince, show 'em!"

"I'm out ya way O.G.," Larry laughed, backing up with his hands in the air. Then he sat back down with Bright and talked for the remainder of the evening.

****

"Bright, Nicole is driving us over to Lil Boo's white pool party, so hurry up and get dressed, she'll be here in an hour!" Treasure yelled through the phone.

"Nicole," Bright sighed. "I didn't feel like being bothered with her fat ass, but fuck it, we off school ground. She say some fly shit tonight, I'm on her ass," Bright replied.

"Knock it off already, Bright, y'all made up, and besides, that shit is old! Nicole is the homegirl and I ain't gone let y'all get into it," Treasure said, hoping for a good night.

"Ya okay," Bright said. "I didn't know y'all was big kicking it buddies now...but don't worry, I won't fuck wit ya friend," Bright said in a jealous tone.

Treasure laughed. "Stop it, you know you're my best friend, Bright, so stop letting that baby make yo ass all sensitive and stuff," she laughed. Though Treasure wasn't interested in having a baby, she was excited about becoming a godmother, and she planned on spoiling her new godson or goddaughter to death.

"Whatever, I'm getting dressed, and don't worry, I'll be a good girl," Bright laughed, then hung up the phone. Bright slicked her hair in a side ponytail that hung down her back, she dressed in a short, all white spaghetti strap fitted dress, with a white two-piece bikini underneath, she wore burgundy trendy heels, and burgundy accessories. She knew it was an all-white pool party, but because they were going to a Piru party, she wanted to represent to the fullest and grab lots of attention, especially from Lil Boo in particular.

Bright walked into her mother's room where her brothers and sister Ryonna were watching movies. "Cordell, I'm about to go to the party with Treasure for a few hours, please no going outside or having company while I'm gone. Y'all got snacks in there, so no store runs a'ight?" Bright said, giving her brother direct eye contact.

Bright had been helping her mother keep snacks and drinks stocked up in the house, since they were always the first to go. She also used the snacks as bait to keep her siblings in check. When her mother would question her about the whereabouts of her money, she would tell her that Larry had given it to her.

"I told you I was gone hold the house down, Bright, so don't worry," Cordell said.

"Don't let me down, Cordell, I really wanna go to this party, and plus I already gave you twenty dollars to be on ya best behavior."

"Bright, I'm fourteen years old, I'm almost a grown ass man, I gots this," he said, waving her off.

"I'ma mess you up, boy, keep on cussing!" Bright laughed as she made her way out of the room and to the front door. Once Bright made it down the stairs of her apartment, Nicole pulled up in a black BMW on twenty inch rims. Treasure was glowing in the passenger seat.

"Hey Nicole, damn! Treasure, you look fucking beautiful, bestie, straight DNBB baby!" Bright said, approaching the car.

Nicole smiled and waved at Bright while Treasure blushed. "You look super cute too, bestie," Treasure replied. "But check out Nicole, thirty pounds smaller from the last time you seen her," Treasure bragged.

"I try, I try," Nicole said as Bright climbed in the back seat of the car.

Bright had to admit to herself that Nicole looked amazing, but since she still wasn't feeling her from their last incident, she wasn't going to tell her that. In Bright's mind, Nicole thought she was better than her, and now that she was big kicking it with her best friend...only made matters worse.

On the ride there, Bright indulged in the small talk from school to boys and was on her best behavior.

"Look like it's on and popping over here!" Bright said, snapping her fingers and winding her upper body from side to side.

"It does," Nicole agreed. "Look at the flashy cars parked out here," Nicole said, backing her brother's B.M.W in between a burgundy and white low-rider, and a Hummer on twenty four inch wheels.

"That's Lil Boo low-rider, that muthafucka is fresh, ain't it?" Treasure said.

Both of the girls agreed. When they stepped out of the car, they gained the attention of every eye in the street as they made their way to Lil Boo's front door.

"Hey sexy ladies, come on out back," Lil Boo signaled once he had seen Treasure's face. Treasure lit up like a light bulb.

"Cuteeee," Nicole smiled and said under her breath at the same time.

Treasure laughed, "I told you."

Once they made it to the back door that led to the garage where pool and dominoes were being played, Treasure introduced her girls to him.

"Hey you," Bright smiled, extending her hand. "Nice to finally meet you, I've heard so much about you."

Lil Boo grabbed Bright's hand and planted a soft kiss on the top of it. "Nice to meet you, Bright."

Then he said, "Oh you must be Nicole, I told you when I saw you I was gone bite you, for clowning on the phone the other day." He laughed, then he wrapped his arms around her and gave her a big hug. "Now I can put a face with that sweet voice of yours," he said releasing her from his hug.

Bright's horns instantly came up; she thought, *what the fuck did I miss?* Treasure read Bright's facial expression, then immediately felt the need to explain.

"Nicole called me one day I was kicking it with Lil Boo, and he told her to call me back, and girl, they got to clowning," Treasure said briefly, filling Bright in.

Bright put on a fake smile, "Oh yea, cuteeee, I'ma go make me a drink," she replied nonchalantly. Then she walked in the direction of the open bar.

Lil Boo had outdone himself throwing his end of the summer, all-white pool party. The butlers were dressed in white tuxes with red ties, and the female servers dressed in white skirts, low cut white tops and wore white heels. The tables that sat alongside the pool were candle lit and draped elegantly with white tablecloths. The girls inside the pool all wore white two piece bathing suits and the guys wore either white trunks or basketball shorts.

After a few drinks, Bright got over her jealousy and asked Nicole and Treasure to get inside the pool with her. Standing in front of Treasure, taking the last sip of her drink, Bright caught a glimpse of Lil Boo and his boys staring at her, so without further notice she pulled her white dress off as seductively as she knew how then dove in the pool.

"Come on, Nicole!" Treasure said removing her dress to get inside the pool.

"I gotta go put my bathing suit on, where's the bathroom?" Nicole asked Treasure.

"I'll take you," Treasure said, leading Nicole inside. Then she yelled out to Bright that she'd be right back.

"You having fun?" Lil Boo asked Bright as he took a seat and lit a blunt by the side of the pool.

"Yeah, but I can think of a lot more fun and freaky shit that I could be doing right now though," she gave him a seductive smile then winked at him.

"Damn!" Lil Boo said. "Is that right?"

Bright laughed. "A wet pussy always needs something fat to fill it up and keep it tamed," she flirted.

"You's a little dynamite, huh?" Lil Boo's penis began to rise.

"Shhhhh, don't tell nobody," she said, pressing her index finger seductively on her lips. Then she dove back under the water to swim.

"You getting in, Lil Boo?" Treasure asked as she and Nicole made their way back to the pool.

"Naw, you ladies have fun, I have a party to host," he said, then sat back and watched the show that Bright was putting on in the pool.

After the party started clearing out, Treasure was too drunk to go home, so she decided to stay the night with Lil Boo. "I'll take you home, Bright, you ready?" Nicole asked her.

"I don't wanna leave my girl," Bright said, more infatuated with the idea of kicking it with Lil Boo a little while longer.

"Y'all go ahead, I got, her," Lil Boo said, hugging a drunken Treasure.

"Yep, I'm good right here with Boo," Treasure slurred, smiling at her friends.

"I'ma stay with her, she too drunk," Bright told Nicole, looking in the direction of Lil Boo and Treasure.

Nicole laughed, "Girl please, you know she about to get her some," she whispered in Bright's ear. "Roll with me; Treasure is cool with Lil Boo, he got her," she assured Bright.

"Naw, I'ma stay here wit my homegirl," Bright said, wrapping a dry towel over her cold body. "I'ma stay wit you!" Bright yelled to Treasure as Lil Boo picked her up to take her to his bedroom. "Is it cool for me to stay over?" Bright asked Lil Boo.

"Yeah, it's all good, mama." He smiled; he knew Bright wanted to fuck him.

After everybody was gone, Lil Boo gave Bright a T-shirt and towel and told her she could shower in his downstairs bathroom. Bright stripped butt naked in front of him, then pointed to his bathroom. "That one right there?" she asked, swinging her bottoms on her index finger.

Looking at Bright's fat pink pussy, Lil Boo was unable to think with his right head. He grabbed a condom off the top of his fireplace, then took his pants off. Before he could put the condom on his stiff member, Bright had dropped to her knees and crawled to him, begging to taste it. Bright held his penis with both of her hands and filled her throat up to capacity.

"Get that shit, baby," Lil Boo said as he popped his penis in and out of her drip ping wet mouth. After she gave him her infamous head job, she rolled the condom on his penis with her mouth.

Lil Boo picked her up and slammed her up against the wall and blew her insides out. Her pussy was looser than Treasure's, but Bright put on a wilder performance. He liked the way she slid his dick from her pussy to her ass hole in one quick motion.

Bright liked the way Lil Boo bit on her nipples and spread her ass cheeks apart to make sure every inch of him was inside of her. He was putting in work.

Lil Boo had fucked Bright into his kitchen, then threw

her over the sink and hit it doggy style until he came. Though he was enjoying the moment he had to make it quick, because he didn't want Treasure to wake-up and catch them. After he pulled his pants up, Lil Boo left Bright leaning over the sink, and then he walked upstairs to his bedroom without saying another word to her.

"That shit was bomb," Bright said to herself, then she took a shower and went to sleep.

****

The next morning, Nicole came to pick Treasure and Bright up from Lil Boo's house to take them home. Bright had thirty minutes to get home before her mother made it home.

"Push it, Nicole, I'm tryna beat my mama home," Bright said.

"We'll be there in ten minutes," Nicole said.

"I was so drunk last night, I didn't even get none," Treasure said.

"Damn," Nicole laughed.

"I was faded and passed out too," Bright said.

Treasure looked back at Bright with a look of disappointment on her face. "And you shouldn't of been drinking last night Bee...you're pregnant!"

"I'm straight, Treasure, I'm only in my first trimester."

"Which are the most important stages too, Bright...I agree with Treasure," Nicole added.

Bright sighed, then looked out the window. She wasn't in the mood or trying to hear it, especially from Nicole.

Once Nicole dropped Bright off, she ran up to her apartment, checked on her brothers and sister, then climbed in her bed before her mother made it home.

"Fuck, last night was wild," Bright said to herself, then she fell back asleep.

****

Bright hadn't heard from Terrence in weeks. He hadn't called her for her birthday or returned any of her calls, and she had been leaving him urgent messages a few times each day. *Maybe his wife died or he's in jail or something.* In the middle of her thoughts, her newly downloaded Biggie Smalls "Get Money" ringtone alerted her, indicating that Terrence was calling her. Bright dashed for her cell phone and quickly answered.

"Hey boo, where have you been, I've been calling you?" she said in one breath. After a few moments of silence and no response from Terrence, Bright asked him if he was alright.

"Naw, not really...my wife passed away." he said, trying to avoid tears. He had been messed up in the head to say the least. Tameka had asked him for ice cream and when he returned with it, she was dead.

Bright sighed in pain. "I'm so sorry to hear that, baby. Come pick me up and let me be there for you, Terrence."

"I need time to clear my head right now, Bright."

"I understand, baby, take all the time you need, I'm here for you. But you think you can at least drop me off some money for school clothes?" She hoped she didn't sound too inconsiderate, but she was broke.

"My homeboy, Pee Wee, owe me a couple grand, I'll tell 'em to meet up with you in about an hour by Starr King. That should hold you up for a minute, I'll call you in a couple days." Then he hung up.

Bright hooked up with Treasure to walk with her to

Starr King to meet up with Pee Wee. Pulling up in a souped-up Monte Carlo, Pee Wee gave Bright an envelope full of money then exchanged numbers with Treasure. Before parting their separate ways, Treasure and Bright went to the nail shop to get their nails and toes done and their eyebrows waxed. Then they went home.

****

"Hey Suge, let me call you back, babe, my little sister, Deja, just got out of juvenile!" Bright yelled excitedly into the phone, then hung up.

They all drove two cars deep to the juvenile to pick up Deja and to take her out to dinner. Her mother didn't have the money she was expecting to throw Deja the BBQ and water fight bash she had planned too, and Bright got the money too late from Terrence to throw the event. So after Bright finished with all of her school shopping and had a few hundred dollars left, she gave her mother one hundred and fifty dollars extra to help treat everybody to lunch at Lucille's at the Long Beach Town Center. Deja had gotten a little heavier and her hair had gotten as long as Bright's hair. She was different too, more quiet and reserved, not the talkative Deja that she used to be.

"My baby's just growing up," Rosette said, smiling and eating.

In the middle of everybody laughing, eating and talking, Larry walked up to Bright, and on one knee, he proposed to her in front of her whole family.

"My Pretty, Bright, the love of my life and girl that I want to spend the rest of my life with, and not a day less...will you marry me?" he asked rubbing the palm of her hand, and looking deep into her eyes.

Bright was speechless. "Yes, I'll marry you, Larry.

You're the man of my dreams, Larry Lane," Bright said and then kissed him softly on the lips. "I love you, Larry," she said as he slid a gold band on her wedding finger.

Rosette chimed in with a smile on her face. "You sure can marry her after she's eighteen, Larry Lane," then extended her arms out to hug him. She was happy for her daughter. Larry brought the best out of her, and to her that was what real love did.

Bright was so caught up in the moment, that she began speaking without thinking. "Ma, you gone be a grandmother too," she said before she could catch herself. The once loud and happy table immediately fell into complete silence. Larry stood frozen where he stood. He and Bright had agreed they would tell her privately. *What was she thinking?* He thought.

"You're what!?" her mother said, slamming her fork in her plate."

Bright just stared at her mother, speechless.

"I'm-hummm, I'm, I'm pregnant, Ma," Bright stuttered.

Rosette's eyes filled with tears. "I knew the day would come that my failure in parenthood would show in you, I just didn't know when," she said with her arms folded across her chest, rocking and nodding her head. "I should of been there for you more, Queen Bee, this is all my fault," she cried. "I took ya youth straight from under your feet." Rosette was filled with guilt.

"Oh, Rose, don't say that, girl, you are a wonderful mother," her friend of many years, Gale, said as she gave her a comforting pat on the back.

"No I'm not, Gale! I put my work over my kids, and Bright damn near had to raise herself and her sisters and brothers," Rosette said, wiping her tears away.

"Hey, you think you a bad mother because you work, Rose?" Gale asked with a look of disbelief on her face. "And because you don't mind working damn hard to take care of your children? To keep a roof over their heads and to keep food on the table. Look at me," Gale said, turning her friend's face to hers. "You give your last to your children, you provide for them the best you can by yourself, and you're always there for them!" Getting misty eyed and emotional Gale continued. "Bright did this because she's growing up, Rose. We did the same thing, remember?" she was hoping to bring her friend back down to reality. "And I know I had me a good Mama...God rest her soul!" she remembered telling her mother that she was pregnant at the tender age of sixteen. "So we not gone go there with the blame game, Rose, you only did what any other mother would have done: work hard to take care of her children. And I say you did a damn good job at that!"

She wiped Rosette's tears, then gave her a long, tight hug. After the two friends shared a hug, Bright knelt down beside her mother.

"Mom, you've always done the best that you could do with us, so please don't blame yourself, listen to Gale," Bright said nodding her head. "I got pregnant because I wanted too, me and Larry both wanted this baby," she cried.

Larry knelt down next to Bright and chimed in, "I'm gonna always be there for, Bright and our baby, Moms," he said, giving her a sincere look. "And that's on my life," he promised.

"Well, I guess, I'ma be a Grandma," Rosette said, forcing a smile on her face as she hugged her daughter.

"And Larry, I'ma hold you to your word too," she assured, making direct eye contact with him.

"I'm a man of my word, Moms," then he joined in on the hug and kissed both Bright and her mother on the forehead. "When I get drafted to the NBA your daughter and grandbaby are gonna be set for the rest of their lives...just watch."

Back to School
"2005"

Part Nine

After, Larry dropped Bright off at home, he secretly headed out to look for a part time job so that he could contribute and start buying the baby things. Bright didn't want Larry to work; she wanted him to keep his head in the books and work hard toward his career in basketball. Bright told him that she could afford to take care of them until he was drafted to the NBA. She had lied and told him that she received a healthy monthly lump sum from her father's estate.

Before, he didn't mind her treating and splurging on him and keeping money in his pockets, but now that she was carrying his baby, he knew that it was time to step up to the plate and take care of his responsibilities like a man should. But because he knew Bright would fuss, complain, and stress about him seeking employment, he decided that it would be in his best interest to keep it a secret from her.

Larry had been all over the city looking for well-paying work, but with no real work experience, the only opportunity he had was a job at fast food restaurant. So when the manager at McDonald's hired him on the spot, Larry took the job and ran with it. The job was thirty minutes away in the valley, so he was confident that Bright wouldn't find out. And he planned on saving every last dollar that he made for Bright and their unborn child. Larry knew that with school, basketball, and work that he would have less time to spend with Bright and that she would complain, but he knew that his hard work and efforts would pay off in the long run, and that he was doing the right thing.

****

After spending Terrence money on her boyfriend and their baby, Bright and Treasure decided to have lunch at Subway in the Lakewood mall. Treasure had met a new boss baller named Rafael (a.k.a. Monster), that kept her pockets fat, hoping he would get her in bed soon. He gave her money every time she mentioned she wanted or needed something.

"What you gone tell Ice about you being pregnant, Bright?" Treasure asked curiously.

"That it's his baby, what you thought?" Bright said, swallowing a huge chunk of her tuna sub. "Can't just be giving up money," Bright said, pulling a bankroll out of her bra.

"You said y'all used protection all the time, though, Bright," Treasure said, confused. "So how you gone pull that off?" she wanted to know.

"I ain't but four weeks now, so when I see him I'ma let him hit raw dog and then four weeks later, I'll tell him I'm pregnant. That simple," Bright said, feeling good that she had come up with a master plan.

Treasure nodded her head. "I hope this brilliant idea work out for you, girl," Treasure said in between sips of her Diet Coke.

"It will. I'll almost be eighteen by the time I have the baby, and me and Larry plan on getting married and moving in together on my birthday. So I'm not trippin', I'ma dump Terrence, tell him the baby is not his, then get on," Bright summed up. She had been going over the plans all night.

"You better hope and pray that fool don't kill you, Bright," Treasure said with a serious look upon her face.

"He gone have to find me to try to kill me," Bright laughed.

"Alright, it's your life," Treasure shrugged.

"I personally think you got yaself a good dude in Larry and that you should just stop fucking with Ice, now," she said, giving Bright direct eye contact. Ice had a reputation for being crazy, and she didn't want Bright to get hurt or chance losing Larry.

Bright stood to dump her tray. "Trust me, Treasure, I gots this," she said confidently. After they caught the bus back to the Norfside of Long Beach, Treasure and Bright went their separate ways.

****

"Hey baby, how are feeling," Bright asked Terrence sympathetically once she answered her phone.

"Where you at?" he asked her.

"Just walked in the house from shopping." She put her bags on her bed, then took a seat to rest her feet. "You sound a little better baby, does that mean today has been a better day for you?" she asked again.

"I wanna fuck, can I come pick you up?" he asked. Bright sighed with an attitude. "Terrence, why are you coming at me like that, and why the hell are you avoiding my question?"

"Look, I'm alright, Bright." He paused. "I wanna see you and I wanna fuck, now can I come pick you up?" he asked, getting straight to the point.

He was heartbroken and messed up in the head over the passing of his wife, and he just didn't want to talk about it; he wanted to fuck. Bright was ready to snap, but reminded herself that he had just lost his wife, so she rolled with the flow. "Pick me up down the street from my house in about an hour, daddy."

"I'll be there in an hour," Terrence replied, then hung up.

Quickly, Bright hopped in the shower and threw ona pair of booty shorts and an "I Love Hot Guys" fitted T-shirt. She fixed her side pony tail, threw on her sandals, and then left out the door. It was her mother's off day, so she didn't have the responsibility of her siblings that day.

Terrence pulled up in his truck, looking physically and emotionally distressed, and Bright could tell from his weight loss that he hadn't been eating. She wasn't gonna make him feel bad about it, but she was definitely gonna get him back together, starting with washing and braiding his hair, then she planned on fucking the life back into him. And with Larry's tight schedule, she knew she'd have the time to do so.

"Hey, Daddy," Bright climbed in and said in a comforting tone, then she reached over and hugged him real tight and planted soft kisses all over his face.

Terrence forced a smile. "We gone go back to my place," he said, pulling off her street, bumping his music. Bright nodded her head in agreement and tried reaching for his hand, but he pulled it away.

Terrence's mood was so dark that he couldn't see the light. He tried breaking out of it by reminding himself of Tameka's last words to him: "I'm not afraid to go, I'm hurting here and I'll be in a much better place," but nothing helped. He knew she had to go, but he just wasn't expecting her to go before he came back with her ice cream.

On the ride to his house, Bright tried her very best to comfort and cheer Terrence up, but he kept drowning her out with his music, which caused her to fall asleep. When they arrived at his house, he awoke her by squeezing on her pussy.

Inside Terrence's four bedroom luxury suburban home, Bright thought, *Wow this would be my life if I didn't have, Larry.* His house was decked out modernly and he had all the newest house appliances and electronics, his all-white living room suit looked as if it was hardly ever sat on. Terrence sat on the couch and flipped the television on, then began to roll up a blunt. "Want me to roll it for you?" Bright asked, wanting him to be able to relax and clear his head.

"Bright, I'm good, don't start treating a nigga like no baby and shit," he said, looking in her direction. "That's the last thing I need right now, just chill out," he said, then got back to rolling the blunt.

"Say no more," Bright said, backing off with her hands in the air. "Now, where's your bathroom? I'ma run you a good bubble bath." She paused, looking at him. "Can I at least wash you up and give you a massage, Daddy?" she smiled seductively.

"That's more like it! Go upstairs, down the hall and to the right. I'll be up there in a minute." He hoped getting some pussy and head would relieve a little of his stress.

"Bring the blunt up too!" Bright yelled down to him.

After rolling the blunt, Terrence went upstairs and climbed inside the hot bubble bath that Bright had drawn up for him, then they shared a blunt. Bright gave Terrence a good bath. She washed him up, massaged his shoulders, and even climbed inside for foreplay. She rubbed her fingers through his hair and passionately kissed him like she never did before while she straddled him. Once they got out, she dried him off from head to toe, then landed on her knees where she used her mouth to suck a nut out of him.

"Oh shit, Bright!" he moaned. "That shit feel so good," he said, holding the back of her head. Bright worked him, causing him to explode in her mouth. "Swallow it," he looked down and told her. As instructed, Bright swallowed it then licked her top lip, hungry for more. Then he led her to one of his guest rooms. In bed, Terrence climbed on top of Bright without using protection, just as she hoped he would. Then he penetrated her hard and fast, making the headboard slam up against the wall with each pump.

"This shit feel so good, Tameka, make slow soft love to me, Teddy Mama, just one mo time" he moaned with his eyes closed.

Instantly, Bright was turned on hearing Terrence call her another woman's name, so she grinded her magic on him soft and slow, gripping him as if her mouth was on him. Nice and tight. "Oh, Tameka!" he said, burying his head in the pillow with Bright's legs held high over his shoulders. Bright kept at this rate until he begged her to go faster, and seconds later he came inside of her. She felt bad for letting him come on top of her baby's head, but it was all a part of her plan.

After a few more, rounds Terrence told Bright to cook him something to eat. She fried up a batch of chicken strips, made a couple of loaded baked potatoes, and boiled some corn on the cob. When he finished eating, he gave her props on her cooking skills, hit it once more, then took her back home. Before she climbed out of his truck, he passed her a roll of money.

Terrence liked spoiling his women; it made him feel good, and kept them loyal to him. At least, that's what he thought he was doing with Bright. "Buy you something nice," he told her, feeling better than he was before he picked her up.

Bright smiled, "You know I will." Then she closed the door and made tracks in the direction of her house.

Stepping out of the courtyard, Cordell spotted Bright getting out of Big Ice from the east side's Escalade. He wondered, what *is Bright doing with Ice?* Then he hit the corner to catch up with his partners.

****

"Hurry up, Bee," Treasure said after their first day back to school. "Nicole gone meet us at Burger King then drop us off at home." As usual, both girls were the best dressed females on campus, representing the Norf's baddest. Every guy in school had their eyes on them, and the females hated.

"Nicole, Nicole, Nicole," Bright said in an irritated tone. "Didn't her ass graduate from high school, or can't she find any friends in college?" Bright hissed.

"Bee, quit being like that, Nicole is the homegirl. Besides she tutors me in algebra. I'm tryna get a scholarship, so I gotta keep a high grade point average," Treasure replied.

"Fuck a scholarship when you can have a balling ass nigga worship the ground you walk on and take care of you," Bright said catching up to Treasure. "I'm just tryna graduate from high school...and that's just for my Mama," Bright admitted honestly.

Treasure just shook her head at Bright. It was funny to her how Bright was still the same, and how in many ways she herself had changed. Education had always been important to her, but now she was really interested idea of messing around with different ballers in hopes of being their main chick was no longer her M.O.; she was feeling the idea of finding and falling in love with a guy that would love her for her. She had even kicked Larry's friend Reggie to the curb for seeing her as nothing more than a booty call. Her priorities were falling in line, and she wanted to be respected for more than her body, big behind and a pretty face; but more so respected for her intelligence and mind.

"What's up with you and Lil Boo?" Bright asked curiously as they crossed the street.

"We still cool, I just been on some other shit lately,"Treasure said like his name left a bad taste in her mouth. "And plus that nigga been acting funny ever since that night we stayed over his house. Maybe he mad cause he ain't get none, I don't know!" Treasure said, waving the conversation off.

Bright thought, *Yeah that nigga ain't get no ass alright, but he was all up in this, and matter of fact I'ma put that nigga on my list just in case Terrence start tripping!* She laughed. "That's cause you slippin' in ya pimping, pimpin'!" Bright yelled, elbowing Treasure. "That nigga 'pose to be filling them pockets up, why you playin'?" She said seriously.

"I'm cool on all that," Treasure said nonchalantly.

"But what I'm about to do is pimp these fucking books so I can get a damn scholarship, pimpin'!" She shot back. "Besides that my little friend Monster stay paying the lady...and he still ain't hit it."

"Yeah, you definitely been hanging with Nicole," Bright said with her lips twisted up. "Cause one thing for sure, and two for certain, a bitch with good looks and a bomb ass body can get and have whatever the fuck she wants from a nigga, so why go to school when you don't have to? That's for ugly hoe's," she laughed, hoping to get Treasure back on track.

As Bright was preparing to get more information on money-man Monster and ask Treasure when she was going to finally introduce them, Treasure interrupted her thoughts.

"There go Nicole right there, Bee," she said, waving to her friend. "Her brother gave her the Beamer as a graduation present, wasn't that nice?" Treasure said, happy for Nicole.

"If her brother giving away them kind of presents, I may need to meet him," Bright laughed. "He's married," Treasure said.

Bright laughed, "And what is that supposed to mean to me? Married men money is the best money, cause they'll do anything to keep a bitch mouth shut so they can fuck."

"You're pregnant, Bee, no more niggas and sponsors for you!" Treasure warned, then grabbed Bright's hand to run across the street.

After having a snack at Burger King, Nicole dropped Bright off at home, then they headed to Treasure's house to study. Once Bright made it inside the house, her mother passed her the phone.

"Right on time, it's your little friend, Suge," she said.

Excitedly, Bright grabbed the phone. She hadn't talked to Suge in a while; they had been moving her from house to house, making it hard to keep a number on her. "What's up, Young? How you been?" Bright smiled.

"Hi, Bright," Suge laughed, just as excited to speak to her. "You know I miss y'all, but since they been moving me around so much, I haven't been able to call as much as

I would like to," Suge said.

"I understand, Suga mama," Bright took a seat on the living room couch next to her mom. "So tell me, what's been up, and how you been doing, girl? And they better be treating you right over there too," she said seriously.

"At first, I thought it was a bad idea, but it's better now. I'm gonna be placed with a really nice Muslim family. The lady is real nice and, she seems like she's really interested in me too, so things are looking up," Suge said.

"A Muslim family?" Bright said as her smile turned into a frown.

Suge laughed. "Yes, a Muslim family, Bright, they seem like wonderful people, and they have a daughter my age too," she smiled.

"Well, as long as you happy," Bright said, "I just don't wanna catch you on Long Beach Blvd. selling bean pies," she teased.

"Yeah right!" Suge said.

After talking for an additional ten minutes, Suge told her that she had to go. Then Bright called Larry to ask him for help with her homework, but he didn't answer. "That's odd," Bright said to herself as she dialed his number again. He hardly ever seemed to answer her calls lately. *Is he cheating on me?* She thought. After calling him back to back a few more times with no answer, Bright fumed with anger.

A Month Later

Lately, things seemed to have changed between Bright and Larry. They hardly ever had time to spend together; he was either always too busy or too tired. And for the first time in their relationship, Bright felt neglected. Approaching four and a half weeks since Bright had first slept with Terrence without protection; she dialed him up to follow through with her plan to tell him that she was pregnant. As the phone rang, Bright prepared herself to cry and act afraid; she was even preparing herself to tell him her true age.

"What's up, beautiful?" Terrence said after turning his beat down.

"I need to speak to you in person, daddy," Bright cried into the phone.

"What's wrong, baby?" Terrence quickly asked in concern.

"Just come pick me up from my house, it's important," Bright cried.

"I'm on my way," Terrence said, then hung up the phone.

Five minutes later, Terrence was in front of Bright's building blowing his horn repeatedly. Terrence figured since Bright turned eighteen, there was no reason for him hiding or picking Bright up down the street from her house any longer.

"Who's that?" her mother asked, looking out of the living room window.

"That's, Treasure's cousin, Ma. He's dropping some of her stuff off to me, since she's not home," Bright said, heading to the door. "I'll be right back, Ma," she said, then ran down the stairs of her apartment.

The second, Bright climbed inside of Terrence's truck, he immediately asked her what was wrong.

"I'm pregnant, baby," Bright cried.

"You are?" Terrence said excitedly. "What you crying for then, girl? You don't wanna have my baby or something?" he asked her with a disappointed look on his face.

Bright just continued to cry.

"After everything I've been through lately, a baby would be the perfect thing in my life right now," he said turning, Bright's crying face to his. Two of his baby mama's lived out of state, and the other one made it difficult for him to even see his son. With Bright, he knew that things would be different.

Bright looked at him through tear drenched eyes, "I do wanna have yo baby, but-but-but," she cried, "I haven't been as honest with you as I should have been, Ice," she said, putting an award winning performance on. "But it was only because I wanted to fucking be with you," she explained.

"You fucking another nigga, Bright?" he asked, pulling into the gas station parking lot, on Artesia Blvd. and Cherry Ave.

Bright turned and looked at him, "No, baby, I would never cheat on you," she cried. "Never!"

Growing impatient, Terrence spat, "Well, what is it that you ain't been honest with me about, Bright?" he asked her once he parked next to the pay phones.

Deciding that the timing was right, Bright let it out, "My age, Terrence; I'm not eighteen, baby, I'm only seventeen years old." she cried. "But I still love you, and wanna be with you, and have your baby though," she pleaded.

The blow from Bright's revelation was dazing, and all he could do was sit there and stare at her for a few moments. "So you mean to tell me that I was fucking a sixteen year old, and that all this time you've been lying to me?" he said angrily.

"I only lied because I wanted to be with you, Terrence," she said, looking directly in his eyes. "I love you, baby, and that's why I'm telling you the truth now," Bright said, wiping her tears away.

Feeling as if he had been stabbed in the back, Terrence began to speak in anger. "No, you telling me now because you're fucking pregnant!" he said, unable to look at her. "I can't believe this shit," he said, nodding his head. "I been fucking a little ass girl all this damn time," he said unbelievingly.

Bright hadn't planned or expected for things to get this dramatically out of hand. She thought, *Seventeen, eighteen, what's the big difference?* Looking at him like he had lost his mind, Bright said, "So what does a fucking number have to do with what we share in our hearts and how we feel about each other? I'm seventeen, I love you, you love me and now we about to have this baby," she blurted out with slight attitude. "So what's up, Ice? You got me or not?" she asked him.

With mixed emotions running through his blood,

Terrence was unable to think or respond logically. "I'ma always take care of my kids, that's not the fucking problem!" he yelled. He took care of all three of his children financially, even if he didn't see them as often as he'd liked. "You got me on fire right now, Bright, and I'ma take you home before I end up doing something crazy to yo ass!" He started his truck up and pulled out of the gas station parking lot.

Bright thought, *This nigga is really tripping.* Getting pissed off that things weren't working out the way she had planned they would, she spat, "Well if that's how you're feeling, then you can give me some money for an abortion, and I can be on top of that like tomorrow morning," she said, hoping to strike a nerve.

Terrence swerved into the next lane, almost causing an accident. It took everything in him not to slap the fuck out of Bright for her comment. Slamming his fist on the dashboard of his Escalade, he said, "I wish the fuck you would abort my baby, girl!" Bright had him boiling inside. "Matter of fact, let me hurry the fuck up and drop yo ass off right quick, because you really about to make a nigga slap the dog shit out of you," he said, driving sixty miles per hour down Artesia Blvd. "And trust me, I don't mind slapping the fuck out of a bitch either!"

"Oh, so you wanna slap me now? Okay then." She sucked her teeth and rolled her eyes.

Pulling up on her street with brakes that could stop on a dime, he quickly stopped in front of her building, causing his tires to screech. "Get out!" He said, unable to look at her.

"Fuck it!" Bright said, then climbed out of his truck.

The second her feet touched the pavement, Terrence burned rubber off of her street and onto the Blvd. Bright was so furious that she was ready to pick a fight with anybody who looked at her the wrong way. Walking up the stairs of her building, she took deep breaths to contain herself, then she opened her apartment door.

"It sure took you a long time to get back, and where the hell are Treasure's things at?" Her mother asked her once she entered the apartment empty-handed.

"I asked him to take me to the liquor store, and on our way back, Treasure called, so we stopped over there," Bright said, walking down the hallway to her bedroom.

"Yeah, I bet," her mother said before Bright closed her bedroom door. She knew there was more to the story, but since she planned on enjoying her day off from work watching football, she lit a cigarette, cracked open a can of beer, and enjoyed the game.

Inside her room, Bright called Treasure to tell her what had just happened. In the middle of their conversation, Larry beeped through on the other line. Practically hanging up on, Treasure, Bright answered his call. "Larry, where have you been and why haven't you been answering my calls?" Bright immediately asked him.

"Babe, calm down with all the questions, I was at practice, then afterwards I rode with my Moms to the valley," Larry said convincingly. However, the truth was that he was unable to answer his phone when he was on the clock at work, and since he only had another five minutes left on his first break, he had to talk quickly.

"So what that mean? You couldn't answer your phone are something?" Bright stood up and put her hand on her hip. She had already had enough for one day.

"Babe, come on," Larry whined. "I've been so busy with school and basketball lately that I haven't even had to the time to get much rest," he complained. "I rode out there with Moms and slept the whole way there and back." He was hoping that Bright would cut him some slack.

Bright smiled; she could tell that Larry was being sincere.

"Sorry, Daddy Lane, I know you have a full plate, but at least try to answer most of my calls, okay baby?" She said in her baby voice.

Instantly, Larry felt relieved. "Ok, baby, and stop

stressing ya'self over small stuff, we want our baby to be as healthy as possible," he said sincerely with a smile on his face.

"I promise, Daddy Lane," Bright said then blew him a kiss over the phone. "Now come pick me up! I miss you." Bright said happily.

"I can't right now, baby. I have a ton of homework and a lot of studying to do right now," he stressed.

"You never minded having me over while you did ya homework any other time, Larry."

"I have a history test coming up, so why not study together?" Bright suggested.

"Babeeeee, I can't...when you're around me, it's hard for me to focus on my work. And I need to focus right now," he felt a headache coming on. "I'll call you later okay?" He said, running out of time to talk. He hated hiding his job from her, but he felt he had no other choice.

"Yeah, alright," Bright said with a puppy-like expression on her face then hung up. It was funny how at first she couldn't keep Larry or Terrence up off of her, but the tables had seemed to turn, and they had no time for her.

Feeling lonely and depressed, Bright took a shower, did a little homework, and then went to sleep for the remainder of the night.

Part Ten

Working the drive thru, with only twenty minutes left on his shift, Larry spotted Bright's uncle in the drive-thru. After he took his order, he threw the idea around in his head on whether or not he should introduce himself to him. Bright was carrying his child, and her mother loved and accepted him wholeheartedly. *So why shouldn't I introduce myself to him?* Larry thought. He wasn't afraid of him, and he wasn't going anywhere so he thought, *Fuck it, I'ma introduce myself to him after I pass him his food.* Once Terrence pulled up to the drive-thru window, Larry passed him his food with a pleasant smile on his face, but before he could introduce himself, he complained about having cold French fries on top of the wrong order.

"I'm sorry about that, sir; let me correct that for you," Larry said reaching his hand out the drive-thru to retrieve the bag.

Mad at the world, Terrence spat, "Yeah, that's what you better do!" He said, tossing the bag at Larry. "I ordered a fucking ten piece nugget, and I specifically asked for fresh fucking fries, not this cold as shit y'all just served me!" Terrence yelled.

Trying to make the best out of the situation, Larry apologized. "Again, I'm sorry about that, sir." He didn't understand how one could get so upset over such a small mistake, when he assured him that he'd take care of it.

"A'ight well fucking do that shit, man!" Terrence said, looking at him like he was ready to kick up some dust.

Larry's patience was running short. He didn't appreciate the tone and the way Bright's Uncle was talking to him.

"Aye, my bad, my man, calm down, I'm tryna get it right for you." Larry walked away from the window, trying his hardest to compose himself from going the fuck off on him.

"My man!" Terrence repeated. "Muthafucka, you don't know me well enough to be calling me yo mans and shit, nigga, just call me muthafucking sir!" Terrence yelled, ready to fly off the handle and attack anything that walked, talked, or moved in the wrong direction. He had lost his wife, his bitch was pregnant and had lied about her age, and on top of that, he had just lost twenty thousand dollars in the game. So to say the least, Terrence was more than mad and upset, he was pissed off at the world.

Larry had taken enough of his shit and was about to snap, but luckily his manager stepped in just in time to resolve the issue. He patted Larry on the back and said, "Don't worry, I'll take care of it, he's just another bitter asshole, mad at the world," he teased.

"You can say that again," Larry steamed, walking into the dining area to pick up trash and sweep up. Not allowing Bright's Uncle to rob him of his day's joy, he put a smile back on his face and decided to make the best out of the rest of his work day.

****

It had been over a week since Bright had heard from or seen Terrence, and since her pockets were getting low, she called a cab to take her to his house so that she could talk some sense into him. After Bright paid the cab driver the last of the money she had, she climbed out of the cab, and then walked up and knocked on Terrence door. After knocking and ringing the doorbell a few more times, he finally answered. Looking her dead in the eyes, Terrence just stood there trying to understand how he had such strong feeling for a girl her age.

With a lifted brow, Bright said, "You gone just keep staring at me, or you gone let me in?" She asked, trying to let herself inside.

Terrence smiled and nodded his head. He had calmed down and was really just about to call and apologize for the way that he treated her. They had gone too far, did too much, and now that she was carrying his seed, he figured there was no use in holding any grudges or crying over spilled milk. It was what it was.

Bright waited for Terrence to close his door before she began to speak. "So what, you cool on me, now? You saying fuck me and the baby over a punk ass number?" she demanded to know with her hand on her hip.

Not appreciating her tone in his home, Terrence snapped. "Look, sit yo ass down, and don't be coming over here stirring up no bullshit when you was the one in the wrong in the first fucking place," Terrence pointed out. "And besides all that, I like my house to stay peaceful, just as it was before yo light bright ass walked up in here!" Then he walked in the kitchen. His home was a place of tranquility, relaxation, comfort, and a place where he could think clearly. And he didn't welcome, allow, or invite drama, chaos, nor the street into his comfort zone.

Bright was mad, pregnant, and broke, and regardless of what Terrence had just said to her, she was still gonna vent and say what was on her mind. "Well, I don't give a fuck right now, Terrence! I been at home stressed the fuck out, crying, no money, no dick, no man, no nothing cause yo ass is on some bullshit," she said, winding her neck and pointing at him. "Did you ever think about me while you were out on ya guilt trip? Huh?" she asked, standing in his face.

"Look, I said calm down with all that noise, Bright." Terrence was trying to keep his cool, but Bright was beginning to irritate the hell out of him.

Ignoring him, Bright continued to fuss, "No, you think it's fucking okay to lie and hurt me, but when the fucking tables are turned, you just bail out on me, like that!" Bright said, ready to argue and get her point across.

Terrence slammed the glass he was drinking out of on his kitchen counter. "Lie and hurt you, are you fucking serious?" he asked, looking her dead in her eyes. "I make sure ya black ass keep food in ya mouth, have money in yo pockets. I even pay them bills that ya mama can't fucking seem to keep up with, and on top of that, I keep ya ass fly in all them designer clothes! So I don't wanna hear none of that bullshit you talking right now girl!" Terrence yelled back in his defense.

Bright bucked her eyes and snapped her neck. "Oh, so it's all about money now huh?" she huffed. "Yeah, you keep me paid and fly and yes, you've given me money from time to time to help my Moms out with the bills, but that's what you're supposed to do, if you my man!" She yelled with attitude. "But my feelings can't be paid for, Terrence, you've lied and hurt me before too, and way worse than what I've ever done to you!" she cried, more sensitive from her pregnancy than anything.

Dumbfounded, Terrence asked, "What the fuck have I

ever did to you Bright?" he was confused.

"You fucking lied to me about being married to that bitch..., But before she could get another word out, Terrence slapped her so hard that she spun around twice. " Don't you ever fucking mention or disrespect my wife's name ever again!!!! You fucking hear me?!" Terrence was ready to fuck something up. His wife was a very sensitive issue, and his scars were still very fresh from her departure. He wasn't going to allow Bright, or anyone for that matter, to speak negatively on or disrespect her as long as he was alive.

Instantly feeling regret from her words, Bright palmed her stinging cheek and cried. She remembered Terrence saying that he didn't mind slapping the fuck out of a bitch before, but she didn't think that included herself. Sliding down the kitchen counter and onto the kitchen floor, Bright cried, "I love you, Terrence, why you doing this to me, baby?"

Terrence looked at Bright on his kitchen floor telling him how much she loved him in between sobs. He hated to do her the way he did, but he needed her to understand that Tameka was off limits. Feeling she had learned her lesson, he picked her up off the floor, hugged her tight, and told her he loved her too.

"I'm sorry, Ice, I never meant for it to come out like that, baby, you know I would never intentionally disrespect your wife like that," she cried harder and harder. "I know she meant the world to you too, I just wanted you to understand the hurt and pain that you've caused me in the past. And if I've been able to accept you for your imperfections, baby, then why can't you find a place in your heart to forgive me for mines?" Bright cried, holding on to him for dear life. She needed to be back in that special place in his heart; he was her security blanket.

"I love you baby," Terrence said to her as he lifted her face off of his chest to kiss her lips, then he wiped her tears away. "You my boo, you know I got you, baby," he said, wrapping her legs around his waist, then continuing to kiss her pretty face.

"Make love to me, Ice," Bright moaned, calling him by his street name to make him feel empowered while she pulled his shirt off and grinded her body up against his. One thing leading to the next, they ended up having sex in the kitchen, into the living room, up the stairs, and finally into his bedroom. Afterwards, Bright laid there with a smile on her face, not from the sex, but because she knew she was back on payroll.

"Cook ya nigga somethin' to eat!" Terrence rolled over in bed and said.

"Whatever you want, baby," Bright said, getting out of bed. After stretching her sore body, she went inside the bathroom to shower before preparing Terrence a home-cooked meal. Deciding to make beef, bean and cheese burritos, Bright cooked both her ground beef and refried beans on a low fire, while she chopped lettuce, tomatoes and onions, then grated sharp cheddar cheese. In the middle of draining the grease from the ground beef, Bright received a call from, Nicole. *What the heck she want with me?* Bright thought.

"What who want with you?" Terrence said, coming down the stairs.

"This bitch name Nicole, nosy Ice," she teased, then she put the pan back on the stove and answered her phone. "What's up?" Bright said, adding taco seasoning and a half of a cup of water in the ground beef.

"You busy right now?" Nicole asked her.

"Naw, what's up?" Bright asked again, preparing to combine the seasoned ground beef and refried beans in one pot.

"Well, I'm just gone come right out and ask you then, before it get back to Treasure." Nicole cleared her throat. "Did you fuck, Lil Boo?" she asked seriously.

"Did I what?" Bright repeated almost choking on her own spit.

"Did you fuck, Lil Boo?" Nicole asked her again.

"Hell naw!" Bright responded defensively. "Why would you even ask me some shit like that, Nicole?" she asked, feeling her heart beat a mile a minute.

Nicole explained, "I talk to one of Lil Boo's homeboys, I'm not saying his name, but he slipped up and told me that Lil Boo told him that after everybody left his house that night of his white party, and while Treasure was in his room asleep, that you threw the pussy at him, and y'all fucked," she said, not skipping a beat. She wanted to call and tell Treasure what she knew right away, but decided to go directly to the source first.

Bright's mouth fell wide open. *No that nigga didn't go and run his mouth like a little bitch,* she thought. "Well that's a lie, Nicole, and that's on my mama!" she said in a defensive tone. "Treasure is only my best fucking friend in the whole wide world, so never that, and whoever told you that can miss me with that crap," Bright said, trying to regain her cool.

Nicole sighed, "I'ma keep It real wit' you, I was gone tell Treasure after I heard it myself, cause she's my girl too. But I decided it would be best to speak to you first," she said honestly.

Bright was relieved that Nicole hadn't told Treasure,

and she was gonna try her best to convince her not to mention it to her either. "I mean tell her, I can care less, because I know like Treasure knows that I would never do anything like that to her," Bright said convincingly. "But to me, it's like, why even mention some false bullshit to her when she ain't even messing with dude like that no more. That would be like going an extra mile to add confusion to our friendship, especially when it's not true," she hoped, Nicole would keep her mouth shut.

Nicole wasn't buying it. She knew Bright was hiding something and that she was trying to keep her from telling Treasure; she just nodded her head. "That's why I called you first, because I'm not messy like that. But then I got to thinking back to that night, and I remembered how persistent you were about staying over there with her. I know Treasure was drunk and when she told me she crashed right away, that kind of messed my head up, because you were wide awake, Bright."

"First of all, it don't sound like you called to ask me anything, seems like you called to accuse me! And second off, I ain't ever gone leave my homegirl nowhere by herself, drunk! Plain and simple, we ride together!" Bright said, taking her tone up a few notches. She couldn't stand Nicole's ass, because she knew she was only trying to steal her best friend. Seeing Terrence walk in the direction of the kitchen with a concerned look on his face, Bright quickly tried to collect herself. "Anyways, Nicole I'm chilling with my dude right now, I'ma hit you later." Then she pressed the end button on her phone to end the call.

"What was all that about?" Terrence asked, grabbing a glass then opening the refrigerator to get something to drink.

"This fat, hater bitch tryna come in between me and Treasure," Bright fumed rolling his burrito up.

"That's that messy ass female shit," Terrence said, taking his plate from her hand. "Y'all friends don't let the fakes and haters come in between that," he said, then took seat on the couch to eat. Not having much of an appetite, Bright ate half of her burrito, and then asked Terrence to take her home. She had already missed two of Larry's calls, and since Treasure was blowing her phone up back to back, she knew it was time to go home.

On the ride back to her house, Bright played asleep so that she could think of ways to get herself out of the jam. She was sure that Nicole had told Treasure everything and that it was the reason that she was blowing her cell phone up. But no matter what, Bright was gonna keep a straight face and deny the whole thing. Approaching her street, Terrence shook her to wake her up then tossed her some money. Pulling up on her block, Bright noticed both Treasure and Nicole posted in front of her apartment complex. She thought to herself, *Fuck, this bitch couldn't wait to run her fat ass mouth!*

Terrence pulled in front of Bright's building, then rolled his window down to speak. "What's up, Treasure?" he said, peeking Nicole out. She was thick and sexy to him.

"A gang of, bullshit, Ice," Treasure said, nodding her head.

"Yeah, that's what Bright was telling me too, but I'ma tell you like I told her, don't let them fakes and hater's come in between y'all friendship, y'all been friends for too long," he said seriously. Treasure nodded her head in agreement, and instantly, Nicole's smile turned into a frown. She knew that comment was aimed at her, but since she knew she was neither a fake nor a hater, she brushed it off and gave him a nasty look.

Bright blew Terrence a kiss goodbye. "A'ight boo, I'll talk to you later before my mama come out here trippin'," she said.

Terrence kissed his lips back at her. "A'ight, baby, hit me," then he drove off her street.

Bright directed her attention to Treasure, "So after a long stressful ass day, I have to come home to some punk ass bullshit, huh?" Bright said, nodding her head with a disbelieving look on her face.

"That's what I'm saying," Treasure replied, giving Bright the same disbelieving facial expression. "So did you fuck him or what?" Treasure came right out and asked her.

Bright looked from Nicole then to Treasure with a nasty look upon her face, then said, "So hold up, Treasure, you mean to tell me you gone come at me sideways, in front of this fake ass bitch right here?!" she said pointing at Nicole, feeling betrayed.

"Bitch!" Nicole said feeling froggy. She had warned Bright in the past about coming at her foul, and she wasn't gonna take it today. "I done told ya ass, Bright!" she said stepping to her.

"Hold on, Nicole," Treasure interjected, jumping in-between the two. "Let me talk!" Looking at Bright she explained. "Bee, I asked Nicole to come since she was the one that brought it to my attention. She told me y'all talked and since I didn't wanna be getting nobody's words twisted up, I thought it would be best to have her here."

Removing her eyes from Nicole, Bright spoke, "So basically, you believe this shit right, Treasure? Cause if you didn't, we wouldn't be having this conversation right now," she shot.

"Naw, I'm trying to ask you yo side of the story, Bee," Treasure replied, slapping her fist into her hand. She was looking for the truth in her friend.

"No! I didn't fuck him, end of the story," Bright said nonchalantly, with a dumb expression on her face.

Treasure was confused and didn't know what to believe. After a few moments of silence, she said, "Well, why would he be telling people that?"

Frustrated, Bright stomped her foot into the ground and snapped her neck. "I don't know! Call that nigga and ask him why him and his little friend is lying on me. Maybe they both wanna fuck me! She finalized, rolling her eyes at Nicole, with her hand on her hip.

Treasure sucked her teeth. "Oh don't trip, boo, I called him," she said with a smirk on her face. "I'm just waiting on him to return the call," she shot back.

Not feeling Nicole's presence or Treasure's vibe, Bright decided it would be best to say her last words and part ways before things got ugly. "Well since it look like you done already picked sides, and you believe this shit, I guess it ain't no need for me to be standing here any longer," Bright said, getting teary-eyed, then she headed in the direction of her apartment. Though she may have been wrong, she knew that Nicole just wanted to steal her best friend from her.

Treasure yelled after her, "Bee, I never said I believed anything or anybody yet, that's why I'm here talking to you, and not here tryna whip yo ass!" she barked defiantly. She wanted to believe Bright, but her gut was telling her differently.

The words "whip yo ass," were all Bright heard. She didn't like to be threatened, and she was far from a punk, and furthermore, she didn't like the way the words sounded coming out of Treasure's mouth. It made her feel as if Treasure was trying to challenge her. "Whip my ass!" Bright repeated, turning back around to face her. "What, you tryna catch a fade with me or something, Treasure? Why you out here fronting on me in front of this fake ass bitch, Nicole?" Bright yelled, stepping up.

Nicole became fed up; she was tired of Bright's verbal assaults. "Fuck that, I ain't gone keep being no more of yo bitches, bitch!" Nicole yelled, running up on Bright, ready to catch her fade.

Immediately, Bright dropped her things to the ground and put 'em up. "What, y'all bitches wanna jump me now?" Bright said with her guards up, ready to fight.

Without further words, Nicole two-pieced Bright in the face: one to the nose, and the other to the chin. Slightly dazed, Bright began to swing like a madwoman, swinging and pulling at Nicole's hair. Treasure tried breaking them up.

"Y'all stop it, she's pregnant, Nicole!" she yelled, trying to pull them apart. Seeing Nicole get the best of her best friend created a natural reaction in Treasure, and before long, she and Bright were both whipping Nicole's ass.

"What the fuck?" Nicole screamed, bearing more than she could handle at one time. The forces of them together became vicious, Bright working her from the front and Treasure getting her from the back. Nicole lost her advantage on Bright when Treasure jumped in the fight. She couldn't believe that Treasure was jumping on her, especially when she had been nothing but a good friend to her.

Regaining her strength, Nicole grabbed Bright by her hair, pulled her down, and started taking blows to her head. Bright used her free arm and kept punching Nicole in the side of her face and ear. From behind, Treasure dragged Nicole to the ground, afraid that she may have made Bright miscarriage. Bright fell on top of Nicole and continued to give it to her in the face, each fist after the next; Bright wouldn't stop.

Eventually, neighbors begin to come outside, and Bright's mother and siblings ran outside of their apartment to break up the fight, or aid if they had too. Things were out of hand and Treasure began to feel bad for her part in the fight and pulled Bright off of Nicole. Bright yelled, kicked, and screamed.

"Bitch, if I lose my baby, I'ma kill you, BITCH, I'ma fucking kill you!!!" she threatened.

Once her mother was able to get Bright upstairs, she called the ambulance, seeing that Bright had blood on her. She went outside to find out what had happened. Without telling Bright's mom that they spent the night at Lil Boo's house, Treasure explained everything to her. Shortly after the paramedics and the police arrived, Bright pressed charges on Nicole, and then she was rushed to the emergency room. After having many different tests run on her, Bright was relieved that she and the baby were alright. The blood that her mother spotted on her was from Nicole's nose and blood from her scraped up knees from falling on top of Nicole. In the situation, Bright wouldn't have pressed charges, but since

Nicole was trying to steal Treasure away from her, so she decided jail would be the perfect place for her. Waiting to get released from the hospital, the doctor walked in with her file open.

"Is everything alright with the baby?" Rosette asked the doctor, seeing the look on his face.

Passing his chart to the nurse the doctor responded, "I guess that all depends," he said, looking from Bright to her mother.

Giving him a suspicious look, Bright said, "Don't tell me something's wrong with my baby, Doc?"

"There's not just one, but two babies," he informed her, "And they're both alright," he assured her. Both Bright and her mother's eyes almost popped out of their sockets.

"TWO!?" They both repeated at once.

The doctor laughed, "Yes two, Miss Sheldon," he said, looking at Bright.

The doctor's revelation of twins hit Bright like a ton of bricks in the back of the head. She was prepared to have one baby, but two seemed to be a bit much and scared the life out of her. On the ride home, Bright called Larry to tell him the news, but as usual, he didn't answer. *He's probably with his new girlfriend,* Bright thought.

Slowly, depression began to consume her, and she felt like crying. Instead she tried to call Treasure, but her grandmother told her that she wasn't home. Desperately needing to hear that everything was going to be okay, Bright looked to her mother for comfort. "Mom, two babies," was all she could manage to say.

Stopping at a red light, her mother turned to her and said, "Two babies that will have all the love in the world, Queen Bee," she said, holding her daughter's hand.

"Everything will be just fine," she said, hoping for the best.

Part Eleven

Nicole had ignored all of Treasure's calls and had eventually changed her number to avoid her calls. Treasure felt bad for her part in the fight and couldn't help feeling like she had lost a really good friend. Her spirits were down, and she was unable to shake the lingering depression that had set in on her. She had even begun to question her and Bright's relationship, and though Bright swore she never slept with Lil Boo, it just seemed funny to her that first Chrome accused her of trying to get with him, and now Nicole hearing from Lil Boo's homeboy that she kicked it with him the night of his all white, end-of the-summer pool party.

Thinking back to that night, Treasure did recall Lil Boo joining her in the bed way after she had fallen asleep. And when she asked him where he had come from, he told her he had smoked a blunt with Bright and then given her towels to bathe with and blankets to sleep with. Treasure didn't think anything of it at the time, but now it was suspicious to her because Bright never mentioned them smoking a blunt at all. When she spoke to Lil Boo, he denied it and then started ignoring her calls. A sly smile appeared across Treasure's face. She had a trick up her sleeve, and if she found out that Bright slept with Lil Boo, she was going to kick her ass and end their friendship for good.

****

"Yeah, whatever, Larry!" Bright complained, walking up the stairs of her apartment with Larry. They had just come from the movies and were having another argument about Larry never having enough time to spend with her. The only reason he had taken her to the movies was to celebrate them having twins. "Every time I ask to come over, I can't. If I ask you to take me out somewhere on the weekend, you're too busy or tired. So what the fuck, Larry, are you cheating on me?" Bright asked, stopping in her tracks.

Larry wanted to tell her he had a job, but the other night when he joked about working at Mc Donald's, Bright burst into laughter. She told him that she'd rather see him sell drugs before he worked at such a low-paying job. It didn't bother him that Bright was a materialistic girl; he actually thought it was cute that she set standards high. His problem was with gold-digging type of females that were only out to get money, but in their case, he knew that Bright would give him her last. She practically provided him with a whole new wardrobe, bought him every new pair of tennis shoes that came out, and kept money in his pockets just to keep him from working.

"Don't worry about a job, boo, I got plenty of money for the both of us until you get drafted to the NBA," she would always tell him. And for that, all Larry wanted to do was, marry Bright, spoil her and make her happy. But her thinking of him as a loser for working at Mc Donald was just something he couldn't accept or handle, so he'd just have to continue to lie to her until he got his big break.

"Do you think I'm cheating on you, Bright?" Larry asked her in a disbelieving tone. "Because I'm not." He looked deep into her beautiful green eyes. He was head over heels in love with her and just wanted to do the right thing.

"You said it, not me!" Bright spat, holding back the tears in her eyes. She felt that because she was pregnant and had gained a little weight that Larry had lost interest in her. It was always the babies this, the babies that...it was never about her anymore.

Larry kissed her on her lips then hugged her tight. "I keep telling you, baby, that you mean the world to me, Mama Lane, and that everything that I do is for us. And one day, the only thing you gone have to worry about is what Prada and Gucci is coming out with next," he laughed. "Spend money, take care of our children, and live the fucking fabulous life!"

Bright wiped her eyes then smiled, money always made her happy. "Don't forget my mansion and all my fancy cars," she added.

"Oh shit, how could I have forgotten that?" he teased, kissing Bright on her lips once more. "But I have to do what I have to do right now, to assure that Pretty Bright get what she wants," he smiled.

Bright laughed. "Pretty my ass, I'm drop dead gorgeous," she snapped playfully.

"Yeah baby, you are all that...But you'll always be my Pretty Bright." He wrapped his arms around her waist then winked at her.

"Pretty Bright" she sighed. Bright believed her looks were above Pretty, but since he was always calling her the name, she wanted to know why. "How you figure?"

"From the first time I laid eyes on your pretty face I thought, damn, she has the prettiest face I have ever seen in my entire life, so I call you my Pretty Bright," Larry said truthfully.

"Well, Pretty Bright it is," she smiled, rubbing her index finger softly down the side of his smooth chocolate skin. It was one of the most heart-filled things a guy had ever sincerely said to her.

Getting back to their original conversation, Larry said, "So you gone quit being so hard on a brotha then, right?" he held her face with his hands. He had a lot of stress and needed her to be there for him instead of adding to it.

"I promise," Bright said, wrapping her pinky finger around his, and then she grabbed his hand to lead him into her house. Being pregnant and in love with Larry was changing Bright. She'd avoid Terrence as much as possible or until her pockets got low. And even then, her performance wouldn't be so great and Terrence would complain that the pregnancy was bringing the worst out of her. She dreaded climbing in bed with him and was turned off by everything that he did. It had gotten so bad that Terrence had backed off to give her space, he had grown tired of Bright's nagging and complaining. But when he dropped money off to her, he requested that she drop to her knees and at least give him head.

"Hey Moms," Larry said, giving his future mother-in- law a tight hug.

"Hey son, how's my UCLA M.V.P. doing?" She teased. During basketball season, the media would blow Larry's name up on the news and in the newspaper as being one of the best in the league. They were practically having a bidding war over Larry Lane in the NBA, so it was now only a matter of time.

Larry laughed as he rubbed through the sea of waves in his head. "I'm a'ight Moms, you on your way to work?" he blushed, flashing his million dollar smile.

"Yeah, I'm on my way out for work," she said, grabbing her lunch out of the refrigerator. Noticing his big smile, she said, "What you smiling so hard for, M.V.P.? You and Queen Bee ain't ran off and got married or anything like that now?" she teased. "We made an agreement that we weren't keeping anymore secrets from Moms," she said, placing her hand on her hip.

"No more secrets, Moms," Larry smiled. "You be making me blush, calling me M.V.P. and everything," he replied truthfully.

"You have a lot to be proud of, and I'm very proud and happy for you," she smiled looking at Larry.

Larry nodded his head. "I guess I do, I just wish your brother would cut me some slack," he said, looking back at Bright.

"My brother?" Rosette snapped with a puzzled look upon her face.

"Yeah, Bright's uncle that she's scared to death of," he teased.

Bright quickly changed the subject, while her mother eyed them both suspiciously. "Uncle!" she said. She had sisters, but they both lived in Cincinnati, and her brother's life had been claimed by cancer before Bright was born.

"Yes mom, uncle," Bright said, whisking Larry into the hallway. "Give me a second to speak to Larry alone, Ma," Bright said, hoping she wouldn't be busted.

In the hallway, Bright whispered to Larry. "Please don't mention my uncle to, or around my mother. They got into a real bad argument, then they disowned each other, and haven't spoken to each other in years. But if she finds out he's been around here, it'll upset her and then she'll get angry with me because I keep in contact with him," she lied persuasively.

Covering his mouth, Larry said, "Oh, my bad, I'm

sorry, baby, I didn't know," he said regretfully. "I see ole Unc like running around like he the big bad wolf or something," he said, getting serious. "But I told you though, he ain't gone run us," Larry said like he had a bad taste in his mouth. And he meant that.

Hearing her mother's footsteps coming closer to their direction, Bright said, "Okay baby, but please don't mention him to Mama, it will only upset her," she warned. Larry hurriedly nodded his head in agreement. "Got you baby."

Joining them in the hallway, Rosette said, "Now what's going on with all this you're afraid of your Uncle stuff that Larry is talking about?" she said, looking in between the two of them.

"Ma, Larry was talking about his uncle," Bright said, looking at the time. "Aren't you gonna be late for work?" she asked.

Rosette looked at her wristwatch. "What, he bothering you or somethin'?"

"No, Moms, everything is alright, Bright's just afraid to meet my uncle because I told her how mean and grumpy he was," Larry said, covering up for Bright. "Everything's all good though," he assured her.

Changing the confused expression on her face, Rosette grabbed her work and lunch bag then proceeded to the door. "Y'all had me going for a minute there, because my brother is dead and has been even before Bright was born," she affirmed, then opened the door to leave. "I'm gone, Queen Bee; take care of my babies," she said, proceeding to exit the apartment. Then before closing the door behind herself, she remembered what she wanted to tell Bright earlier. "I don't know what's going on with Deja and Cordell, but they both done turned into street runners. When they get home, tell 'em I want them to stay in. I don't want them getting into any trouble."

However, what Rosette didn't know was that the trouble had already begun. Cordell and Deja were officially out experiencing street life.

Though Bright had noticed how they had both begin to spend more time outside of the house then they did in, she figured they were probably hanging with friends. "Got you, Ma," she said, then she closed the door behind her mother.

"Isn't that wild?" Bright said, directing her attention back to Larry. "She swears she's never talking to her brother ever again in life," Bright said with a sad face, nodding her head in disbelief.

"Wow," Larry said, "if you hadn't warned me, I would of believed Moms didn't even have a living brother."

"Yeah, I told you," Bright said, leading Larry to the kitchen to make him a plate of her mother's dinner: smother chicken, rice, and fried corn.

After dinner, Larry helped Bright straighten up the apartment, rubbed her sore feet for a while, then left to go to work. But he told her he was going home to study.

"I love you Larry Lane," Bright yelled out her front

door as Larry made his way down to his Mustang.

"I love you more, Pretty Bright," Larry yelled back up to her, then he got in his car and sped off before he was late for work.

****

At five months pregnant, Bright laid on her back in Terrence bed with him on top of her pumping away. Disgusted, Bright wished he would hurry up and bust a nut so that he could give her some money and take her back home. Being pregnant made her hate having sex with Terrence; she felt degraded. The only man she wanted inside of her was Larry, but it was the money that kept her in and out Terrence's bed and on her knees in his truck when she was too lazy to fuck. Bright wanted to cry; his every stroke, kiss, touch, and moan made her skin want to jump off of her and crawl away. But how else would she buy the things that her babies and Larry needed? Or keep fresh clothes on her back and money in her pockets? She had outgrown being broke and had become accustomed to having lots of money in her possession.

She didn't want her babies to lack anything, and she certainly didn't want her future husband working a low-paying job that would demand his time from her, school or basketball practice and end up losing his chances at getting drafted into the NBA. She couldn't let that happen, so instead of dumping Terrence, Bright decided to hang in there just a little bit longer. *Hurry up!* she cried to herself.

"What the fuck is up with you?" Terrence climbed off of Bright and stared at her. *This bitch is always crying about something,* he thought.

"I told you since I've been pregnant that it hurts me to have sex and you don't care, all you wanna do is bust a nut," Bright whined. The truth was that her pregnancy made her see the ugly truth that was called her reality, and it hurt her deeply to lay in bed and let Terrence nut on her and Larry's babies' heads. She wished she could just suck his dick and get it over with, but he just had to have the pussy, no matter how much she complained it hurt her. She even went as far as telling him that she had a high risk pregnancy, and that the doctor told her to abstain from having sex to avoid having a miscarriage, but Terrence didn't care. All he wanted was pussy, pussy, and more pussy.

"A'ight beautiful," Terrence sighed, seeing that Bright was really being affected by having sex. "If the dick is too much for you to handle right now, a nigga can jack off until we have the babies," he said disappointedly. "Nigga still like his dick sucked though," he smiled, stroking himself. It turned him on knowing that he was tearing the pussy up.

Bright nodded her head in agreement. "This shit ain't no joke, Ice." She called him his street name to stroke his ego. "I love making love to you and everything baby, but I don't wanna lose the babies over it either. So we went have to take it easy." She acted as if she was in pain.

"You alright, baby?" Terrence asked, then tossed two bundles of money to her on the bed. "I bet that'll make you smile," he said, holding his dick in his hand, ready to get it sucked. He knew that money would shut her up.

As usual, Bright lit up like a Christmas tree and smiled. "I can suck it, but the coochie needs a break baby," Bright climbed across the bed to let her mouth meet Terrence's rod. Bobbing her head up and down his penis, she devoured him until he yelled, moaned in ecstasy, and came inside her mouth. After she spit it out, she took a shower, then Terrence drove her back home.

The second Bright stepped foot out of Terrence's truck, Treasure yelled out her name as she made her way up the street. "What's up, bestie?" Bright responded once she closed Terrence's truck door.

She hadn't kicked it with her girl in a minute and was in desperate need of catching up and smoking a blunt. She had such a sickly pregnancy, and the only time she could eat or hold anything down was if she smoked a blunt. She just kept it a secret from Larry because she knew he'd flip out. He had already told her that he didn't want her consuming any weed or alcohol while she was carrying his babies. Terrence, on the other hand, didn't mind Bright smoking weed while she was pregnant. His mother smoked her whole term while pregnant with him and he turned out fine and didn't have a problem with it. It was alcohol that he had a problem with, and he and Bright had an agreement that she wouldn't indulge until after she had the babies.

"I been missing in action, so I decided to come holler at you, since you been too busy for me," Treasure teased with attitude. "And you know you the only friend I have since Nicole and Suge been out the picture," she added.

Bright hugged Treasure tight. "Girl, I been missing you," she smiled. "But every time I called your house you were either asleep, busy, or gone, so I thought you were too busy for me, BF," Bright teased. "I spoke to Suge the other day too and she doing good!" Bright smiled.

"I got a lot on my mind," Treasure said, pulling a bag of Kush out of her purse.

"You know I need some of that too," Bright said,

walking into her courtyard. "My mom getting ready to go to work so give me a minute so we can get high!" Bright laughed.

"Yeah, but you really need to stop smoking weed, Bright," Treasure said out of concern for her unborn babies. She had told Bright time and time again, but she never listened.

Bright turned to look at her with a pitiful expression on her face. "Girl, I told you this is the only way I can eat, and I gotta feed the babies," she said, carefully climbing the stairs to her apartment.

"Yeah you always sick...Or crying," Treasure added, falling into laughter. "Straight drama queen."

Once inside the apartment, Rosette said, "Queen Bee, make time to catch up on some of the class work you missed while you were out of school last week," she said the second her daughter walked inside the apartment. She didn't want Bright using her sickly pregnancy as a reason or escape from finishing high school.

Bright flipped her hair behind her shoulder. "Already done, Ma, me and Larry had a study date last night and he helped me with all the work I needed help with," she said proudly.

Rosette smiled. "Good...I sure love that boy, he's awesome," she said, nodding her head. "Hey Treasure, baby," she greeted with a warm smile on her face.

"Hello, Miss Rose," Treasure greeted back. Treasure liked Rosette, her spirits were always up even when things were down.

"Well, you girl's gone on ahead and do whatcha do, I'm taking the night off, Queen Bee. I've been feeling awful, so I'm calling it a night. But when Vince get here, just send him to my room please," she said,making her way down the hallway.

"You need to go to the doctor Ma," Bright said to her mother. She had been under the weather for three days now, and Bright was growing concerned.

"Just over-exhausted and not enough rest, I'll be alright," she said, then closed her bedroom door.

"I told her the same thing," Deja added, coming out of the boys' room with her new running buddy, Veronica. "She was throwing up and complaining of a headache earlier, not to mention she losing a lot of weight." Deja was concerned too.

"This is getting serious," Bright said, storming off to her mother's room. Then she opened the door without knocking. "Ma you're going to the doctor tomorrow, and I'm staying out of school to go with you," she said with her hand on her hip. Seeing her mother slumped over on the side of her bed with her eyes closed, Bright freaked out. "Maaaa!" she yelled running to her side to see if she was breathing. "Help, call 911, Mama needs help!" Bright yelled, pulling her mother's eyes open and checking to see if she had a heartbeat.

Quickly, her mother snatched her head out of Bright's hold and caught her breath. "Girl, are you crazy or something? I'm just saying my prayers," she said, snapping out of an intense prayer.

Holding her chest, Bright sighed of relief as she tried calming herself down. "Well Ma, you scared the crap out of me, I ain't ever see you pray on your knees before," she took a seat on the corner of her mother's bed.

Rosette laughed to herself looking at her frantic child. "Well that's probably why I always feel like I'm drowning out here, so I decided to pray a couple of times a day. I'm even considering seeking a home church," she smiled proudly.

"Oh Lord, Sister Clark is on a mission again," Bright laughed, then took off out of her mother's room before she started preaching the word of God to her. Because Bright didn't understand God and his laws, she didn't like having spiritual conversions because it scared her to death. The only thing that she did understand was that she was a sinner, and that her punishment was waiting for her in the pits of hell. So when it came to God and religion, Bright avoided talking about it as much as possible.

"Close my bedroom door back, Queen Bee!" Her mother yelled after her.

In the hallway both Treasure and Deja were on the floor in tears busting up laughing at Bright's reaction to her mother praying.

"Whatever, bitches," Bright gave them the finger, then went to close her mother's bedroom door.

After changing her clothes, Bright sat with Treasure in the front of her building, talking and smoking a blunt. "So what's been up with you, Treasure? You still cool on Reggie?" Bright asked, passing her back the blunt.

"I speak to him every once in a while, but that's it." Treasure was over dudes that just wanted to fuck.

"You just being stingy with the coochie," Bright teased, since she knew Treasure was on this new celibacy kick. "When I'ma get the chance to meet this Monster cat, though?" Bright asked, choking on the weed.

Treasure no longer felt comfortable bringing Bright around any guy that she had interest in; things always seemed to get crazy when she was around. So whenever Monster would try to get her to hook his homeboys up with her friends, she would always tell him she didn't have any friends. She was really starting to feel him too. "Monster is cool, he respects my celibacy and still enjoys being around me," Treasure smiled. "He's out of town right now though."

Bright cut her off laughing. "What you won't do, the next female will, so you better quit playing and give yo man some of that good ole coochie before you lose him," she said with the flare of the eyebrow. "And I can bet my last dollar that another bitch is already throwing that shit at'em," Bright said seriously to her friend. She didn't believe in all that sex after marriage celibacy crap, but what she did believe is that the gold mine between her legs kept her paid.

"Naw, I'm cool, I'm saving this good cooch for the dude that I commit to and settle down with. Ain't like I'm having orgasms like that anyways, Lil Boo was the only dude to ever make me cum, but after all that shit he said about you, I'm cool on him too," Treasure said. She wanted to get down to the nature of her visit and fish for answers.

Bright snapped her neck. "Did that nigga tell you that mess?" Bright asked with attitude and a flared up eyebrow.

"I mean, no, he didn't admit it, he said no, but why would Nicole just lie?" Treasure said, guiding the conversation right where she wanted it.

"Cause that bitch was tryna steal my bestie, that's why!" Bright snapped. "Ole fat jealous bitch," she added then hit the weed.

Treasure put out a fake laugh. "So what did happen that night after I went to sleep anyways?" she asked.

"Treasure, I didn't fuck him, on my life, on my Mama, I wouldn't lie to you," Bright said persuasively, looking directly in Treasure's eyes.

Treasure smiled, "I believe you, Bee." I just want to know what happened after I went to sleep. I was faded, remember?" she added.

Bright squinted her eyes to recall the evening, then a smile appeared across her face as she thought about all that good dick Lil Boo had served her that night. "Lil Boo gave me a blanket and towels to shower with then he went back upstairs," she shrugged. "That was it?" Treasure asked, holding back the mug that Bright's response had given her. Lil Boo said y'all smoked, so why would he lie about that? *This bitch is lying,* Treasure thought.

When the ring tone, Ghetto Superstar, blared from Bright's cell phone, indicating that it was Larry, she hurriedly answered the phone. Treasure had caught her off guard with her question, and since she didn't know what Lil Boo had told her, she was happy to have gotten the interruption. "What's up, Daddy Lane?" She answered in a flirty tone. Bright smiled, "Wait, hold on baby, let me tell Treasure bye." She removed the phone from her ear. "I'ma hit you later, bestie, I been waiting to talk to baby daddy all day," she smiled.

Treasure thumped the last of the blunt to the ground then stood up. "Call me when you get off the phone, I wanna finish talking to you," Treasure said.

"Soon as I get off the phone," Bright said, nodding her head. Once Treasure made it off of Bright's street, Bright went inside the house, washed her face, brushed her teeth, and then laid in her bed talking to Larry. Treasure had called her twice, but Bright ignored her calls, and she planned to do so until she personally spoke to Lil Boo.

****

The next day Bright and her mother went to Universal Care Clinic in Bellflower for her mother to get a doctor visit. "I don't like you missing school for me, Queen Bee, so afterwards, I'm dropping you off to school," Rosette said.

"That's fine, Ma, I just wanna make sure you're alright," Bright said, pulling her mother's car into the clinic's parking lot.

"You're a pretty good driver, too," her mother laughed. Rosette had been teaching Bright how to drive ever since she was eleven years old, and she was proud of her expert driving skills.

"I get it from my mama," Bright laughed, remembering the few times she had to drive her mother and siblings home when her mother was too drunk to drive from one of her friends' get-togethers.

Inside the doctor's office, they discovered Rosette had high blood pressure, and that was the cause of all the headaches she complained about. After the doctor prescribed Rosette some blood pressure medication, he told her to back off smoking cigarettes and drinking beer and recommended that she get more rest and exercise. Back inside the car, Bright asked her mother if she could drop her off at home and then pick up her missed work from school since the school day was almost over.

"Well, I guess so," Rosette said, relaxing her head on the headrest of the passenger seat. "I'm tired, but you be careful, you have a permit, not a valid driver's license yet and I can't afford to have my car impounded," she said, then closed her eyes.

"Ok; you not going to work tonight, are you Ma?" Bright asked.

With her eyes closed Rosette shifted in her seat. "Well, who else gone pay the bills? Of course I'm going to work," she answered quietly.

Bright looked at her poor tired mother. She worked around the clock and even though it made it easier for her to do what she wanted to do, she didn't like to see her overworked and burnt out. "Ma, why don't Vince help you out sometimes?" she asked, starting the car up.

"He didn't father any of y'all, so I don't put my responsibilities on him. Besides that, I don't like asking men for money because then they start thinking they own you," she replied, trying to get back comfortable in her seat. "Been there, done that, and I hope you understand that," she added, opening her eyes, to give her daughter direct eye contact.

Rosette had lived the high-roller lifestyle. She had been the mistress to a rock star for many years and had Bright. She had been the girlfriend of a big time, Mexican drug-dealer, and had birthed Deja and Cordell...And he used to beat the shit out of her. Finally, there was Ramon and Ryonna's father, who thought he owned her. So after all that, she figured that if she relied on nobody but herself, she could avoid suffering any further mental anguish. But now her independence was wearing on her health and she knew she'd have to make some changes in her life...And quick.

"Ma, that don't mean he can't help you out a little bit; he is your so called man," Bright snapped with attitude. She couldn't believe her mother would sleep with a man as long as she had been with Vince and still allow herself to be broke the next morning.

"Well he does when I ask him to! Now leave me alone so I can shut my eyes, Queen Bee!" her mother snapped back. "All up in my business like she got some damn money to foot the bills," her mother mumbled out loud.

"Well how much do you need, Ma?" Bright asked driving down Artesia Blvd.

"Give me five hundred dollars and I'll stay out for the rest of the week, Mrs. got-all-the damn-answers," she sat up looking at Bright.

Once they approached the red light on Orange Ave, Bright grabbed her purse and pulled out five crispy one hundred dollar bills then passed it to her mother. "And there is a lot more money where that came from too," Bright said, then put her foot to the gas once the light turned green.

Shocked, her mother said, "Where did this money come from, Bright?" She wondered where and how her daughter had gotten her hands on that type of money.

"Calm down, Ma, I got it from Larry," she said, looking from her mother to the road. "He gives me money every other week, and I been saving it until after I have the babies," she lied.

"Well, I won't take it!" her mother said. "That money is for you and my grandbabies," she said, ending the conversation.

"Ma, take it, I have a lot of money, Larry's family has cheese and he really has it to give away. So I'm giving it to you, I already have everything I need for the babies. Don't you see all that stuff in my room?" she asked. She had been preparing for the babies and buying things weekly, not to mention all of the items Terrence had been surprising her with.

Rosette didn't like the idea of taking money from her daughter, but since she had it to give, she was gonna accept it. "Okay, but just this one time. I don't want Larry taking care of my responsibility. Matter of fact, I'm giving it back, every red penny, you hear me?" she said, tucking the money in her bra.

"I'm not taking it, Ma, and when me and Larry get married, you won't ever have to worry about working ever again either! Larry thinks you and his mother both deserve a permanent break from work, and I agree!" Bright said seriously.

Rosette smiled. "Thanks, but no thanks." Then she climbed out of her car once Bright pulled up in front of the apartment building. "Hurry back with my car too!" Then she headed in the direction of her apartment.

****

Bright had no intentions of going to pick up school work; she needed to borrow her mother's car to go holler at Lil Boo. She needed to know exactly what he told Treasure before she ended up getting caught up in a lie, so she drove herself to Compton to speak to him. On the ride over, Terrence was blowing her phone up, but she didn't answer. She had enough money, and she wasn't in the mood to fuck or suck him off.

Pulling up on Lil Boo's street, Bright was happy to see his cars parked in his driveway. After parking on the street, she climbed out of the car, walked up his driveway, and knocked on his door. He answered the door looking breathtaking. He was dressed in all-white linen and Gucci tennis shoes, and her vagina immediately became moist just thinking of the wild sex they had had.

"To what do I owe the pleasure of ya fine as just popping up at a nigga door without first calling?" Lil Boo said, undressing her with his eyes. Pregnant and all, she still looked good to him.

Bright smiled. "Can I come inside?" she asked with her hand on her hip, checking him out.

"Yeah, you can come inside," he said softly, then licked his lips.

Bright followed him inside, swinging her ass left to right as sexily as she could, then she took a seat on his couch. "So what you tell Treasure?" she wanted to know. "I ain't tell Treasure shit, my big mouth homeboy spilled that shit on Piru," Lil Boo said, taking a seat next to her on the couch. "When she asked me that shit, I told her we smoked a blunt in the backyard then I gave you bath towels to wash ya ass with, and a sheet and blanket for you to sleep with," he said honestly.

Bingo, he told her we smoked a blunt, Bright thought. "Why you tell yo homeboy, though?" Bright asked. "You know you messed up a beautiful thing, right?" Bright would have crept with him a few more times if he would have had a tighter grip on his mouth.

"Yeah I did," Lil Boo smiled. He knew Bright was referring to herself, but he was going to work his hand at another shot of her superb head and a chance of sticking his dick back in her soak in wet pregnant pussy. "A nigga do miss Treasure too, with that sweet tasting ass pussy of hers. I can't even get baby girl to come through no more...with them beautiful eyes." He knew if he disregarded Bright and showed her little interest that she'd go out of her way to demand his attention by giving it up. He knew hoe's of her caliber - *Straight slut,* he thought as he looked at her.

Bright laughed. "Yeah okay, but anyways, that was all I came through for, seeing that I'm not missed or wanted around here," she stood preparing to leave.

"You a lie," Lil Boo quickly said, taking a different approach. Now that she was in his house, he wanted her butt naked and in his bed. "I miss you too. Too bad we couldn't all come to some type of understanding, cause I got enough dick for the both of y'all fine asses."

Bright chuckled, "Nigga you ain't got enough dick for me alone, paleaseeee!" she sighed, stretching and poking her breasts out to reveal her hard nipples.

Seeing hard nipples, Lil Boo reached out and grabbed them both. "Let's try again," Lil Boo said, then grabbed his swollen penis. "I hear pregnant pussy is the best pussy too," he smiled.

Bright pushed him on the couch, took her clothes off, and then sat on his lap. "How you want this pussy, boy?" She asked him seductively as she straddled him.

"You like riding dick?" He asked, slapping her hard on her ass. Then he leaned over and grabbed a condom out of the jar full of condoms that he kept on his end table. "Put that on for me," he said, passing her the Magnum condom.

Bright carefully moved to her knees, unwrapped the condom, then placed it in her mouth and on his fat penis. Then she stood up with his penis in her hand and gently guided it inside of her wet tunnel. Giving Lil Boo a ride doggy style he played with her clit and made her cum quicker than she had expected. Moans began to escape from her mouth and she began to tremble. Lil Boo grabbed her by the waist and slammed her up and down his penis until he came. Then he pulled her by the hair and whispered in her ear, "I have plenty of dick to go around."

Bright smiled, "How much money do you have to go around, though?" She stood up to put her pants back on.

"Enough," Lil Boo said, waiting on her gold-digging ass to ask him for some.

Bright threw her right hand out and said, "Can I have some?"

Lil Boo laughed. "I don't pay bitches to fuck, they pay me. Now if you don't mind, I have business to take care of," he said, walking to the bathroom to wash his dick off.

Bright felt not only degraded but disrespected. *How could he, she* thought. "Oh shit, it's like that?" Bright smiled to keep from crying.

"Yeah, just like that," Lil Boo said, followed with a smile. "But hey, come again, I'll be available next Tuesday," he said, walking her to the door.

"Pleaseeee! Yo broke ass ain't never gotta worry about hitting this again!" Bright said, looking him up and down, allowing her emotions to show on her face. She couldn't believe he played her like that.

"That's cool too," he said as she walked out of his door.

"Because yo homegirl got better pussy than you do anyways, you trick ass bitch!" Then he slammed his door shut and fell into laughter. He dealt with top of the line females and only fucked with hoes when he was lonely. And on Tuesdays, all his females were at work and Bright came right on time.

"No, this broke ass nigga didn't," Bright said, walking down his driveway. Then she grabbed her mother's Honda car key and went to town on both sides of his Benz. After she was satisfied keying his paint up, she yelled, "Yeah nigga, now the cost is on ya car, bitch!"

then she hurried to her mother's car and made her way back to north side of Long Beach.

Part Twelve

At school, Bright found excuse after excuse to leave early. She hated being there and since she had a sickly pregnancy. It was nothing for her to throw up a few times and get sent home. She was tired of school, and suddenly began to hate being pregnant. She felt fat, ugly, and was tired of everybody making a bigger deal over the babies than her. It was always "the babies this" or "the babies that". Larry was so afraid of accidentally hurting them that he hardly ever had sex with her and when they did it, it was extremely boring. After being excused from school for the day, Bright called Larry to pick her up.

"Baby, come pick me up from school, I'm not feeling well," Bright said into the phone once he answered.

"You're not feeling well again, baby? Is that normal? Are the babies okay?" Larry asked in a panic.

Bright rolled her eyes. "Yes boo, the babies are okay, it's me that's not feeling well," she snapped with attitude. "It's not always about the babies, you know?"

"Quit being jealous, Pretty Bright," Larry teased.

"Go to Burger King, I'll pick you up in fifteen minutes," he said, then ended the call.

Bright went inside of Burger King, ordered a chicken salad, then sat and waited for Larry to pick her up. Ten minutes later, she saw his mother's van pull into the lot. She couldn't stand riding around in the old minivan, but she figured at least she'd get some alone time with him today. Outside, she was surprised and disappointed to see Larry's mother pull in front of the restaurant, smiling and waving at her to get in. Bright liked Larry's mother, she was a very nice lady. However, because she was a religious woman, Bright tried to avoid her as much as possible, because she was always quoting scriptures from the Bible and asking Bright when she was going to church with her.

"Hey Mrs. Lane, I didn't know you were coming to pick me up, thanks!" Bright said, pretending to be happy to see her. She was hoping to spend some quality time with Larry.

"Larry was busy studying, so he asked me to pick you up," she smiled. "Are you alright?" she asked Bright.

"This pregnancy keeps me sickly," Bright replied, getting inside the van.

"I know the feeling, Larry kept me sick as a dog too." She gave Bright a comforting pat in the knee then drove out of the parking lot.

"So where am I taking you?" she asked kindly.

"I guess home, since your son never has time for me anymore," Bright complained.

Mrs. Lane said, "Oh, don't feel that way, sweetheart. You and the babies are the reason my son pushes so hard," she said sincerely. "He says he's gonna be everything that his father was to him, a good father." She laughed. "That man died with a dream and vision and was a good man, and I'm so proud that Larry is following his father's footsteps," she smiled.

A father was something that Bright had never had. When she was a kid and would fall and skin her knee, she'd always hope that when she looked up, that her father would be there to pick her up, kiss her wounds, and make everything better. Something about being a fatherless child did something to Bright and made her feel empty inside.

"Tell me about your father, Bright?" Mrs. Lane asked.

Bright put on her pretend face and begin to speak. "My father was a very wealthy and well-known rock star. And he used to make the biggest deal over me," she sighed. "My life used to be like a real fairy tale before he passed away," she lied, because the truth hurt her too much.

Once Mrs. Lane dropped Bright off at home, Bright went inside and tried to make herself eat the salad she bought from Burger King. As usual, her appetite was spoiled, so she went and grabbed her stash of Kush weed out of her bedroom closet and rolled up a fat blunt. Since Bright didn't have a lighter and her mother wasn't home, she lit the blunt on the kitchen stove, then quickly ran through the living room and to the front door. Opening the front door, Bright was caught off guard with Suge's presence; she was about to knock on the door.

"Sugeeeeeeeee!" Bright yelled, hugging her friend, while inhaling and balancing the blunt that dangled from in between her lips.

"Hey preggo Bright," Suge said, just as happy to see Bright as she was to see her. "What you doing smoking while you're pregnant?" Suge asked with a disagreeing look on her face.

"Girl, I can't even get an appetite if I don't smoke,"she answered truthfully, hitting the weed once more.

Suge nodded her head. "That's all bad," she responded, then extended her hand for the weed.

Bright hit it again then passed it to her. Suge hit it once and then choked on the smoke. "Damn, I ain't had no weed in a minute," she said hitting it again, then passing it back to Bright.

"How's it been at your new home?" Bright asked, putting the blunt out.

"I really like my new foster parents, like I told you. They Muslims and all, but they cool as fuck! Sister Mohammad takes me to the mosque with her and spends a lot of time talking to me about me and how I feel," she smiled happily. Her mother never took such interest in her.

"That's good, Suge, I'm really happy for you," Bright said, walking back into the apartment. "Don't go all bean pie and on pork strike on me either," she teased.

Suge laughed. "I've honestly never been a big pork fan anyways, so it's not like I'm missing it," she replied. "You heard from that bitch?" Bright said, referring to Suge's mother.

"Yeah, a couple weeks ago she called me and I listened, end of story," Suge quickly said.

"No, she didn't have the nerve to call you! What, she want you to come home?" Bright said in disbelief.

Suge shook her head no. "She called to apologize to me and tell that she loved me," she giggled. "And I actually believed her, well, at least after talking to Sister Mohammad, I believed her. She told me she was going to counseling and everything."

"Fuck her and her apology!" Bright said, heading to the restroom to freshen up.

Suge laughed, "I know, right! But I forgave her anyways, Bright; Sister Mohammad said that forgiveness is the key to new and successful beginnings."

"Sister Mohammad is getting on my last nerve already, with her self-righteous self," Bright teased, drying her hands. "How 'bout after I have the babies, me, you, Treasure, and Sister Mohammad go jump that hoe?" Bright said seriously. "And I know Treasure would be down for that," then she, rubbed lotion on her face, arms, and hands.

"People do messed up things when they ain't right, Bright, so no, we won't be jumping on my mother," Suge said nonchalantly. *Like how you fucked Chrome, Suge* thought.

"Well, let me know if you change your mind," Bright teased.

After a few awkward moments of silence, Suge begin to speak. "Bright, I wanna talk to you about something that I found in your room the last time I was here," she said seriously.

"Holla," Bright said, taking a seat on the living room couch.

Suge sat down on the couch across from Bright then said, "Well, one day I was in your room, and I dropped your cell phone behind your bed, and when I went to grab it, I found a letter from Chrome to Treasure and my curiosity got the best of me and I read it," she said, giving her friend direct eye contact. "And I was wondering why you forged a letter to him in Treasure's name?"

Being a great liar, Bright was prepared to answer the question. "Because he kept bothering Treasure, writing her every other week; and after everything he had done to me, I was sick and tired of hearing his damn name. So I decided to write him back pretending to be Treasure, hoping that he'd leave her the fuck alone!" She became angry thinking about the way he had beat her.

Getting straight to the point, Suge asked, "Did he really rape you Bright?" She wanted to know the truth.

With a disbelieving look on her face, Bright spat, "How

dare you even ask me some shit like that, Suge! What, you think I just fucked the nigga?" she snapped. "Treasure's my best friend - I would of never did no shit like that to her!" she said offensively.

Before Suge could reply and remind her of the words she wrote on the letter, their conversation was interrupted by a knock on the door. "Who is it?" Bright asked, walking to the door.

"It's me, Treasure!" Treasure yelled from the other side of the door.

Before opening the door, Bright gave Suge a sign for her to keep her lips sealed. Suge nodded her head in agreement. "What's up, bestie?" Bright said, opening the door for Treasure.

"Why you leave school early today Bee? I was looking for you," Treasure said, landing her eyes on Suge. "Hey Suge, look at you!" Treasure said, meeting her halfway for a hug. "I was missing you boo!" Treasure sang happily.

"I been missing you too Treasure," Suge said, becoming emotional. "What's been up though?" She asked.

Treasure took a seat on the couch with Suge and said, "Drama girl! Did Bee fill you in on the Lil Boo and Nicole issue yet?" She asked, looking at Bright.

Bright spoke up, "No, we've been talking about Suge and her new home life," Bright smiled, hoping to change the subject. "And I wasn't even thinking about that drama and them meaningless ass people. Fuck both of 'em," she said irritated.

"What happened?" Suge asked curiously, looking from Treasure to Bright. She had a feeling that Bright was trying to cover up something and she wanted to know what it was. After Treasure told her the complete story, Suge's mouth was hanging wide open. "Not Nicole, she was the homegirl, why y'all jump her?" Suge asked.

"I know, I feel bad now too," Treasure said, "but what was I supposed to do?"

"Fuck Nicole, fat hater nation ass," Bright was annoyed at how Suge was taking up for her. "That bitch was tryna keep up mess between me and my bestie, and she got what she deserved!" Bright barked.

"I know, but dang, Nicole was cool...maybe y'all should of talked about it, is all I'm saying?" Suge replied. "Cause it wasn't like she made it up, she just said what Lil Boo homeboy said, right?"

"Suge you trippin', all on that bitch's nuts like she somebody," Bright said with attitude.

"She's right though, Bee," Treasure said, agreeing with Suge. "She only told us what she heard, which was the same thing I would have done had it been you or Suge. And to this day, I wish shit didn't go down the way it did cause Nicole was nothing but real to me," Treasure said regretfully.

"What the fuck ever, poor Nicole!" Bright snapped, yelling at the top of her lungs. "I wish I would of just went home that night instead of staying to watch yo back. Then maybe none of these lies would of surfaced, and you would still have your precious Nicole!" She vented.

"It's not even like that." Treasure was growing tired of Bright always playing the victim.

"What happened after she went to sleep, Bright?" Suge asked.

The million dollar question, Treasure thought.

"If you must know, Detective Suge," Bright snapped,

"Lil Boo gave me blankets and towels to shower with, then we smoked a blunt and he went back upstairs, and I took a shower and went to sleep!"

"So y'all did smoke a blunt, Bee?" Treasure asked.

"Yeah, I told you that, remember?" Bright lied.

"No you didn't, but Lil Boo told me y'all smoked a blunt. He told me y'all smoked one then he came up and got in bed with me, but you never mentioned it."

"I thought I did," Bright lied, acting as if she was puzzled. Treasure knew Bright didn't have Lil Boo's number stored in her cell phone, because she had gone through it several times after the incident. Convinced that Bright and Lil Boo were telling the truth, Treasure removed herself from the couch and hugged Bright tight. "What you hugging me for?" Bright asked, playing dumb. She knew that small detail would save their sinking friendship and clear her name.

"Because you never told me about the blunt, Bee, and that was why I didn't know who or what to believe." she admitted.

"Treasure!" Bright shouted disappointedly, "You believed that I would stoop that low and screw yo boyfriend, boy-toy or whatever that nigga was to you?" She asked as if she was truly hurt by her comment.

"Forgive me, Bee," Treasure said honestly. "But first it was Chrome, and then Lil Boo, so I guess I was just a little messed up in the head."

Shedding a few tears, Bright said, "Oh my God, Treasure, I'm your true friend and I would never intentionally do anything to purposely hurt you. You're my bestie, and I love you," she said, speaking from her heart. Though, Bright's actions didn't show it, she loved Treasure like a sister, but when that hoe in her came out to play, she just couldn't control it or contain herself. The two hugged and vowed to never let anybody, male or female come in between their friendship ever again.

Suge, on the other hand, knew a little more than Treasure, and wasn't so convinced. She knew in Bright's world that Bright got what Bright wanted, and it didn't matter who she had to step on to get it. Later, after the house started to fill up with Bright's siblings, Suge called for her foster mom to pick her up, and Treasure went home.

3 a.m. Tuesday Morning…

After coming back from the strip club with his boys, Terrence desired some head, so he called Bright up and told her to meet him outside.

"Terrence," she whined, "It's three o'clock in the morning, baby. I'm sleeping."

"You know what, I been noticing how you been real heavy on complaining and trying not to satisfy yo man," he barked, "And I'ma do the same thing the next time yo ass ask me for some money," he said, then hung up on her.

Pissed, Bright called him right back. She couldn't afford to be off his payroll, especially since she was helping her mother out a lot more around the house. "Ice baby, why you hang up, boo? Come scoop me up right quick so I can take care of you, daddy," she said sweetly into the phone, but had a bitter expression on her face.

"That's what I'm talking about, just come outside in a robe…no panties on," he said, then hung up. Ten minutes later, Bright was creeping down the hallway to the front door.

"Where you going?" Deja asked, heading to the bathroom. She could tell she had startled Bright.

"Mind ya own and you'll live long," Bright replied quietly. "I'm 'bout to step outside real quick, don't lock the door."

"A'ight, Deja said stepping closer to Bright. " Who baby is that, Larry's or Ice's?" Deja asked.

Bright almost choked on her spit. "It's Larry's baby, and what you know about Ice?" she asked curiously, since she had never mentioned him to her.

"You'd be surprised what I learned in juvenile," Deja said. "Your secrets are safe with me, but I have one for you though. Ramon is gay. I caught him sucking another boy's weenie yesterday in his bedroom closet, and I haven't been able to sleep ever since," Deja explained, feeling as if she was about to throw up again. Bright's eyes were bucked, and her mouth flew wide open; she was speechless. Deja said, "I know, right, imagine how I felt, I fucking seen the shit," she whispered.

Bright's phone vibrated in her pocket and after looking at the caller ID and seeing it was Terrence, she told Deja that she'd be right back. She didn't know what else to say. Outside Bright climbed inside of Terrence truck. Since he knew she would be unable to stay out with him, he didn't see any use in getting a room or taking her back to his place, so instead he drove a few blocks down from her apartment and parked. Bright got on her knees and tried to please him as best as she could, but because her little brother was on her mind, it made it hard for her to satisfy him.

"Damn, what's the problem?" Terrence asked, frustrated.

"I'm uncomfortable down here, my stomach is getting too big to be on my knees in your truck," she lied. Though she was approaching the second trimester of her pregnancy, her stomach was still pretty small for twins.

"Let me hit the booty hole then," Terrence said, helping her off of her knees. "A nigga need to get this one off."

Knowing she wouldn't be able to get out of pleasing him, Bright lifted her robe up and carefully placed herself on top Terrence. Aiming straight for her booty hole, Terrence found his way in. "That booty is tight," he moaned, squeezing her breasts and biting on her back. Wanting him to hurry up and be over with it, Bright made loud fuck noises, held on to the steering wheel and slammed her ass up and down on his penis until he erupted inside of her. As she climbed off of him, Terrence smiled. "I'ma need some of that booty more often."

Pretending she enjoyed it, Bright said, "Yeah, I enjoyed that too, baby." Then she smiled and asked him to take her home before her mother noticed she was gone. Terrence dropped Bright off without breaking her off. She didn't bother asking him for any money either, her brother weighed heavily on her mind, and all she wanted to do was finish talking to Deja about it.

Back inside the apartment, the sisters sat in Bright room talking as quietly as possible.

"You didn't tell, Ma, did you? Bright asked.

"I wanted to, but I just couldn't do it," Deja shrugged.

"Fuck, what are we going to do?" Bright asked, covering her face with both of her hands. It had finally hit her why Ramon had become so distant and why he was always locked up in his room.

"The question is, what can we do?" Deja said nodding her head. "This makes me wonder if somebody has ever touched him before."

Bright went numb for about ten seconds then said, "Maybe we should find him a girlfriend or something." Deja nodded her head. "I can't even believe were even having this conversation! Ramon never showed any signs of being gay," she said, still in shock.

"So you opened the closet and he was on his knees sucking the boy's dick?" Bright asked, trying to get a visual.

"Yes!" She answered in a loud whisper.

"Well, what did he say after you caught him?" She wanted to know.

"He didn't say anything because I closed the closet door back and walked out the room. I didn't know what to say! But then later that night he asked me not to tell, and told me that he would never do it again."

The sisters spoke until the sun came up, and then they both dressed and went to school. At school that day, Bright felt like she had ADHD because she was having the hardest time concentrating. At lunch, Bright went inside the nurse's office and took a nap. She was all messed up in the head thinking about her little brother, and all she wanted to do was erase and block the whole thing from her memory bank, but because Deja was in on the secret too, she knew she had no chances of escaping it.

Part Thirteen

After cooking dinner, Rosette went to her room to grab a little rest before going to bible study. She had found a nice church off of Long Beach Blvd. that was helping her to find peace, and teaching her how to survive her insanity. Life was hard for Rosette; she worked too much, got paid too little, and more importantly, she had a house full of children that needed more of her time then she could afford to give them. So when Bright offered to pay her a few hundred dollars every month to help out with the rent, bills, and additional money for groceries, she accepted the offer with open hands. She figured Bright had it to help out, so why not accept it? She had her own room, and was about to have twin babies in a few months, so why not let her help out more around the house? For the best of her health, Rosette quit her second job so that she could be home at night with her children, she even planned on going to the county building to apply for food stamps and cash-aid. Things would be a little tight, but she felt she owed it to her children. Climbing in her queen-sized bed, Rosette said a quick prayer then rested her eyes.

Walking in the house after a long day at school, Bright grabbed the weed from her stash, rolled up a blunt, then went outside to hit it a few times before the rest of her siblings made it home. Once she put the blunt out, she went back inside, took a shower, and then stretched out on the living room couch. Ten minutes later the house filled with her siblings.

"Ramon got in another fight at school, they jumped him this time," Deja said once she entered the apartment.

It seemed like he had been getting in fights every other day since she had caught him in the closet. She felt sorry for him, but he wouldn't talk to anybody or let anybody in.

"Yep, he got a busted lip too," Ryonna said, pointing at him. She always took up for her brother when the kids at school teased him and called him a faggot for playing with girls.

"I told him to take me to the dudes that jumped on 'em, but he don't want to," Cordell added. "So I figured he like getting his ass kicked," he said, then slapped Ramon on the back of the head.

"Lower y'all voices, Mama is in her room resting," Bright ordered, then she directed her attention to Ramon. "Who jumped on you, Ramon?" she asked examining his face.

"Nobody jumped me, I told them," he said storming off to his bedroom.

"Yes, they did," Ryonna said; they both went to the same school so she knew everything. "They been calling him faggot's at school and be picking on him all the time," Ryonna said, speaking up for him.

"No they don't, you liar!" Ramon yelled from his room.

"I said keep y'all voices down, Mama is asleep!" Bright said with authority.

Cordell came out of the kitchen laughing. "I knew cuz was gone be a little faggot, hanging out with girls all the time," he said nodding his head. He had been noticing a lot of gay traits from Ramon, starting with his little friend that he always seemed to be locked in the room with and the way he twisted his lips and laughed.

Bright walked over and slapped Cordell across the face.

He was about to slap her back until Deja approached, ready to flex. "I wish you would hit her!" Bright stared at him. "If I ever hear you call him a faggot again, I'ma snatch yo nuts off, you hear me?" She asked in a firm tone.

"Man, fuck both of y'all," Cordell pushed his way past both of his sisters. "I ain't no little kid no more, so y'all better keep yo hands to yourself," he said as he opened the front door.

Hearing all the noise, Rosette couldn't sleep any longer. "What's all the commotion about?" she asked after getting out of bed. The room fell silent; her children all stared at her. Seeing that Ryonna was about to spill the beans, Bright gave her the "don't say anything expression," then she stopped speaking in mid-sentence.

"Is anybody gonna say something?" Rosette yelled, looking at each of her children for an answer.

Standing in the door's entrance, angry at his sisters, Cordell yelled, "Yo son is a faggot, Mama, and he got beat up for it at school today," he said mean-mugging both Bright and Deja.

"He's not a faggot!" Bright said defensively, ready to slap the living daylights out of Cordell again.

"Yes he is, Mama," Cordell responded, nodding his head, then he stepped closer to his mother so that she could see the truth in his eyes. "And not only that, but your oldest daughter is a hoe, Mama. She's not only pregnant, but she screwing this old nigga name, Ice too!"

Angry he planned on revealing everything that he knew. "Oh, and Deja, she having sex too," he laughed, looking in her direction, "But the funny thing about her is that she up on tape with hers. She got a train ran on her by three different dudes - her and her little slutty ass home girl, Veronica!" he laughed. "Oh and me?" he stressed, hitting his chest, "I'm just a Crip from the Norf," Mama. "I figured with two hoe ass sisters, a faggot ass brother, a workaholic mama, and a daddy serving a life term in prison, that it would be in my best interest to get put on the hood, so that at least somebody could have my back," he said throwing his arms in the air.

Cordell was hurt and angry about his current life status. He hated that dudes from the hood whispered about his sisters disrespectfully when he passed them…the half breed hoes. He hated the fact that guys called Bright a gold digger and high-priced prostitute, and that Deja was on tape, and labeled as a hood rat in the neighborhood, and that they called his little brother soft and said he acted like a punk. He didn't have any positive influences in his life, nobody to talk to, or to teach him how to be a man. So being from the hood was the next best thing in store for him - he'd have his OG's to teach him how to be a man, have street brothers to have his back, and a crew to rely on when he needed them.

Bright and Deja couldn't believe the information that Cordell had just revealed, or furthermore, that he knew all this time without saying a word to them about it. Deja wanted off with his head for putting her on blast like that. She didn't ask for what happened to her. She stormed in his direction and began to swing on him.

Snapping out of her shock, Bright joined Deja, getting her licks in too.

Standing there, Rosette wanted to break everything up, but she couldn't. She was stiff, and she felt like someone had knocked the wind out of her. Ryonna screamed at the top of her lungs for everybody to stop fighting. Unable to take the chaos that was going on in the house Ramon ran out the front door with his backpack on. Rosette's speech slurred when she tried telling them to stop. She tried catching her breath, but it felt like she was suffocating. Then she began to feel dizzy and had double vision. Suddenly, numbness began to take over her arms and legs. Not able to help herself she slid down the wall and onto the floor.

"HELPPPPP, MAMA JUST FELL ON THE FLOOR," Ryonna cried at the top of her lungs, jumping up and down. She was so scared and afraid that she peed on herself. If she knew that giving such information would turn the house so mad, she would have kept it to herself. Immediately, everyone stopped fighting and directed their attention to their mother.

"Call 911, Deja!" Bright yelled. Cordell got on the floor with Bright to aid their mother.

"What you want me to do, sis? He asked on the verge of tears.

"Help me lay her on her back, then go grab a pillow to put under her head," she said, trying to remember everything she learned about stroke and heart attack victims. After carefully helping his sister lay their mother on her back, he ran inside her room and grabbed a pillow.

"Mama, you okay?" Cordell asked, gently tapping her on the face. She was going in and out of consciousness, and he was really afraid. "Stay awake, Mama," Cordell continued to say, seeing her fluttering eyes.

"You're gonna be alright Ma, the paramedic is on the way," Bright said with tear-stained eyes.

"Is she having heart attack?" Cordell asked his sisters.

"It looks like she's having a stroke," Bright said,

examining her mother. "Lift her neck a little, Cordell, to make sure she has a good airway for breathing." Bright tried her best to keep calm.

"Hurry the fuck up!" Deja said, pacing the floor, looking out the window for the paramedics. Ryonna bit her nails, crying and looking nervously around the room. Bright couldn't contain her sniffles as she sat on the side of her mother, trying to keep her comfortable.

"Y'all see what we did to Mama?" Cordell said. "We can't keep stressing her out like this, man," he said, unable to hold his tears back. "Cause if we lose Mama, who we gone have?" he said, looking at his sisters.

"Mama is strong, she's gonna be alright," Bright replied. "Her heart is still beating and it sounds like the paramedics are close."

"Go outside and show 'em up, Ryonna," Cordell ordered, hearing them getting closer and closer in the distance. Ryonna ran down the stairs, while Deja stood in the doorway looking from her mother to her little sister Ryonna as she stood out front waiting for help. "Keep fighting, Mama," Deja cried, then she bent down and kissed her on the cheek.

"She's hangin' in there," Bright cried, wiping the drool away from her mother's mouth with the back of her hand. "Mama's gonna be alright, aren't you, Ma?" Bright cried, looking into her mother's zoned out eyes. "You have grandbabies on the way," Bright said, nodding her head, trying to force a warm smile on her face. It was hard, Bright knew she had to be strong for her siblings and display a positive attitude.

Cordell held his mother's hand. "You promise, Bright?"

"I promise," Bright said, then wiped the tears from

her brother's eyes. "Mama's gonna pull through this, she's a fighter."

"Here they come," Deja yelled. "Does she still have a heartbeat?" Deja asked, holding her hands on each side of her face. She was so nervous that she could just about rip the skin off of her face.

"She does!" Cordell replied after lifting his head from his mother's chest. Once the paramedics came inside, they took her vitals and confirmed that she was having a stroke. They laid her on the stretcher and then rushed her to the hospital. After the paramedics left, Bright grabbed her mother's car keys and then drove her and her siblings to the hospital. After discovering that Ramon was missing, Bright later received a phone call from her mother's second cousin, named Shanna, explaining that Ramon was at her house. Because they had only heard of Shanna, but never been formally introduced, Bright was curious as to how Shanna and Ramon got in contact, so she asked.

After clearing her throat, Shanna responded, "Gale is a good friend of both your mother and me, we all grew up together," she smiled. "But to make a long story short, Gale called and told me that little Ramon had come over to her house alone, and that he was very hysterical. She said she tried getting in touch with you guys and wasn't able to get a response. And since she had to go to work, she asked if I could pick him up, and keep trying to get in touch with you all...so I did just that," she sighed. "I do hope I haven't crossed any lines or boundaries, but I just couldn't say no," she explained. "And he's in really good hands here too," she added.

"No...No, there's no problem at all, we actually appreciate it," Bright said in a tone of appreciation. "We were only concerned because we didn't know where he was at," she said, happy to hear that her brother was in good hands. After filling Shanna in on her mother's condition, Bright ended the call, then explained everything to her siblings. With the burden of their missing brother being lifted off of their shoulders, they all sat, silently awaiting the doctor's update on their mother's condition.

****

"Mom, why do we really have to go to visit cousin Rosette in the hospital in the first place? It's not like y'all get along, or ever speak to one another," Ryan said, having morning coffee with her mother on her bedroom patio.

"Well, her son is still here, and from the looks of things, she could use some family support," Shanna said, smoking her cigarette, looking into the morning skies, lost in deep thought.

"Well, I'm not going, I'm staying here," Ryan pouted, tucking her arms inside her pajama shirt to warm them.

Breaking her daze, Shanna gave her oldest daughter direct eye contact. "If you're not going with me, then you're not staying here, because I can tell that you're itching for a piece of crack, and this time you won't be removing anything from this house to get it," she snarled.

Ryan rolled her eyes in the back of her head. "Oh wow, I did that one time, and you're gonna seriously continue to hold that against me?" she said seriously.

Shanna stood up and drank the last of her coffee. She wasn't in the mood to argue with Ryan, nor was she gonna put any more energy into it. "I'm going to shower and dress, and I advise that you do the same," she said, dumping the remains of her cigarette in the ashtray, then walked inside her room. Ryan stood up in a tantrum, then went to take a shower. *Fuck, I wanna get high,* she thought as she drew herself up some bath water.

****

Bright kissed her mother on the forehead. She was happy that she was okay, but the doctors did tell her that her memory may be a little shocked - short or long term.

"How you feeling, Ma?" Bright asked her mother the next morning as she laid comfortably in her hospital bed. They had all stayed overnight in the hospital worrying about their mother, and Ramon stayed the night with Shanna. Rosette opened her eyes and looked at the strangers surrounding her bed. When the young beautiful girl asked her how she was feeling, she was unable to get her words out right properly. "I'm…k," she struggled to say.

"It's alright, Ma, just relax," Bright said, seeing her mother trying to lift herself up in bed. The others all agreed.

"Just lie down and get better, Mama," Deja added, then kissed her on the cheek.

It had been a long night for them all. Barely able to sleep in the waiting area, they were all really tired, and after they all kissed her, they decided to go home to get some rest. Before they could step out the door, Bright was slapped with the presence of her reflection and a woman who she assumed to be her mother's distant cousin Shanna. She told Bright that she would stop in to visit her mother and drop Ramon off. Bright looked the girl up and down, both of them amazed at how much the two of them resembled each other.

Ryan said, "Wow, this is really freaky, Mom, she looks more like my sister then Kesh," she said, covering her mouth in shock.

Ignoring the statement, Shanna stepped in front of Ryan then cleared her throat. "You must be Bright," she said, extending her hand to shake.

Bright smiled and shook the hand of the beautiful, crippled, but well-put woman before her. " And you must be cousin Shanna," she said, shaking her hand. Then Bright introduced the rest of her siblings to them. After the introductions, they all walked back inside the room, and Bright walked back over to her mother's bed side. "Ma, your cousin Shanna and her daughter came to visit you," she said, removing her hair from her face. Her mother never told them much about her and her cousin's relationship, all they knew was that she didn't like her very much.

Shanna moved closer to her cousin's bedside with a warm, friendly smile on her face. "Hello, darling Rose, even a stroke couldn't deny or take away such beauty," she said, then bent down to kiss her on the face.

"Is she alright?" Ryan chuckled, looking at her strangely. Rosette looked confused.

"She's good, her memory is just a little off from the stroke," Bright said, then quickly rolled her eyes at her. *How dare this bitch walk up in here and look at my mother like that, in her sick bed,* she thought. It was evident from their expressions that Deja and Cordell were wearing on their faces that they had both picked up on to Ryan's tone and the funny look on her face.

They must think they uppity or something, Deja thought, looking Ryan up and down.

I see why Mama doesn't fuck with they funny acting asses,

Cordell thought, mean mugging Ryan.

Shanna cleared her throat, looking into Ryan's direction, then lifted her brow. Ryan laughed. "I didn't meant it the way it came out, I was asking because she looked confused, that's all, no disrespect intended," she said to everybody, recovering from laughter.

"I don't see nothing funny, though cuz," Cordell said, getting an attitude.

"Neither do I," Deja said.

"I didn't catch on to the joke either," Bright chimed in. Though they fought and bickered with each other, it was clear that in their household they fought and rode together up against anybody who wanted it, cousins and all.

"I told you I should have stayed home, mom," Ryan said, feeling like she was being attacked. "Because people are always misunderstanding me," Ryan started to walk out of the room. "I'll wait for you in the waiting area," she said, then exited the room.

"I think that might be best," Bright said, following her out of the room with her eyes.

With her arms folded across her chest, Shanna said, "Please excuse her; I'm sure she didn't intend to offend anyone, she is really a very sweet girl." She smiled, then she directed her attention back to her cousin. An awkward silence filled the room as the siblings exchanged expressions of dislike for their newly introduced family.

"NOOOOOO," Rosette yelled, snatching her arm away from her cousin Shanna. "OUT," she said in a loud and firm voice. Though she was out of it, she knew that the lady standing in front of her had done something very wrong to her, and she didn't want her around. The siblings all gave each other puzzled looks.

It's okay," Shanna smiled. "I'm your cousin, Shanna. I'm not here to hurt you, I'm actually very concerned about you!" Shanna spoke as if Rosette was deaf.

Rosette balled her fist on top off her stomach, turned her face away from Shanna, then mumbled, "No."

"You getting her upset," Cordell said. "Maybe you should roll and come back another time," he suggested, stepping to his mother's bedside. He didn't like his mother's response to Shanna.

Bright felt bad for Shanna, but she agreed. "Yeah, she had a rough night and is probably very tired," she said looking at Shanna.

Ryonna clung on to Deja, nodding her head in agreement. She didn't want her mother to be bothered after everything she had just been through.

Holding her head high with pride, Shanna swallowed hard. "I understand, but if you need anything, please call me, I'm always willing to help family," she said, preparing to leave the room. Then she stopped in mid-step and looked back at them. "I tried to bring little Ramon here with me, but he just didn't want to leave. He's at my house with my son, he's really very shaken up too, maybe one of you should come over, talk to him...then take him home," she said, with a genuine look upon her face. All she really wanted to do was help out, she thought; *after all these years, does Rose still really hate me that much?*

Bright nodded her head. "I'll have my boyfriend bring me, can you text me the directions to your house?" she asked.

Looking as if she wanted to release a few tears of her

own, Shanna said, "I'm not really good with texting, but my son Jasper Jr. is. I'll have him text you as soon as I get back to the valley." Then she exited the room. After making sure their mother was comfortable they all kissed her again then went home. They were all really very exhausted.

****

"I don't like them, Mom, family or not," Ryan pouted on the ride back home. "They remind me of ghetto trash, and my God, I can't believe how much Bright and I look alike!"

"Yeah, you're definitely family," was all Shanna said as she thought back to the good and not-so-good times she and her cousin Rosette shared together.

Shanna's biological mother had passed away while having her, and because her mother was a known prostitute in Southern California, her father went unknown and could have been anybody. At the age of two, Shanna was removed from a foster home and adopted by an older couple in their late forties named William and Marlene Johnson, upstanding residents of Compton California who were unable to conceive children of their own. Though from a happy home, by the age of ten, Shanna realized just how boring it was being an only child. She would tell her parents she wanted someone to play with, and she started bringing her second cousin Rosette Clark around every weekend and practically the whole summer up until their late teens. After that, the girls were inseparable, and would be seen together all the time, up until sometime late in 1976 when things took an unexpected turn.

It was 1975 when eighteen-year-old Shanna and her

Seventeen-year-old cousin Rosette went along with Shanna's white suburban friends to a rock concert. Neither had ever been to one before, so when they were presented with the opportunity, they figured why not? It was free. Inside the concert, they had a blast, partying like real rock stars, yelling and screaming at the top of their lungs. Both girls were acting wild and crazy and were having a good time.

Growing an immediate attraction to the lead rocker, Rosette yelled in Shanna's ear, "White boy is outta sight, and boy is he gorgeous!" She said, melting in lust with him.

"Out of sight, alright," Shanna said, looking at her cousin like she had lost her mind. "I do black, now where they at?" she teased seriously.

Rosette laughed then directed her attention back to the show. Getting wild, Rosette lifted her blouse and shook her breasts with her hands in the air, as she yelled and screamed. "OUCH!" she yelled once she gained the lead rocker's attention. He winked at her and Rosette almost passed out. "Oh my God, Shanna, did you see that? He noticed me!" she said, snapping her fingers, trying to gain his attention again.

"Yuk!" Shanna said acting as if she was gonna purge. "I think we're looking at two different people,"she said, nodding her head at her cousin.

Rosette laughed, "He's beautiful, so I guess we aren't looking at the same guy," Rosette smiled, admiring his long blonde hair and golden tanned skin. He had ripped his shirt off and revealed his small, but muscular build. The way he performed onstage turned Rosette on; she just had to meet him. Happy that they had backstage passes, Rosette went to the ladies room to make sure she looked good. Rosette believed in showing lots of skin because she always got complimented on how she had the body of a super model. Shanna, on the other hand, dressed more on the conservative side. After making sure her soft curls were in place, she freshened up her lipstick then shot out of the ladies room to go backstage with the girls.

Backstage was a whole different world than the world she grew to know. It was the rock star lifestyle at its finest: sex, money, and drugs! Shanna, not being as drug prone as Rosette was, kept a close eye on her. She had seen the excitement in her eyes when she saw the rich and famous sniff up top-of-the-line Peruvian flake cocaine. When it came to partying, Rosette partied hard; she wasn't like Shanna, who was known to hold the wall up at parties.

"Beautiful Nubian Queen," the lead rocker said as he crept from behind them, squeezing a chunk of Rosette's ass. Rosette smiled seductively, then purred like a cat.

"Is it true what they say, about black pussy, that it's sweet, huh? He said with a foreign accent. "You'll never know if you don't try it for yourself," she whispered in his ear.

The lead rocker smiled, "I like the sound of that! How about you meet me back in my room in about an hour?" After he gave her his room information, he walked away. "By the way, great tits!" he winked.

Rosette smiled, biting down on her bottom lip, and then winked back at him. An hour later, Rosette was in the hotel room with the lead rocker whose name she later found out was Bret Sheldon, high on cocaine and feeling above the clouds. He had bought in two white girls to join them in bed; he told Rosette he wanted to see if black pussy was better than white pussy. Up for the challenge and willing to fight for the lifestyle that Bret offered, Rosette did many things that night that she never imagined she would ever do. Hours later, he put the two white girls out of his room and declared black pussy as being the best type of pussy in the world, and from there, he and Rosette would have made history.

Jealous wasn't even the words to express how Shanna felt about Rosette and Bret's new relationship. They hardly ever hung out together and besides that, Rosette had turned into a real cocaine addict. She dressed like the singer Tina Turner, lots of times with short skirts and no undergarments. And because she had a light complexion, he asked that she wear blond wigs sometimes when they went on the road to avoid racial tension. Many people in passing thought she was white, so it worked to their advantage. Bret Sheldon couldn't get enough of Rosette, and he took care of her fruitfully, labeling her as his Black Rose.

A year later, sex, drugs, money, and rock and roll was Rosette's new lifestyle. Life was great. She had met many respectable entertainers being Bret's latest girl, but the good times came crashing down when racial tension caused them to keep their relationship under the scope. Bret lost money and fans over his open relationship with her until he made a statement that hit newspapers worldwide. "She was nothing more than a bed monkey, and something that I like to call, a little fun in rock and roll!"

Devastated, Rosette contemplated committing suicide. Her heart had been broken for the first time in her life, and Shanna was there to pick up all the pieces and get Rosette back on track. Deciding it would be best to visit her older sister who had gotten married and moved to Cincinnati, Rosette caught the next flight out. A few days after Rosette's departure, Bret had just got back to the states off of a very successful tour, and he wanted to make things right with his Black Rose. He actually loved Rose more than any woman he had ever been with, but because of times and politics on interracial dating, he had to say and do things that he wished he could take back.

In searching for his Nubian queen, he only had luck in locating her cousin Shanna. Desperate to speak with his Black Rose, he gave Shanna five hundred dollars and a note to where Rosette could meet him at, but she never came. It was a stormy night and after his concert, Bret laid in bed alone with Rosette weighing heavy on his mind. Moments later, he got a knock on the door. Ex- cited, thinking it was his Black Rose, he got up to open the door only to see Shanna standing before him. Seeing something in her eyes that he had never seen before made things happen between the two. It was a night that Shanna wasn't proud of, but it was the same very night that they conceived her first born...Ryan. So not only were Bright and Ryan cousins, but they were blood sisters too.

****

Later on, Bright and Larry rolled to the valley to pick Ramon up from their cousin Shanna's house. She had a huge house, and the inside was decorated tastefully. After they made it inside, she was introduced to Shanna's other children, Jasper and Keisha. Jasper was fine, and had she not known he was her cousin, she would have definitely given him her digits. However, Keisha's presence was on a Mafioso status; she seemed like a no nonsense type of person, and only spoke when she was spoken to. She was a very beautiful, mysterious, looking hood chick, and Ryan was right they resembled each other more than Keisha did. Keisha had long, dark thick hair, pretty light brown eyes like her bestie Treasure, and she even had a similar body shape as Treasure's. Keisha dressed like she came straight off the cover of high fashion magazine. It was obvious that they were living the good life: big house, fancy cars parked out front, and money to spend. Bright thought, *maybe it was a good thing that I met my new cousins after all.*

"Right this way," Shanna said, breaking Bright's train of thought as she led her up the stairs and into one of the rooms. Larry stayed downstairs so that she could talk to her brother in private.

"I came to get you and take you home, Ramon," Bright said as she sat next to him on the bed he was resting on.

"Do I have to?" He asked, avoiding eye contact with her.

"We miss you, and nobody is gonna be calling you anymore names," she said, rubbing the back of his head.

Ramon eyes watered up, then he looked at his sister in her eyes, "Am I a faggot, Bright?" he asked.

Bright shook her head no. "Not at all; you're just misunderstood," she said falling into an emotional mode.

"If I'm not, then why does everybody treat me bad, and say that I am then?" He asked curiously.

Bright was lost for words and didn't know what tosay. "We'll talk when we get home, Larry is waiting for us downstairs," she said, standing up from the bed.

Grabbing his back pack, Ramon followed his sister out of the room and down the stairs. He was confused as ever and needed her to help him understand what was going on with him and why people treated him so poorly. They picked on him and called him horrible names just because he liked boys. He didn't ask to be the way that he was, and he just wanted to be treated kindly and given a fair chance.

Part Fourteen

Back at home, things had changed for the better. The siblings had bonded in a closer relationship, and showed more respect toward each other for the sake of their mother, who was slowly recovering from her stroke. Since Rosette couldn't work for the time being, and refused all of Shanna's contributions to help her out, Bright worked overtime milking Terrence to keep up with the bills. Preparing to leave the house, Bright called Cordell to her room to speak to him before she left.

Earlier that day, Bright talked to Deja about her situation, and Deja admitted that she deeply regretted her actions. She told Bright that her and her homegirl had popped E pills with their so-called boyfriends, and after that, everything took a wild, unexpected turn for the worse. Not only was she on tape, but she had missed her period and was afraid that she was pregnant. Deja told Bright she wasn't ready to be a mother and that if she was pregnant that she wanted Bright to take her to get an abortion. Bright promised her that she would be there for her and would support any decision that she made.

Ramon, on the other hand, was opening up more to their mother than anybody else in the house. Bright was at least happy about that. However, he did shy away from Cordell because he was always trying to teach him how to be tough and macho. Cordell didn't mean any harm by it. He was only trying to teach his little brother how to be a man the best and the only way he knew how. Ryonna was still such a little lady and angel and remained the same sweetheart through it all.

"'Sup wit it, Queen Bee?" Cordell said, thinking he was super swagged out.

Bright closed the door after him. She wanted to explain her situation to him, since he already knew everything, but she wanted to correct him about one thing. "I called you in the room because I want to talk to you about me and Ice's relationship. Yeah, it's true I been fucking with him for almost a year now, he cool peoples. He been breaking me off, but I'm not a hoe. Who you think was helping mama to keep a roof over our heads? And how do you think she was able to take the time she had taken off from work before she had the stroke? Who you think was paying to turn that cable and the phone "right" back on when it got turned off? Or helped keep y'all favorite snacks stocked up in the kitchen? Yeah," Bright said, nodding her head, seeing that her brother was getting the point. "All of that has been because of me, so just know that I been doing this not only for me, but for all of us," Bright said, becoming emotional. "I love Larry with all my heart; he's the man I'm gonna spend the rest of my life with. And when he get drafted to the NBA, we plan on buying Mama a house, and moving far away from Long Beach, and after that I won't ever have to deal with Ice ever again. It just works for me right now... for us," she stressed.

"I love mama with all my heart, because she means us well, and would give up her last dollar for all of us...but I can't be like her," Bright said, shaking her head no. "Here mama is, not even in her fifties yet, and she has all these health conditions: high blood pressure, migraine headaches, and now this stroke. They're all stress related conditions," Bright said, getting teary- eyed. "Mama has been with this fool Vince all these years and he can't even help her out around here. And I just refuse to live like that when I can be getting money from these fools to alleviate all the bullshit. So instead of thinking of your big sister as a hoe, think of me as more of a business woman who ain't gone let a nigga fuck with me or waste my time for free."

Cordell couldn't do anything but respect his big sister after what she had just told him. He just wished she didn't have to do it, and that Larry would hurry up and get drafted to the NBA. "I hear you, sister, and I can't do nothing but respect you for it," he stood up to hug her. "And if that nigga Ice ever treat you bad, or put his hands on you, just let me know, because I got some homies that are ready to put that burner to him and rob his balling ass blind," he said hugging her tight.

Bright pushed him off of her. "Boy, please, Ice is crazy about me, and he cool people. He's just not the one for me," she admitted truthfully. "So you and yo little Crips need to back it on up," she teased. Raised in Long Beach, the gang life was a common thing, and almost every dude in the city was from a hood. Since she knew there would be no way of talking Cordell out of the gang life, she hoped that getting them out of the city would change his role as a gang member before he got in too deep, or that he would at least be more like Terrence and be about his paper.

After wrapping her conversation up with her brother, Bright checked on her mother, then stepped out of the apartment to handle her business with Terrence, and get some more money. She had rent, bills, and mouths to feed. Once Terrence picked her up, they grabbed a bite to eat at Red Lobster, did some baby shopping, then made a quick stop to the sex shop before going back to his place.

On the ride back to his place, he asked Bright how her mother was doing.

"She's getting better, her memory is still a little blurry, so she hasn't been able to work." Bright paused and looked at Terrence. "I'ma need your help again this month, Ice, to take care of the rent and bills, I can't be on the streets," she said seriously.

"I'm starting to notice that whenever you want something from me, I'm always "ICE," he laughed. " But you already know that I got you, Beautiful, especially since you about to have my babies and shit." Then he reached over to rub her belly.

"Thank you, Ice," Bright teased, then sensually bit him on the neck. "Bet you can go for some bomb-ass head right now, huh?" she asked him, allowing her mouth to fill up with saliva.

"You know a nigga always like getting his dick sucked on, especially while driving," he watched Bright as she unzipped his pants and pulled his penis out. When she began to suck on it, he was careful to keep his eyes on the road.

Closing her eyes, Bright pretended she was having oral sex with Larry. Sucking, biting, and slurping all over his knob, she moved her head in a very passionate motion, she appreciated him. "It tastes so good," she said, looking up at Terrence with his penis in her mouth.

"Kiss it baby, kiss it!" he moaned, on the verge of a quick orgasm. With Bright bobbing up and down on his penis at full speed, Terrence couldn't help but to release in her mouth, then he held her head down until she sucked out every last drop of his cum. "Swallow it," he asked her when he finally let her come up for air. Unable to stomach it, Bright felt as if she was about to throw up and used her hand to cover her mouth. Seeing that, Terrence passed her the few napkins that he had in the console for her to spit up on.

"My stomach weak baby, you know I can't take much down," she said, happy that he didn't press her to swallow it. "The only reason I was able to eat was because you smoked that blunt with me earlier," she pouted.

Terrence exhaled then rubbed her head like a pet for a job well done. "Baby, you the best," he moaned, anxious to get back to his place and get fucked and sucked on all night long.

After reclining her seat, Bright kicked her legs up on the dashboard and fell into a quick nap. Back at Terrence's house, he had Bright working like he did when they first kicked it. He fucked her every way possible in both holes, not including her mouth, and he titty-fucked her too. Terrence got his last nut off, while Bright rode him on the edge of his bed. She had worked him and he was barely able to keep up. Dripping profusely with her nipple in his mouth, Terrence slapped Bright on the ass and told her to take the dick. When he finally came, they both fell sound asleep. Breaking Bright's rest was her vibrating cell phone. Reaching over to look at the caller ID, she quickly climbed out of the bed to take Larry's call. Once she made it down to the living room, she answered his call.

"Hey, Daddy Lane," she answered in a sleepy mode.

"Baby, baby, baby!!!!!" He yelled into the phone. "Yo baby daddy did it, Pretty Bright! I've officially been recruited to the muthafucking NBA, baby!!" Though he knew his day would come, he couldn't help releasing tears of happiness from his eyes thinking of how proud his father would have been on this day for him.

Bright had to catch herself from screaming at the top of her lungs, but it didn't stop her from jumping up and down and telling him how much she loved him, and how happy she was for him. "I'm sooooo happy for you, Larry Lane," then she began, blowing kisses into the phone.

"Who is that?" Terrence said, walking down the stairs, he was unable to sleep from all the noise Bright was making.

Bright immediately powered her phone off then said, "Crap, my phone just went dead."

Terrence gave her a stern look, "Was that some nigga you was just blowing kisses to on the phone?" He asked her.

Bright laughed. "No silly, that was my cousin he just got drafted to the NBA," she said excitedly, "And I'm happy for him!" She hugged Terrence tightly. She was so happy at the moment that she had to share and express the love and emotions that she was feeling with Terrence.

Terrence smiled. "Well tell dat nigga I said congratulations," he was happy for her cousin. "And tell 'em we like sky box seats too," he teased. After talking about her so-called cousin and the NBA, Bright asked him to take her home so that she could check on her mother. After a quick bath, Terrence drove Bright back home.

"I been noticing something about our relationship, and I know if I've been noticing it that you been noticing it too," he said in a deep mindset.

"What's that? Bright asked, looking at him curiously.

"I just feel like we been on a different level then we used to be, when we first hooked up," he said, not wanting to sound too much like a simp. "It's been a hard year for me, I lost my wife and on everything, and that's been a major issue for me to deal with, so I just been wilding out on some different type shit. And now that I've kinda come back down to reality, I feel like I've been neglecting you and treating you like a hoe, on some booty call type shit," he expressed honestly.

Bright sighed and thought, *Please don't go falling in love with me right now, Terrence, cause I'm on some other type shit right now, baby.* "I understand, Terrence, it's been a hectic year for the both of us, and with everything going on, it's just been taking a lot of our time. Me being pregnant, and my mother wanting to put you in jail," she teased, "And now with her health and everything," Bright said nodding her head. "I've just been at home, tryna do the school thing, looking out for my brothers and sisters, and now I even have to take care of my mother and keep our household going until she gets back on her feet. So trust me, I don't feel neglected at all 'cause my plate has been full too," she said.

Terrence held tight to her hand. "I'ma make you my wife, Beautiful Bright, I'ma be a good father to my kids, and more importantly," he paused, "I'ma be a good nigga to you and make you happy. You been there for me mentally and physically, and I ain't gone let you slip away from me like Tameka did while I have you in my life." Terrence was used to having a woman at home to cook and clean for him, to have his back and to listen to him when he needed to be heard. Tameka being gone made him realize just how much she meant to him and how important her role was in his life...and Bright was the next best thing in line.

Bright thought, *Wow, is this fool really simping right now? I ain't about to be yo wife, marry you, and I ain't even pregnant with yo kids! Brace yaself for the next lost playa, cause this game is about to end!* She laughed to herself. "I know you will, Terrence," is all she said.

"You think I'm playing, huh?" Terrence asked her, seeing that she didn't take what he was saying seriously. "Open the glove compartment, there's something in there for you," he insisted.

Bright sighed then opened the glove compartment, seeing a black ring box inside she took it out and opened it up. Surprised, her mouth flew wide open. Terrence pulled over on Artesia Blvd., leaned over, and then kissed her on the lips. "I love you, Bright; will you marry me and let me make you happy, and raise our kids together?"

Happy seeing the platinum three-carat diamond ring that he had bought for her, Bright yelled, "Yes!" No one had ever given her a ring as beautiful as the one he had given her. And even though she wasn't gonna marry him; she was taking the ring, because she knew it was worth more than ten thousand dollars.

Happy, Terrence tongue kissed her, told her he loved her, and then told her once she turned eighteen that he was going to buy her a house of her choice. Thinking of the life she and Larry would share together once they got married brought tears to her eyes. Terrence wiped her tears away and told her she would never have to worry about another unhappy or sad day ever again.

****

Inside the house, Bright spread the news about Larry being drafted in the NBA. Everybody was so happy for him, and her mother even released a few tears of joy.

He did it," Rosette said, sitting up in her bed. She was

almost back to her norm and regaining her memory back. "Is he stopping by today?" She asked Bright. After Bright explained to her mom that he had a few errands to run and that he would be over later, she got out of bed to shower. "I wanna cook my son-in-law dinner, then," she smiled.

"I can cook dinner, Ma, I want you to just kick up your feet and relax," she said insisting, that her mother get back in bed.

"I promise you I'm feeling fine, and besides that, I feel like I was confined to the bed too damn long," Rosette was starting to feel like a patient. "It would actually make me feel I'm of some use around here Queen Bee; you've done enough, and I thank you baby," Rosette extended her arms to hug her daughter, then she went to take a shower.

Bright gave Ryonna twenty bucks to clean the bathtub out for her so that she could take a nice hot bubble bath. Though she took a bath at Terrence's house, she still felt the need to scrub him off of her in preparation for Larry's arrival. When Bright got out of the bath tub, the smell of smothered pork chops and onions lingered throughout the apartment. It was one of Larry's favorite meals, and Bright was happy that her mother remembered, it proved to her that she was having a speedy recovery. Bright went into the kitchen, preparing to help her mother out.

Rosette turned to Bright and told her that she wanted her to go back to school in the morning and get caught up in her school work. She had received a call from the attendance office letting her know that Bright had been missing a lot of school. Rosette explained to them that it was due to her illness and now that she was back on her time she needed to catch up.

"Ma, I'm way behind from all the days of school I've missed so far, I just decided to drop out and get my G.E.D.," she said honestly. She thought school was no longer of any importance to her, especially since she was about to get married, have twins, and be set for life.

Rosette raised her eyebrows. "It's better that you just finish off your senior year, Queen Bee. A high school education is so much more respected in the work place then a G.E.D.," she explained to her daughter.

Bright laughed. "Ma, Larry just got drafted to the NBA, do you hear yourself? I'm never gonna have to work a day in my life, and neither are you," she said. "Not only are we getting married, but these babies are going to ensure that," she smiled confidently.

Deja added, "Yeah Mama, Bright done struck gold!" she yelled as she and Ryonna set the table for dinner.

Rosette stopped what she was doing then grabbed her daughter's hand and held it tight. Looking in her eyes, she said, "A woman's only guarantee and security blanket in life are the ones that she holds within herself, Queen Bee. God forbid Larry gets hurt or injured out there and can't play anymore. He's gonna need his wife to step up to the plate and help out," she said. "Or what if things don't work out the way you hope or plan for them to?" Seeing the look on her daughter's face, Rosette said, "Yes, Queen Bee, all fairy tales don't last forever; and though I hope and pray the best for you." she stressed. "I just want my daughter to be prepared for the best or the worst. I've been in love a million times, have had it all, and have lost it all just as quickly, because it was always at the hands of a man." She paused for a few moments to wipe the tears that had formed in Bright's eyes. "I want you to take my advice, get a good education, and get a couple degrees under your belt. You're a very smart girl," she said to Bright. "I know you can do it."

Bright had never been told she was smart before, so it immediately made her eyes tear up. "I know it may have happened to you, Ma, but I'm not gonna allow it to happen to me ever again," Bright said, then walked off to her bedroom. This was finally her chance at getting both riches and fame, and she wasn't going to allow anyone to stand in her way or stop her from getting it.

Rosette stopped herself from calling after Bright. She wanted her to think about what she had said to her. But what she didn't understand was the last part of her daughter's statement that she wasn't going to allow it to happen to her ever again? Hunching her shoulders, Rosette called Cordell to take out the trash, then she told him to tell Ramon to come out of the room to join the rest of the family for dinner.

Vince stopped by for dinner with a big bouquet of flowers for Rosette. When Bright came out of her room and saw him sitting at the head of the table, eating, laughing, talking, and smiling, she wanted to throw up. Looking at him now, she recognized him for the true loser he really was and resented her mother for tolerating him. *Nigga decided to pop up all of a sudden now huh? Where was he when Mama was down and out?* Bright thought.

"Hey, superstar," he greeted her. "Your mother told me the good news," he smiled, removing meat from his teeth.

"Yeah, nice flowers," Bright said nonchalantly, then "We tried waiting on son-in-law, Queen Bee, but it's getting late. I packed him up a real big plate of food though; it's in the microwave," she said, pointing toward it.

"Yeah, he called and said that he was going to be running late, thanks, Ma," Bright replied. Pulling a wad of money out of her bra, she approached the table. "Here's some money for the rent and bills," Bright passed the money to her mother then looked in Vince's direction. "It's just a little something from me and Larry, we don't want you to have to over-exhaust yourself again."

Knowing his sister's MO, Cordell chimed in, "Now that's what I'm talking about, Larry's the man!" he stressed, putting cables on it. After Bright brought it to his attention, he didn't really appreciate Vince's position in his mother's life either. But because he didn't want to add to his mother's stress, he opted to stay out of her business.

Vince cleared his throat, feeling the tension in the room. Rosette rejected the money. "Vince helped me out with the bills and rent this month," she smiled. "But I thank you guys both dearly."

Jumping in the conversation, Vince said, "Yeah 'cause a man should always help the woman he plans on marrying," then Vince joined Bright in the stare downthat she had started.

Deja reached for the money. "I could use some of that," she laughed. Bright reached to grab the money, then passed all of her siblings each a crispy one hundred dollar bill. Happy they all thanked her, and then she tucked the rest of the money back in her bra.

"Congratulations, Ma," Bright smiled, then kissed her on the cheek. "I wish you both all the happiness in the world and I hope Vince gives you all that you deserve and more importantly, that he's always there for you when you need him." Then she smiled at Vince and exited the room.

"What am I missing here?" Rosette asked puzzled. Vince smiled. "You didn't miss anything, darling baby; everything is just fine," he assured her.

Seeing that everything was alright, Rosette took the money from her two youngest to hold, and told them that she would take them to spend their money on the weekend. While Deja planned on buying clothes with her money. Cordell planned on getting a pack, he was tired of being broke.

Later that night when Larry finally arrived, it was close to midnight. After work, he was supposed to stop by to have a quick meeting with his frat brothers that ended up being a surprise party for him, and it had taken up more of his time than expected. She warmed up his plate then set it on the table for him.

"There goes my future NBA star," Rosette said, coming out of her room. "I wasn't gon' go to bed until I was able to give my son-in-law a big hug and kiss, and tell you how happy I am for you," she said, smiling, with Vince on her trail.

"Congrats man, we're really proud of you son," Vince smiled from ear to ear he had dollar signs in his eyes.

"Awe, thanks Moms, thanks Vince," Larry smiled, standing up to give his mother-in-law a hug, then he gave Vince a brotherly hand shake.

"Bright, sit on Larry's lap so I can get a before picture," she said, struggling to take the picture because the left side of her body was still very weak. Vince was too busy smiling and sucking up to Larry to notice that

Rosette needed his help until Bright brought it to his attention. Then he quickly made his way to her side to take the picture of them. After Vince requested to take a solo picture with Larry, Larry suggests taking a picture with both Bright and Rosette. They finished taking pictures and then they left back to the room so that Larry could finish his meal.

Smiling, Larry said, "I'm happy to see Mom's recovering so well."

"I can't stand Vince," Bright said, nodding her head.

"I thought y'all were cool?" Larry said, taking a bite full of mashed potatoes and gravy.

"We were until I seen how he never pulled through for my mother when she first had her stroke. He didn't bring her any money to help out around here, and don't even mention how many times he came to visit her in the hospital - once!" Bright said, becoming angry. "Now that he hears about your deal, he's talking marriage now, after all these years," Bright said. "I'm no fool."

Larry shook his head. He thought Vince was cool, and he really hoped he wasn't in it to use his mother-in-law. But if he was, he sure wouldn't mind reading the old guy his rights. "Time will tell everything, Pretty Bright, so don't stress over it or stress my babies. Maybe he really has good intentions," he said, trying to turn a negative into a positive.

After dinner, they sat on the couch and fell into a long, intimate conversation about their life while Larry rubbed her belly. Bright thought her life was finally heading into the direction it should have always been: big things and flashing lights.

A Week Later

Though Bright left out the house for school every morning, it didn't mean that she was really going. Her mind was made up and school was no longer an option, she was gonna be paid and set for the rest of her life...what would she really need school for? She liked spending money, not making money, and Larry was fine with that. But in order for her to spare her mother's happiness, she pretended to go to school each day, when in actuality, she was laid up in a plush suite at a hotel that she and Larry used as their love nest. Since the suite supplied a kitchenette, Bright would take pleasure in preparing various meals for Larry.

Still afraid to sex Bright the way she liked him to, Larry would only eat her out and finger bang her when she begged for sex. And when she sucked his dick he wouldn't even allow her to get on her knees anymore, he would tell her to lie on her back and he'd serve it to her. Bright thought all of his precautions were sickening; and she didn't know if it was from all of the attention that Larry was giving the babies, but something inside was causing her to brew a slow hatred for her two unborn children.

On this particular day, Treasure had stopped by the room to kick it with Bright after getting out of school. The girls smoked blunt after blunt, and Bright had even drank a few glasses of red wine. She wasn't expecting Larry for a few hours and figured she'd have enough time to sober up. In the midst of talking and laughing, Treasure received a phone call from Suge.

Happy, she answered her cell phone. "What's up, Suga baby?" she smiled.

Suge spoke low into the phone, "Treasure, I need to talk to you about something very important," she said before losing the courage to do so. "You by yourself?" she asked her.

Hearing that she was speaking to Suge, Bright chimed in, "Tell Suge I said hi!" she yelled across the room.

Responding, Treasure said, "No, I'm with Bee right now, and she said to tell you hi. Now what do have to tell me that's so important?" She asked in a concerned tone as she hit the blunt.

Bright's eyes widened; she hoped Suge wasn't gonna run her big mouth about the letter she had written to Chrome.

In a panic Suge said, "Treasure, I can't holler at you in front of Bright; it's about her," she explained. "So act like we're talking about something else. I don't want her to know that I'm about to tell you," she quickly said.

Seeing that Bright was all up in her mouth, Treasure played the role and followed instructions. "Are you serious, Suge? So what did you do?" Treasure gave Bright several shocked facial expressions.

Sitting up on the edge of the bed, Bright wanted to know what happened.

Thinking of something quick to say, Treasure said, "Girl, why Suge just tell me that the Muslims got to fighting all up in the temple, and had bean pies flying all over the place?" she laughed. "And Suge got hit in the face with one too!" she added.

Feeling a sigh of relief, Bright said, "That ain't funny, Treasure! Ask Young if she want us to come down there and beat them hoe's down?" Then she started laughing.

Continuing to make herself laugh, Treasure said, "Alright then Suge, we'll call you back later; the blunt awaits the lips," she joked, then ended the call.

Treasure couldn't help but feel anxious wondering what Suge had to tell her about Bright.

In the middle of Bright smoking and talking, Larry walked into the room unexpectedly. Catching Bright's lips on the blunt, he flipped out. "I know you not smoking and drinking?" he asked, seeing the bottle of wine on the cabinet next to her.

Nervous, the blunt fell from Bright's trembling lips and onto the floor.

Treasure began to pack up her things. She didn't want to be in the middle of their argument, and was curious as hell as to what Suge had to tell her about Bright.

"I only hit it one time, and drank one glass of red wine, Larry," Bright announced timidly. "And the doctors said that one glass of wine won't kill me and is actually healthy for pregnant woman," she stuttered, hoping he wouldn't explode on her.

"So you gone sit here and lie to me when it's obvious you been in here getting fucked up! I'm looking at your eyes, Bright; they red as shit and you smell like a damn winery," he barked, stepping closer to her. "And I don't appreciate it, not one fucking bit!" he yelled.

Creeping past the arguing couple with her things in her hand, Treasure said, "I'm about to leave, you guys."

If looks could kill, Treasure would have been dead from the look Larry had shot her. "Yeah, you go ahead and do that...godmother. Because I can't believe neither one of y'all trifling asses!" he steamed.

Treasure looked at Larry then back at Bright. She was ready to nut up at him for coming at her like she was the bad guy in the situation.

Bright shook her head no and gave Treasure a

pleading facial expression not to say anything. She could tell that Treasure was about to blow, and she didn't want her boyfriend and best friend to be going at each other's throats.

Treasure took a deep breath and sucked it up on the strength of her homegirl, then said, "I'ma let that one slide for you Bee," then she exited the room.

Falling into a heated argument resulted in another one of Bright's melodramatic moments. "It's always about the damn babies, the babies this, the babies that, what about the babies? Well what about me, Larry, huh? What about me?" she cried. "Are the babies the only reason that you're marrying me in the first place?" She asked, taking her engagement ring off then throwing it to the floor.

She was tired of him always making a bigger deal over the babies than her, when it was supposed to be her that he fell in love with.

Giving her an unbelieving look, he yelled, "No, we're not gone turn this into another 'victim Bright' moment!" he yelled. "You know damn well that I love yo bright ass, and that's why the fuck I wanna marry you!" he continued. "But I'm not gone let you ruin our chance of having healthy babies, because you're being self-centered and irresponsible. Do you even care?" He paused looking at her seriously. He had been noticing the jealousy she displayed whenever he made a big fuss about the babies.

Bright cried, "Why wouldn't I care? I am the mother!" she said, unable to admit it. Depression had gotten the best of her, and at times she contemplated having an abortion. However, since she was too far along for the regular procedure, her only other alternative was a three day procedure. Three days of agonizing pain, suffering, and an even higher risk that she would have to take on her own life, were the only things standing in her way...and she didn't want to die. She no longer saw children fitting in their bright future anymore. She had played mommy long enough, and for once, she wanted to enjoy her young life selfishly without the responsibilities of children. The only worries she wanted were hers and Larry's, and she wanted him to feel the same.

Larry grabbed Bright by the arms, then swiftly but carefully pinned her up against the wall. He was so close to Bright that he could kiss her soft lips. He sensed that something was troubling her soul and wanted to wipe her tears away, but the smell of the weed and alcohol on her breath turned him back to mad. "Well, you better start acting like it now, or it'll be over between us quicker than you know it," he said, then headed to the door.

Bright grabbed his arm to stop him from leaving, but he snatched it back from her and stormed out of the room. She couldn't believe the tone that Larry had used with her over something so small. She loved him more than she loved her unborn babies, but he put them before her. Hurt, Bright begin punching herself in the stomach, crying out loudly. "I hate you, I hate you, I hate you, and I wish I never made you!"

She cried until she couldn't take any more of the pain, then she broke down and cried like a baby.

All she ever wanted was to be loved for her, not for her looks, or because she sucked a good dick, or fucked real good, but genuinely because of who she was. Bright had sacrificed her being, time and time again, to keep Larry looking good, and to keep money in his pockets, so that he could pursue his education and career full time. And here he had put two unborn lives before their relationship, when she had pretty much sold her soul for him.

****

Larry climbed in his car. He was absolutely pissed; he couldn't believe that Bright would jeopardize their children's lives by drinking and smoking weed. Seeing that made him think of the kind of wife and mother she would really be. It was all fun partying before she got pregnant, but now he needed her to grow up for the sake of their children and put them and their best interest first-just as his parents did for him and his siblings growing up. He wasn't going to bend and accept anything less from her, and no matter how much he loved her, he would leave her and take his children away if she did otherwise.

A Month Later

Part Fifteen

After the Christmas holiday Bright was happy that the new year was approaching. November and December had been the roughest two months of her and Larry's relationship, but yet they were able to move forward and overcome their obstacles. Bright knew 2006 would be the year that all her hard work would finally pay off, and that she would soon be living the fabulous life.

Though Bright never made New Year's resolutions, she had made a few for 2006; starting with being a better friend to Treasure. All the dirt that she had done to her had finally caught up to her conscience and for once she felt bad for it all. But since she couldn't take it back Bright planned on being the best friend that she could possibly be to Treasure moving forward.

On New Year's Eve, Bright and her sisters helped their mother clean shrimp and slice sausage in preparation for her savory, spicy gumbo. It was a customary meal that they had every New Year's, and it was also Bright's favorite.

"Count down time, family, where's Cordell and Larry?" Rosette asked seeing that they were within minutes of the count down.

"Him and Larry went to get sodas from the store, Ma." Bright said, "They should be back any second now."

Rosette looked worried. She didn't want them to miss the count down.

"Here they come!" Ryonna yelled as she opened the door for them.

"Right on time," Rosette said excitedly, then she

grabbed the bag of sodas from Larry's hand and told them all to gather in the living room. It was tradition that Rosette and her family bring the New Years in together, while they watched the ball drop in Time Square on T.V. Gathered in the living room holding hands they all counted in unison: "Five, Four, Three, Two, One...HAPPY NEW YEAR'S!" they all yelled happily, blowing their party confetti horns.

Larry kissed Bright on the cheek, "This is our year Pretty Bright; happy New Year's and I love you, baby."

"I know it's our year, Daddy Lane," Bright smiled. "I love you too, boo and happy New Year's, baby." She held his hand tight, then planted a soft kiss on his lips.

For the remainder of the night the family celebrated together, laughing, talking and dancing. Watching, Rosette smiled, then thanked the Lord for pulling her through another year.

****

After the holidays Larry and his mother decided it would be best for him to complete his college education before going into the NBA. He only had a few more months left to get his degrees, and felt he had worked too hard to just let it all go. When he told Bright his decision, she was displeased and she encouraged him to go straight into the NBA and accept his collective bargaining agreement.

Larry wasn't having it, though...his mind was set. Unlike Bright, he believed in a good education and wanted to be there for the birth of their twins. He told Bright that his position was secured and he didn't understand her take on his decision.

But at seven and a half months pregnant Bright was

sick and tired of lying, making fake wedding plans and sleeping with Terrence in order to keep the money flowing in. He was falling too deeply in love with her and she no longer wanted to play the game. The situation was getting too heavy for her to juggle, and all she wanted to do was hurry up and get out of dodge, before her skeletons started falling out of her closet.

Bright lay in the hotel room where she spent most of her school days, sleeping, smoking Kush and master-minding her escape from the city, without getting caught. She received a call from an unknown number in the middle of a good rest. *Who the hell is this?* Bright thought, rolling over in bed.

"Yeah," she answered.

"Baby, I just got hit with a gun case," Terrence yelled through the phone. "I don't have a bond, so I'ma need you to get a prepaid account established on your phone so that I can call you on your cell phone." Then he read a number out loud to her.

"Jail!" Bright said, sitting up on the bed. She was more concerned about him giving her money than him actually being in jail.

"I know, baby, don't trip," he said, hearing the disappointment in her voice. "I'll be out of here as soon as I get a bond, but for now, call that number I gave you and get that prepaid account set up so I can call you and keep you posted." After a few more moments of speaking, Terrence had to get off the phone. Bright was expected to pay her mother three hundred dollars tomorrow, and she wanted to get her mother's bedroom set out of layaway as a surprise for her. *What the fuck am I gonna do now?* Bright thought.

"The ring!" she said out loud, snapping her fingers.

She knew she could get at least nine or ten grand for the engagement ring that Terrence had given her, and if he got out before she got ghost, she would just tell him that she lost it...That simple.

****

"My goodness Suge, what's been up with you?" Treasure asked her when she finally returned her call. "I've been calling you for weeks and no response," Treasure said irritated on her way home from school. She was dying with anticipation to find out what she had to tell her about Bright.

Suge had lost the courage to tell Treasure what she had wanted to tell her for months, because she didn't want to come in between Bright and Treasure's friendship, so she temporarily decided to keep quiet and ignore Treasure's calls. But when she could no longer endure the guilt that was eating her up inside, she made her mind up to call and tell Treasure everything.

"I'm sorry, Treasure," Suge said, then she told her everything, on down to the conversation they had at Bright's house before she had arrived.

"She did what!" Treasure yelled, stopping in her tracks. Thinking on it, she did remember asking Bright to grab the mail for her awhile back.

"Calm down, Treasure, that's the reason I didn't want to mention it to you. But after hearing the whole thing about Nicole and Lil Boo, I thought something was very suspicious about the whole situation, and that Bright wasn't right," she said honestly.

Tears fell down Treasure's face. She felt betrayed in the worst way and by one of the people that she trusted the most, Bright. "So you're telling me that she wrote Chrome back, saying that even if he didn't rape my homegirl, he was still wrong for putting his hands on her and he deserve all the time that was given to him for messing with her in the first place?" Treasure said making sure she was properly hearing the words coming out of Suge's mouth.

"Yup, that's my word, Treasure, and I gain nothing for telling you this. If anything, I'm gonna lose Bright as a friend," she sighed. "I just thought telling you was the right thing to do," she admitted sadly.

Treasure knew that Suge wouldn't lie to her about something like this, so she thanked her. "Thanks for not keeping me in the dark...I love you," she said to Suge.

"I love you too, Treasure."

****

After going to the pawn shop, Bright sold the ring for eighty-six hundred dollars. Then she took a cab to the city of Paramount to search for apartments that she was later going to suggest her mother move into. She had no plans of speaking to or seeing Terrence ever again, and since she had enough money for a security deposit and the first couple of months' rent she decided that now would the perfect time to make her move and get out of Long Beach.

After finding three decent apartments that accepted Section Eight in low traffic areas, Bright took a cab to the liquor store by her house, grabbed some snacks, then made her way home to tell her mom the good news. Her mother had been talking about moving, since the area was getting worse, so she was sure she'd be ecstatic about the location.

Walking down her street, Bright felt as if she had peed on herself. Looking down at the urine-like fluids twinkling down her legs, she panicked. "My water just broke!" she yelled, looking for help. Seeing Rat climb in his hoopty, she called out for his help. "Rat, help me, I'm going into labor!"

Rat quickly drove in her direction. Meeting her at the curb, he laughed in her face. "I guess yo stuck up ass got a problem then, huh? Because you ain't getting yo gold diggin', think you that, entire fake ass in my car you trifling, BITCHHHHH!" then he sped off laughing. He didn't forget easily, and figured this would be a great opportunity to get back at her for treating him like a scrub that day he dropped her off over at her homegirl Treasure's house.

"Fuck you!" Bright screamed at the top of her lungs. Then suddenly, out of nowhere, she began to experience back-to-back pains in her stomach. Falling to the ground, holding her stomach, she cried out for help. The doctor had told her to expect an early labor carrying twins, but she was only seven and a half months pregnant. She had at least expected to make it to her eighth month.

Being noticed by an elderly couple that was driving down the street, they immediately pulled over to help her. Bright told them that she was going into labor, and then asked if one of them could go to her house to get her mother. The man walked over to her building as quickly as he could while the elderly woman tried to help coach Bright's breathing. Confused as to how the proper breathing technique went, she told Bright, "Oh baby, just make sure you breathe," she was agitated that she was of no use to the young girl in need. She hadn't birthed a child in over 40 plus years and had honestly forgotten the whole routine.

Moments later, Deja and Cordell ran out the courtyard

with the elderly man trailing them. "You having the baby?" Deja asked, nervously but was excited at the same time. Cordell picked up Bright's cell phone that was lying on the curb.

"Yes," Bright managed to say in between pains. "It seems like I'm contracting every two to three minutes. Get Mama down here to take me to the hospital," she whined.

"Mama went to lunch and Bible study with Gale,"Deja replied.

Looking around to find his sister a ride to the hospital, Cordell asked the neighbor across the street if he could take Bright to the hospital. "Aye homie, can I throw you a hot dub to take my sister to Long Beach Memorial?" he asked, grabbing a wad of dope money out of his pocket.

"I can't, lil man, my tags are bad," he explained regretfully, then he stepped across the street to see if he could be of any other use.

"We can take her to the hospital," the elderly woman said, looking to her husband, who nodded his head in agreement.

"Cool," Cordell said happily, then he asked the guy from across the street to help him put Bright in the back seat of the car. Before they drove off, he gave the man a twenty dollar bill and thanked him. Deja rode in the backseat with Bright while trying to get in contact with Larry for Bright.

"I called him five times, Bright, he's not answering," Deja told her.

In agonizing pain, Bright said, "Keep calling until he answers."

Finally at the hospital, Bright thanked the elderly

couple for all of their help before being put in a wheelchair and rushed inside. Still with no luck of getting in touch with Larry, Bright became frustrated and cried even more. "He is supposed to be here with me!" She vented, then she told Deja to call his mother's house. Since Bright had dilated over three centimeters, they promptly, admitted her into the hospital.

Moments later, her mother and Gale rushed inside the room. "We having them early, Queen Bee," she said with a comforting smile on her face. She had recovered from her stroke well and was back to her old self minus the drinking and smoking.

Inside the restroom, Gale grabbed cold towels to wipe Bright's face when she heard her continue to complain about being hot. "Ma, where is Larry?" Bright cried.

"I don't know, sweetheart, Deja is still trying to contact him for you," she said, coaching Bright to breathe properly.

After getting the news, Mrs. Lane rushed inside the hospital room, excited to be there in enough time to help." I couldn't get in touch with Larry, Bright, but I did leave a message for him at the university, and I'm sure he'll be here soon. He left his phone on his bed this morning," she said, showing her his phone. Then she kissed her on the forehead and asked her how she was feeling.

"I'm feeling awful because I'ma have these babies without Larry being here," Bright cried.

"Let's just be grateful for all the love that you have in this room at this very moment," Mrs. Lane said with a pleasant smile on her face.

"Praise God!" Rosette shouted, reminding Bright to

remain calm and to breathe.

Once they sent Bright off to the delivery room, the nurse told her that she could only choose two people to come inside the room with her. She chose both her mother and Larry's mother to come in. "But if the father comes, please let him in," Bright instructed in tears of pain and unhappiness. She was really heartbroken that Larry wasn't there.

"I'll be sure to send him right in," the nurse assured her.

Bright had a speedy delivery. Within twenty minutes of pushing inside of the delivery room, she had birthed two premature baby girls that she and Larry agreed to name Lari and Lori Lane. Both weighing four pounds and six ounces, they were almost small enough to fit in each palm of her hand. Unhappy with the way they looked she cried, "Are they okay? Why are they so small?" she asked.

"Twin babies ninety percent of time come out earlier and smaller than normal pregnancies," the doctor told her.

Giving the babies back to the nurse, Bright turned her nose up at the sight of them. They didn't look normal to her, they had wrinkly skin, cone shaped heads, and on top of that, they looked nothing like she had expected them to.

"So precious," she heard Gale say as the nurse made her way out of the room with the twins and to the nursery.

People only call ugly babies precious, Bright thought.

Hearing Gale's comment made tears form in her eyes. It confirmed that Gale thought her babies were ugly too. Mad at how everything was going, Bright closed her eyes and went to sleep.

Moments later Larry arrived. He was furious that he had accidentally left his cell phone at home, and that it caused him to miss the birth of their babies. More importantly he was disappointed for not being there for Bright.

****

Treasure was hot as fish grease. She had not only found out that Bright had fucked Chrome, but Lil Boo had also fessed up about sleeping with her too. He not only admitted to sleeping with Bright the night of his party, but that he had also slept with her again a few months back when she came to his house to find out what he had told her when she confronted him about the situation.

That's why that bitch was avoiding my question all that time when I asked her what happened that night, Treasure thought. And though Lil Boo had only told her the truth because Bright had keyed up his car when he refused to give her money, she was still happy to finally know the truth. Lil Boo didn't owe her anything as far as she was concerned, but Bright did, and for her disloyal act of betrayal, Treasure planned on seeking revenge on her in the worst way. After making it inside of Bright's courtyard, Treasure climbed the stairs, then banged on her front door. When her mother answered with the Bible in her hand, Treasure's tone immediately changed. She wasn't used to her being home at this time of the day.

Giving her a strange look, Rosette asked her, "Is there a reason you're knocking on my door like you're the police?"

Treasure wanted to cuss Miss Rose out and spill the

beans on her hoe ass daughter. However, because she had just recovered from a stroke, and Treasure respected her elders, she had to remind herself that Bright's mother had nothing to do with it. It was between her and Bright. "I'm sorry, Miss Rose, is Bright here?" she asked as humbly as she could in her frame of mind.

With a surprised look on her face, she said, "No baby, you didn't know? She had the babies earlier today. She's at the hospital, and will probably be there for the next three or four days," she said with a happy smile on her face.

"Congratulations, Miss Rose," Treasure said, struggling to put a smile on her face.

Noticing the tension in her face, Rosette asked her if everything was alright.

"Everything is alright now," she smiled. "I'll stop by in the next couple of days or so," she said, heading down the stairs.

"You're not going to go see Queen Bee and the babies at the hospital?" Rosette asked, confused.

Treasure shook her head no, "I'm afraid that I won't be able to," she said, and she left out of the gate.

"What has Bright gotten herself into?" Rosette said out loud to herself. Then she closed the door and finished having Bible study with her two youngest.

****

Terrence was pissed off that Bright hadn't accepted any of his calls, so he had his homeboy call her on a three way for him.

"Hello," she answered in a sleepy tone.

"Where the fuck you at? And why the fuck you haven't been answering my calls, girl?" Terrence yelled through the phone, instantly frightening her.

Happy that Larry had stepped out of the room to grab snacks, she spoke. "You out yet?" she asked nervously. She had already spoken to her mother about moving, so she was praying that he stayed behind bars until they relocated.

"Hell naw, I ain't out yet, and it don't look like these muthafuckas is tryna let me out either!" he fumed. "So I'ma need you to start answering yo damn phone, before you have me fuck something up around here, you understand?" he said with authority.

Without further words Bright ended the call. All she wanted to know was whether or not he was in jail; she didn't care what he had going on, or what he was going through. *Like I really give a fuck!* She thought, then powered her phone off.

****

Larry was happy that he was the father of two healthy little princesses, Lari and Lori, and that they each had all ten fingers and toes. After catching Bright smoking and drinking wine that day at the hotel, he had become concerned about his babies' health, because he figured if Bright was careless enough to indulge in weed and alcohol that day, that she had probably done it many more times before. "Look at all three of my sleeping babies," Larry said sitting next to Bright's bedside, holding his two daughters in his arms.

Her eyes fluttered open, and she instantly smiled seeing Larry there with her. "I love you, Larry Lane," she said, stretching and waking herself up.

"I love you too, Pretty Bright, and guess what, baby? I signed my deal, and as soon as you get out of here, we're going house shopping, you hear me, baby?" he said, then reached over and kissed her on her beautiful face.

"My big house," she smiled.

"Yup, wherever and whatever house you want. I just wanna make you happy," he smiled.

Bright smiled, then reached her hand out to his. "I must be the luckiest girl alive to have a man like you in my life, Daddy Lane. You make every risk or chance that I've taken, done or gone through worth it." She paused. "Now I have no regrets," she smiled, holding on tight to his hand. Her life was finally going into the direction that she had worked so hard for it be.

****

After coming out of the bathroom and climbing back into her hospital bed, Bright asked Larry if he could get her some King Taco. She hadn't really been eating, and now that everything was going perfectly, her appetite had finally come back and she was dying for some of the best tacos in town. Larry kissed his three angels on their foreheads then headed out of the room to grab Bright some tacos.

Wondering why Treasure and Suge hadn't stopped by or called her yet, she dialed Treasure up on her cell phone, but her number was disconnected so she called her house phone. When her grandmother answered, she told her that Treasure wasn't home, so she called Suge up.

"Mohammad residence, Sister Shirley speaking," Suge's foster mother said into the phone.

"Can I speak to Samantha, please?" Bright asked, Suge told them whenever they called the house to ask for her by her real name.

"Can I ask who's speaking?" she asked.

"It's her friend, Bright Sheldon," she said, feeling the need to give her full name.

After a few moments of silence, she said, "She's busy right now; can you call her back tomorrow evening?"

Bright thought that was very odd that she told her to call her back the next evening, instead of later on that day, but she figured, *oh well maybe it's just a Muslim thing,* then she hung up the phone.

****

At King Taco, Larry stood in line a few customers behind Bright's asshole uncle talking big shit about how upset he was at some chick. Larry was gonna step up and attempt to introduce himself for the second time, but he figured his day was going so well that he didn't want to let him spoil it for him. So he patiently waited in line and continued listening to him vent to his friend.

"This bitch don't even know that I'm out right now, but after the way she played me for the last few days I was locked up, on everything, I'm cool on that bitch. I'ma take care of my responsibilities with the twins and everything, but her gold digging ass ain't got shit coming from me!" he stressed.

His boy nodded his head in agreement. "That's why I be telling you, you gotta watch out for these hoe's, because a lot of 'em just be out for the money, homie," he said seriously.

"I can't believe her ass, though," he said, looking at the caller ID on his ringing cell phone. A devilish smirk appeared across Terrence face. "This bitch wanna return my calls now that she see a nigga out," he sarcastically said.

"I thought you said you haven't spoke to her though, Ice?" his friend asked, confused.

"Naw, I haven't, guess she peeped that shit cause I called her from my cell phone earlier," he said contemplating whether or not he should answer her call. "I shouldn't answer this shit but I am I need my engagement ring back. Nigga paid eleven-five for it, so I needs that back like ASAP," he said then answered his phone. "The fuck you calling my phone for, Bright?" Terrence said, stepping out of line and outside so he could cuss her ass out.

Larry thought he was tripping when he heard Bright's name, but it was all beginning to make sense to him now. Dude wasn't her uncle, and that's why she never introduced them, because she was fucking him all along. Something was telling Larry that the story Bright had told him about dude being her mother's brother had seemed too suspicious to be true. He nodded his head in disgust. Bright had been playing him all this time, and was trying to put another man's babies on him. That explained why she was rushing him to take his deal. Angry, Larry stepped out the door and headed to his car. A few cars down, he heard Bright's so called-uncle continue to cuss her out on his cell phone. Larry stood there listening, hoping that maybe there was some sort of a misunderstanding and that Bright wasn't this horrible person that he had just painted her to be in his mind.

"Listen here, Bright, I ain't tryna hear that bullshit you screaming!" Terrence yelled into the phone cutting her off. "I told you that I'ma take care of the twins, but I need that engagement ring back like today!" He demanded.

Larry had heard enough; he was so heartbroken that he couldn't control the shed of tears that fell from his eyes. *I let that girl play me?* He said to himself. Then he thanked the Lord for revealing the truth to him before he wifed her up and ended up raising another man's children. On the drive home, he decided to pack up everything Bright had ever given to him and have it sent to her house. Better yet, he'd drop it off himself. Then he planned on taking the next flight out of state to basketball camp and start training. He had to hurry up and get away quickly before he ended up doing something that he'd live to regret.

****

Bright had been waiting for Larry to come back with her food for over three hours. She had called him, texted him, called his house, and no answer from Larry. An hour later when she called her mother, she revealed to her that Larry had stopped by and left some boxes and a note inside her room. Bright was confused. She didn't know what was going on, or know what to think. *He was fine before he left here, now why isn't he answering my calls?* Bright thought.

Lost and confused, Bright called Treasure's house to see if she could use her mother's car to pick her up from the hospital. The doctor wasn't releasing her until the next day, and her mother told her she wouldn't be picking her up until then. "You must follow the doctor's orders," she told her. Again, Treasure was unavailable, and Bright still hadn't received a phone call or visit from either Treasure or Suge since her trip to the hospital, and now Larry was M.I.A. "Something is very wrong here," Bright said to herself, and the gut feeling that she had in stomach was telling her the same thing.

Day Three

Part Sixteen

After Bright's mother picked her up from the hospital, she asked her mother question after question: What did he say when he came? Did he look mad? How many boxes did he drop off? Tired of answering her questions, Rosette told her that she could see for herself once they got home.

Maybe he just wants to surprise me, Bright reasoned with herself.

Once Rosette parked her car, Bright climbed out and shot up the stairs to see what awaited her in her bedroom.

"Bright, you could at least help me get your babies out the car!" her mother yelled after her, nodding her head.

"Deja, help Ma with the babies for me," Bright said, making her way down the hallway to her bedroom. Seeing the many boxes, she began to tear them open. Inside the boxes were items that she had purchased for him throughout their relationship. Confused, she said, "What the fuck?" Removing the note that was attached on another box, she quickly pulled it off then tore it open, desperate for answers. It read:

I know about your uncle, that really ain't your uncle at all, and how you been fucking him the whole time! And I also know that the twins are his babies not mine!!!! You lied to me Bright, I hate you for it, and I wish I never met you!! I don't ever want to see your face again...you're dead to me now, so just stay the fuck away from me!!!!!

P.S You're not so pretty at all Bright...You're Pretty Poison!!!!!!

Bright cried so long and so hard that she had fallen to sleep, and when she woke back up, she'd cry herself back to sleep again. This cycle repeated throughout the remainder of the night. During her downtime, her mother took care of the twins for her and tried comforting her by reading scriptures from the Bible. Nothing helped, and all Bright wanted to do was crawl under a rock and die. Days later, Bright was so depressed that she tried to kill herself by overdosing on sleeping pills. When her mother found her in her room unconscious with a faint pulse, she called 911.

Confined to her bedroom for weeks, Bright couldn't eat or sleep and she barely moved when her babies cried. Not to mention she didn't feed, hold, or clothe them, nor did she care to. Bright had postpartum depression on top of heartache, and it was eating her up alive.

Treasure had stopped by on numerous occasions, but Bright wasn't accepting any visitors. She blamed everyone but herself for her problems, and felt everybody was out to get her. Looking as horrible as she felt, Bright had dropped fifteen pounds, her hair had fallen out, and nobody could get her out of the apartment for fresh air, let alone her bedroom.

Staying prayed up, Rosette relied on God in her time of need and prayed night and day, hoping that her daughter would snap out of the pit of hell that she had been dwelling in.

****

At school, hiding in the girls' restroom, Ramon cried. He hated that everybody picked on him all the time. He wished he wouldn't have tried to kiss his fifth grade classmate Jake when they were playing hide and seek on the playground a few months back. Now every time he came to school he was getting teased, hit, chased and called a faggot. He had grown so tired of it that he attempted to bring his brother's gun to school and shoot anybody who had ever called him a name or bothered him. But when he looked under his brother's mattress that morning, it wasn't there. So instead, he grabbed the blade he found in his sister, Bright's drawer before leaving out to school. At ten years old, he held so much hurt, pain, anger and resentment inside that murder would have been his only resolution. And his mind was made up that if anybody came inside the stall and bothered him, he was gonna cut their throats.

****

Bright was living her life by the moment. One minute she was trying to get her life back on track, and the next she would be soaking in her own misery. On this day in particular, she was fighting hard to make progress. Sitting on the living room couch with Lori lying across her lap, Bright changed Lari's wet Pamper while she watched the morning news. On her way out the door for work, Rosette smiled because her daughter was showing signs of improvement.

After everything was said and done, Vince had up and disappeared. Rosette didn't worry herself crazy thinking about it; she had learned to put the things she was unable to carry in God's hands. With prayer and faith, Rosette believed that life was full of great possibilities. At work, she was offered a much higher paying position that for once only required eight hours of her time a day. Gale and Lyn stuck by her side like the true friends they had always been to her, and with all of her heart, she appreciated them dearly. Rosette even agreed to have a private lunch with her distant cousin Shanna to try and reconcile and bury the hatchet. She no longer wanted to carry a grudge over people and things that were no longer of importance to her, and she also wanted to thank her for looking after Ramon when she had the stroke. Shanna was thrilled to have the opportunity to reunite with her cousin; she wanted to make up for all the lost time and the heartache she had caused Rosette many years ago

After clocking out from work, Rosette called home to check on Bright, when Bright told her that everything was alright, and she didn't hear the babies crying in the background, she smiled to herself and thanked the Lord for working in her favor. "I'll be home after I make a quick run to the bank... and when Ramon and Ryonna step through the door, tell them to get ready for Bible study," she said in an uplifting spirit.

"I will," Bright replied, falling back into a dazing depression.

****

Punch after punch Ramon endured as the kids stood around kicking and hitting him for being something that even he didn't understand. He didn't ask to be the way that he was, and he didn't understand how God was supposed to love him as much as they told him he did in Sunday school, then turn around and allow these horrible things to happen to him. Unable to grab the blade in time, Ramon tried to defend himself as he swung, kicked, and cried out for help. Seeing what was taking place, a group of parents ran over to break the fight up. Once they pulled him off the ground, the kids continued to call him, punk, pussy and faggot. Angry Ramon sprinted home. He was gonna kill them all and he didn't care about going to jail either. He figured going to jail would be a much safer and better place than school. Now all he had to do was go home get the gun.

****

On her way out the door for school this morning, Treasure received a dreadful call from Bright; she told her to stop by after school to see the babies and catch up with her. Itching to knock Bright's lights out, Treasure called her cousins from Compton and told them to meet her at her house after school so that they could pack her out as they had planned to. Riding the bus home, Treasure thought, *Once I get this bitch outside it's on and popping!* Thinking about everything that Bright had done to her made her run hot; her nostrils started flaring and her fists begin to clench. Stepping off the bus Treasure said to herself, "Won't be any more Pretty Bright when I get down wit ya ass, boo."

****

"This bitch about to make me kill her ass!" Terrence said to himself. He was smashing on the highway, on his way to Bright's house. She had ignored him long enough, and he wasn't gonna take it anymore; he wanted his engagement ring back and he wanted it back TODAY. He had played her little games long enough, and to ensure he got his ring back and to find out what was going on, he brought his cold piece of steel for anybody that stood in his way, including her little brother, Cordell, that ran with the young Northside Crips. With the mindset that he was in... anybody could get it. But one thing for sure, and two for certain, Ice was getting up in that house today, and he wanted answers!

****

Wallowing back into depression, Bright grew angry as tears of pain flowed down her face. She had not only lost her shot at the good life again, but her looks had failed her. She remembered when she was a little girl, maybe no older than five, when she ran into her white grandmother's room and told her that her grandfather Simon was doing nasty things to her. Frantic, Bright climbed in her grandmother's big comfortable bed that was fit for nothing less than a queen and held on to her grandmother tight. Her grandmother had that type of beauty and glamour that even her late age couldn't devour: eyes blue as the deep sea and rich golden hair that hung healthy and full around her thin beautiful face. She grabbed Bright's face then looked her in her eyes.

"With your kind of beauty, sweet darling, no man will be able to resist you, and will have desires to touch you...Even a grandfather," she explained, with the lift of the eyebrow. "So get your practice now, beautiful one, because you're destined to win over the hearts of many men, and will get whatever you want because of it, just as I have," she smiled. "What you have in between your legs is called a gold mine, and it controls men, and makes the world go round," she told her with such seriousness that Bright could feel every word down to her bones. "With looks as dangerously beautiful as yours you will never have to work, or even pursue school and it will guarantee your place at the top. That is," she paused to wipe Bright's tears away, "If you use what you have right."

Bright's heart sank right into the pit of her belly as she adjusted to her grandmother's words. Her revealing this information about her grandfather didn't enrage her or get her upset the way she thought it would. Instead she encouraged it and spoke as if she was giving her valuable information before her time. Scared, Bright didn't want to disappoint her grandmother by not following her instructions and she did want to live a fabulous and glamorous life like her grandmother did...her mind was so crowded and confused. Trying to absorb everything into her young mind, Bright sucked her tears back. This was only the beginning of her hell.

"Now run along and go get your practice, sweet darling." Her grandmother smiled as she helped Bright off the bed. "This will be our little secret," she pressed her index finger up against her lips, "Yours, mine, and Grandpa's," she smiled. Giving Bright that extra push in her step, her grandmother gently nudged her on the back. Bright walked out of her bedroom, looking back at her the whole time, afraid but willing at the same time, until she ended up back down the hallway with her grandfather. She had carried on in that manner countless times until her grandfather died and it never got easier for her. To make matters worse she was never mentioned in his will like he had promised her so many times, and neither did her grandmother. Her father and both her grandparents had gotten over on her. She felt cheated, raped and robbed.

"Bright!" Ramon yelled, trying to gain her attention.

He hadn't waited for Ryonna, Deja, and Cordell like he normally did; he was so mad and angry that he had run all the way home plotting to kill, and he needed Bright to help change his mind. "Bright!" he yelled again.

"They calling me faggot and pussy at school again! I thought you said that I wasn't a faggot and that people would stop calling me names!?!" Standing there with a big busted lip, a bloody nose and a ripped up shirt, Ramon felt alone in the world. "Bright, are you listening to me?" Ramon cried out he was in desperate need of her help.

Stuck in a trance, Ramon's words fell onto deaf ears. Bright was so caught up in the zone that she didn't even hear her own crying babies. Crying, Ramon stormed inside of his room and closed the door. "I'ma kill 'em then!" He yelled, looking under his brother's mattress for his gun. Happy that it was there, Ramon picked it up.

Inside the living room, Rosette found her daughter staring at her crying twins. It was still a mystery to Bright how Larry had found out about her relationship with Ice, but how could he not believe that the babies his spitting images weren't his? How could he just walk away from his own blood? No longer able to sit by and watch Bright grieve over Larry, Rosette made her voice be heard loud and clear.

"Bright! Do something, don't just sit there and stare at your children cry! Pick them up, feed them, nurse them, and be a mother and do something!" She said, grabbing Lori. Bright didn't budge; she just sat there zoned out, lost in deep thought. *He don't care no more, then neither do I,* she said to herself.

Dropping the few bags of groceries she had grabbed after leaving the bank, Rosette walked over to pick up Lari, she had rolled off of the couch. Feeling her granddaughter's soaked and wet Pampers, Rosette shot Bright a disapproving look. "Bright, she's pissy wet!" She yelled, laying them both on the couch then picked up the bag of Pampers that sat next to their playpen. "Change them now, Bright," her mother demanded, looking Bright in the eyes. She was no longer gonna enable Bright to sit on her butt and feel sorry for herself, she was going to see to it that Bright was going to be the mother that her babies needed her to be, if it was the last thing that she did.

Slowly coming out of the trance that she was in, Bright looked at her mother, and tried to figure out what she was saying to her.

Becoming fed up, Rosette said, "Look Bright...whatever you're going through, you better hurry up and snap out of it! You are a mother now, and like me, they need you, and you have to take care of them, Queen Bee," she stared into her daughter's tear-stained eyes. "Larry is gone, baby, and he's not coming back," she cried, hoping she was getting through to her daughter. "It's over now, and I think it's time you finally accept that...it is not the end of the world," she said to her. Bright didn't want to accept the reality, so she ran into her bedroom, locked herself inside and cried.

In the meantime, Ramon held the gun in his hand pacing his bedroom floor, talking to himself. "I told them that I wasn't gon' be a faggot no more and they still just wanna pick on me. And I'm not gon' keep letting them beat me up... and I'm not gon' let them keep calling me names, I'ma kill 'em!" He said, nodding his head then he grabbed his backpack to put the gun inside.

In the next room, Bright packed a duffel bag full of clothes and thought, *Fuck it, two can play this game Larry!* "If he doesn't have to love his own kids, then neither do I...we can both say fuck everything!" She said, becoming more angry than sad. "I made this possible for him, and this is how he repays me? I've been played for the fourth damn time, and I promise there won't be a fifth time," she put him on her mental list next to her grandparents and father. Bright smirked as she thought, *Fuck loving another nigga ever again, I'm about to get what's owed to me,* with the duffel bag in hand Bright walked out of her bedroom.

Heading out of the room with his backpack on, Ramon caught a glimpse of himself in the mirror. Stopping to look at himself, he didn't like what he saw, or understand what he was. Hunching his shoulders, he thought, *how could I expect people to like and understand me when I don't even understand myself?* Ramon dropped his bag to the floor, then looked in the mirror and told his reflection that he hated himself. "I hate you, faggot, I hate you," he continued to say to himself over and over again.

Sitting on the couch, speaking to Gale on the phone, Rosette asked her to come over to give her a hand. She had gotten the babies quiet and needed to get ready for Bible study; Lord knows she needed it. She had found a youth group at church that she thought would be helpful for Ramon, and since Ryonna wanted to join the church choir, she knew that would be enough satisfy and to keep her busy.

Walking down the hallway with a bag in her hand, Bright walked straight out of the apartment door without saying a word. Doubling back, Rosette thought she was seeing things, so she removed herself from the couch and ran over to the front door. Seeing Bright make her way out of the courtyard, she yelled out to her. "Bright, don't you walk out and leave your children like this, Bright! Don't do this to me, I can't do this alone!" She cried. "These are your babies, and you're dead wrong for doing this!" She cried out to her.

Reaching the courtyard entrance, Bright ignored her mother's cries. She knew nobody would understand her reason for leaving, so she didn't explain. She was more harm than good to her babies. She didn't love them, and she didn't understand why. Bright had always heard people say that what didn't kill a person would make them stronger...but she didn't feel so strong at all. She was at the edge; she couldn't breathe and was about to lose her mind. Without looking back, Bright walked out of the gate. She didn't want the life that she was living anymore, and she was going to leave it behind...forever.

Seeing Bright leave, Rosette kissed both her grandbabies. "She'll be back, she just needs a little time to clear her head," she said, trying to convince herself.

Making her way to Treasure's house, thinking of which state she'd relocate to, Bright was met by Treasure and her rowdy cousins from Compton, Lametria and Shantell, on the corner of her block. Treasure couldn't believe how thin and bad Bright looked, but it wasn't gonna stop her from stomping a hole in her ass. "I'm glad I caught you before I left, Treasure," Bright said, nodding her head and wiping the few tears that had fallen from her eyes.

Treasure wasn't concerned about what or why her ex-best friend was crying, or furthermore what she was going through. Stepping to her face wearing a mean mug, Treasure said, "Glad I caught you before you left too, boo."

Confused, Bright took a step back to filter Treasure out; she didn't know what was going on. In this situation, Treasure would have normally just took off on a bitch, but this was personal, and she wanted Bright to know exactly why she was about to beat the dog shit out of her.

"What's goin' on, Treasure?" Bright said, sensing tension and hostility.

Not wanting to waste another minute looking into Bright's sorry face, Treasure got straight to the point. "You a snake, fake, back stabbing ass bitch...and I know yo tramp ass fucked Chrome and Lil Boo, and I'ma beat yo ass!" She yelled with her fist balled and a sour expression on her face.

Just when Bright thought her life couldn't get any worse, it was...and now everything was beginning to add up and make sense to her. Suge had busted her out to Treasure, which explained why she had been avoiding her calls, and why neither of them had come to see her in the hospital. Assuming that Lil Boo had given her up because she keyed his car up, Bright thought, *what a bitch ass nigga!* Dropping her bag to the ground, Bright denied it, even though she knew there would be no way of talking herself out of the jam, especially since Treasure's cousins were with her. "I don't know what you talking about," Bright said, getting herself in fight mode.

"Fucking hoe!" Treasure yelled, taking the first blow, missing Bright's face. Then she aimed to grab her hair. Connecting with the first blow, Bright punched Treasure in the side of the head, making it rock like a bobble-head.

Instantly jumping in, Lametria and Shantell both delivered blows to Bright's face, neck and back. Wanting in, Treasure grabbed her by the hair and started upper-cutting Bright in the face, immediately making blood gush from her mouth and face. "Hold that bitch up for me," Treasure yelled, trying to catch her breath. She wanted to see the damage she had caused to Bright's face. Both cousins held each of her arms and lifted Bright up per Treasure's request. Not happy with the damage that she had caused, Treasure reared back, then swung her leg in full throttle and kicked Bright dead in the face.

"Argggg!!!" Bright moaned in pain.

"Yeah bitch, that's for being a dirty bitch when I was nothing but a real friend to you!" She said, then took another victorious kick to her face. Seeing she had kicked a couple of teeth out of Bright's mouth, Treasure told her cousin's to let her go. "Drop that hoe," she demanded.

Once Bright's body fell to the ground, they all began stomping her out. Bright, having a little fight left in her, continued to try to defend herself, throwing weak punches and kicks in every direction until she couldn't anymore. Still not satisfied with Bright's physical condition while they stomped and kicked at her defenseless body, Treasure went for the brick that she seen laying in the street, and then ran back over and hit Bright in the head with it as the rioter did to the white truck driver, Reginald Deny, back in the 1990's Rodney King riot. Treasure didn't feel any remorse, as she continued to stomp Bright's motionless body, yelling in rage. "Fucking no good ass bitch...you fucking snake!" Treasure reacted beastly; she hated Bright for what she had done to her.

"Hold on, this bitch ain't moving no more," her cousin Shantell said, frantically backing away from Bright's lifeless body.

"For real, Treasure, this bitch ain't moving." Lametria said as she backed away also.

Treasure spit on the ground, then continue to victimize Bright. "This bitch ain't dead, she's probably just unconscious," Treasure said, looking at Bright laid out on the concrete with blood coming from her head. "Bitch gone learn about crossing the lines of loyalty next time," Treasure spat, continuing to kick and stomp her.

Nervous, her cousin Lametria said, "Bitch, let's bounce and go to my house, I have a bad feeling that this bitch is dead Treasure," she said, backing away from the scene. Shantell had to pry Treasure off of Bright. "I fucking hate this stupid bitch!"

"That's enough, Treasure, let's go!" Shantell grabbed her arm and pulled away.

As they were all running from the scene, Treasure looked back at a helpless Bright lying motionless on the ground, bleeding from her head, she started feeling regret. At first, Treasure wanted to follow her heart and confront Bright then end the friendship without having a physical altercation. But her LBC street mentality interfered with that and resulted in her calling her cousins to do Bright in and teach her a lesson. Climbing inside of her cousin Shantell's car, Treasure hoped that Bright wasn't dead, especially when her sole intention was just to stomp her out and teach her a lesson.

****

Before going to Bright's house Terrence decided to stop by her best friend Treasure's house to see if Bright was there first...he knew the two were always together. "Trifling bitch gon' give me mines!" He had popped an E pill and was in the mood to break a bitch neck. Pulling onto Treasure's street Terrence immediately decreased his speed and turned his music down. Her street was swapped with police, paramedics and spectators. Observing the scene he thought, *Niggas already getting turned up 'round this muthafucka I see.* Trying to avoid a run in with the law, Terrence made a quick left off of, Treasure's street and in detour to Bright's house.

****

With two crying babies on her arms, Rosette was happy when her children finally got home. "Ma, we couldn't find Ramon," Cordell said. "And we been looking all over for him," Cordell added, concerned for once. He had heard that Ramon had gotten beat up again, but nobody seemed to know where he was, and they looked everywhere for him.

"Did he come home yet?" Deja asked, walking toward his room.

"I haven't seen him," Rosette said, popping a bottle in Lori's mouth.

"He better hurry up so we can go to church, huh Mama?" Ryonna said, sad but excited about joining the church choir.

"Yeah, he sure better," Rosette managed to smile at her youngest daughter. If she had let any of her children down in the past, she swore she wouldn't let Ryonna down now. It seemed like even in their drama-filled home, Ryonna still held a glowing innocence.

Coming out of the kitchen, Cordell said, "This is strange, Mama, where can Ramon be?"

Out of nowhere Deja screamed, "MAAAAAAA!!!! Get in here!" She jumped up and down in the hallway, screaming and crying her poor lungs out. Her next words were too inaudible to make out, so instantly everybody ran in her direction.

"What's going on?" Rosette said, running to her aid with baby Lori in her arms. Stopping in front of her boy's bedroom, she could not believe what her eyes were seeing. Tears immediately started overloading in her eyes, and she couldn't help the rapid flow of tears that flowed down her cheeks at the sight of her baby boy,

Ramon, hanging from the light fixture with a cord wrapped around his neck...Dead.

No mother should ever have to experience what she was experiencing at that very moment and endure such agonizing and unexplainable pain. She was trying to stand strong for her children, but her knees buckled. Everything and everybody had a breaking point, and Rosette had finally reached hers. Falling to her knees, she let out a sigh of hurt and pain that only a mother could at such time.

"NOOOOOOOOOOOOOOOOOOOOO!! HELP ME JESUS!!!!!" She cried and screamed at the top of her lungs. Rosette cried a river...then everything went black.

The

End

Also by Mimi Renee, Now Available!

Featured Author in,
I'd Rather Be Single

The story continues...

Ink Game Publications
Proudly presents

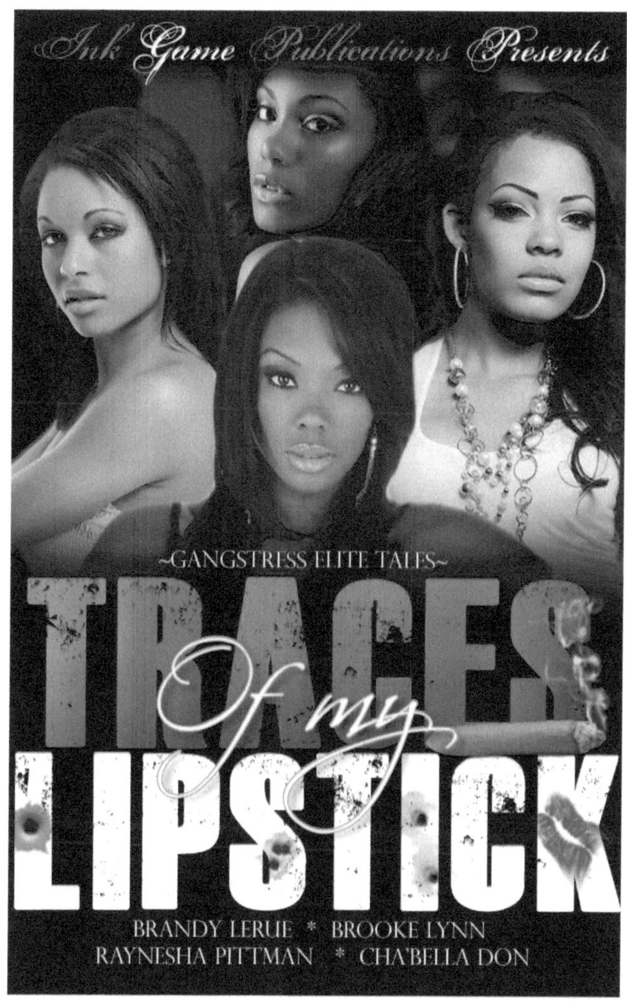

www.ingramcontent.com/pod-product-compliance
Lightning Source LLC
LaVergne TN
LVHW091029080826
845145LV00002B/414

9780615395364